ECOKINESIS

The Ability to Control Nature

CASSIE GREUTMAN

Published by Fully Invested Publishing

Printed in the United States of America

First Printing, February 2020

Second Printing, March 2024

ISBN: 978-1-964185-04-0

CHAPTER ONE

I trudged across the cafeteria toward my normal table. This was so not fair. After everything Dan and Nina had found out about me in the last months, I couldn't believe they were still making me go to school.

Sure, Dan hadn't seen any proof since I couldn't leave Sanctuary without getting grabbed by the fae, but still. My invisible sword sheath should have won me some points. He totally believed Nina of course, but believing and seeing? A little different. And there was a whole lot to believe.

Lucy was already sitting at our table, reading a book. Somehow we always sat together, even though we didn't like each other and didn't talk. There really wasn't much to say. Since I'd almost turned her brother over to the fae to save myself, I felt guilty around anyone from the Martan family. She just had a problem with everybody. I sat down across from her and started in on my lunch. Sad that here in Sanctuary I couldn't eat nearly as much.

Suddenly Lucy looked up, then straight back down. I checked over my shoulder to see what she was looking at. Cray, headed our way, super late. Yep, that was the real reason she always sat with me. As much as she pretended to hate fae, she sure didn't mind being around my kind of, sort of, brother.

"Hi, Trisha." Cray was always so polite. Sometimes it got on my nerves. He nodded toward Lucy. "Hello." He was adjusting better than I would have thought possible. He was like a shy human kid now, not a shy fae kid. Normal clothes and the fact that he'd learned some slang seriously helped. Dan had worked his government magic to get him into school. I wasn't in on the details and I wasn't sure I wanted to be.

"Hey, Cray." I loved saying that. I think it annoyed him, but again, the whole polite thing. He'd never said a word.

Lucy mumbled something but hardly looked up. Real smooth. Ah, just another day at Anthony High. After battling trolls, hyran and fellow fae, it was beginning to feel really dull around here. I wasn't sure yet if that was good or bad.

Even the self-defense classes Nina had put me in weren't that great anymore. It was a lot of work. It had been fun when Nina and I were going together, but they'd moved me up two levels beyond her and now we were in different classes. It made me really glad she was taking them, but I also really hoped she'd never need to use what she'd learned. My foster mom wasn't really the fighting type.

The bell rang. Kids slowly collected their trash. Cray's eyebrows shot up and I laughed, pushing myself to my feet to go dump my tray. "Better chow down on something fast," I said, moving past him toward the trash can.

He groaned and stuffed some noodles in his mouth while following me toward the door.

"Where were you anyway?" I asked.

"Trying to find my way here," he said, his cheeks flushing. Even after a month of school he still couldn't figure out how to get anywhere without help. And I'd thought I was bad.

"I can help you get to your next class, Cray," Lucy offered. "You know, if you want help." Her voice trailed off and her face went beet red.

"Okay then." I drew out the words and twitched up an eyebrow. "See you, guys." I took off, really not wanting to see them. It was just weird. Mostly because Cray was pretty much my brother now, after all we'd been through together, and I still didn't like Lucy. Cray had chosen to do the right thing and help me over being able to stay with his own kind. I was pretty protective of him.

The rest of the school day zipped by pretty quickly. Which was great, because I had self-defense class all night, and I was pretty excited about going and getting knocked around.

I'd also joined basketball, but practice wasn't until tomorrow. Oh the possibilities, now that I could bruise and bleed without insta-healing, or more specifically, not worrying about people seeing me do it. Did I sometimes miss the ultra quick recovery time? Oh yeah, especially waking up after a particularly harsh night at the dojo. But it was so worth it to be able to actually be in group sports now. Sanctuary with its no abilities thing had changed my life.

The whole zits thing wasn't cool though. At all.

But I'd always wanted to be normal, and here it was. Just as amazing as I'd thought it would be.

After my last class, I mashed the books I wouldn't need tonight into my locker and charged toward the exit, waving at a few teammates on the way. So weird to have people wave back. But this was life now. And it was shaping up great.

I always walked home after school. Sure, it was cold, so Nina didn't like it much. But sometimes I did miss being more independent, and somehow she seemed to sense that, so she let me.

I threw my backpack over my shoulder and waved to Lucy, just to make her mad. Rebecca always made her ride the bus, even though she could have walked with me. I didn't mind, it meant I didn't have to spend time with her. And her mom did have reason to be paranoid, after the whole Jaime snatch thing. Having your daughter taken by superpowered creatures from another realm tended to do that to a person. But at least I'd been able to get her back. And get to the point where I could live with myself for getting her into the situation in the first place. Most of the time.

Cray rode the bus too. He said it was because he didn't like walking, but I got the feeling it was more about Lucy than exercise.

I didn't tell anyone that the real reason I walked was a dog that always followed me.

The mangy mutt always showed up as soon as I was out of sight of the school. At first I hadn't liked it. Growing up on the run and then in home after home, I'd never really gotten attached to pets. But this ugly thing grew on me. I'd even started hiding leftovers from lunch in my backpack to feed him once we reached a point no one from the school would see us.

Sure enough, there he was, waiting for me. He really was an ugly dog. Long matted hair covered his body, the color indiscernible because of the dirt and whatever other gross stuff he'd gotten into caked all the way down to his skin. His ribs still stuck out, though that was getting better because of the food I was bringing him.

I felt bad on the weekends, and I didn't know what he did for meals then, but our apartment didn't allow dogs. Nina would probably freak out if I tried to bring him home. Dan would be in my corner on this one though, he loved dogs. Maybe once we got moved somehow Storm would just show up one day, and it would be a complete surprise to everyone, including me.

Yeah, I'd given him a name. Not a great name, but hey, I hadn't really done this before.

Stormy saw me and dashed my direction, tail going a million miles an hour. He jumped up and nearly knocked me over. I shoved him down.

"Hey now, Nina will know something's up if you ruin my school clothes."

He just sat and grinned at me, tongue lolling out like usual.

"What? You think I have something for you?" He cocked his head and went still. I pulled a small piece of hamburger out of my pocket and threw it to him. He snatched it out of the air and it was instantly gone.

"That's all you get until we reach the alley. You know that."

He whined a little, but fell right into step with me when I started forward.

A couple of blocks from the school there was an old alley between two factories. I stopped halfway down it and dropped my backpack. "You ready for this?"

Stormy dropped into a sit instantly, staring me down.

"I'll take that as a yes." I unzipped my bag and grabbed a baggie of food. It was amazing what teenagers threw away. So far no one had seen me rooting around in the trash can. Hopefully it stayed that way.

I tossed Storm the first chunk of burger with no ceremony. No reason to make the poor guy wait.

It was gone just as quickly as the small piece I'd given him earlier. "Hungry today, huh?" I took pity on him and grabbed the rest of the food out of my bag and dumped it on the ground in front of him.

He gulped it down fast enough I worried he'd choke himself.

"Easy there boy. It isn't going anywhere."

I waited until he was done and looking for more before reaching out to scratch his grimy head. I didn't know much about animals, but getting between them and their food when they were super hungry didn't seem like a good idea. At least it wasn't a good idea for other people to get between me and my food when I was starving.

Suddenly Storm's stare jerked from his attention being on me, to him locking onto something behind me. I looked over my shoulder to see what he found so interesting.

A guy. A tall guy, at that. In a big coat, with a hat, and a scarf covering most of his face. It was cold yeah, so it made sense, but it still gave me the willies. In all of our times using this alley, Storm and I had never run into anyone. Ever.

The guy stepped forward, raising a hand.

Storm moved between me and whoever it was. I'd never seen him even grumpy. Surprising with how hungry he'd been when I'd first started feeding him, but he was sure unhappy now. He raised his hackles and a low growl rumbled out of his throat.

Okay, that was a little scary.

"What do you want?" I asked, slowly reaching back to make sure I still had my sword. Check. Even though we were supposed to be safe here, I was paranoid and didn't trust a single fae other than Cray and Jaden, so I still carried it. Yeah, sometimes it got in the way, but better safe than sorry. At least with the invisible sheath Wade had made for me, no one saw it and thought I was a serial killer or anything.

"Trish."

Oh great. I knew that voice. Speak of the devil.

"Sic him, Storm."

Storm didn't even deign to give me a look. He just kept growling without moving. It didn't matter. I didn't actually want him to sic. The idiot standing in front of me might hurt him.

"What do you want?"

Wade pulled the scarf down. "Can we talk?"

Okay, was I curious what he was doing here? Absolutely. Did I really want to talk? Absolutely not. Seeing him made all kinds of bad memories try to push through the barrier I'd built. I knew what it was like to be in a family now, I wasn't the same person I had been, but thinking about the things I'd done before... Nope, better not to think about them at all.

"Nope. We were finished talking when you tried to kill me."

He gave me a weak smile. "And look how that turned out."

I raised a hand in a full on stop signal. "You didn't let me finish. I thought we were done then, but I was starting to feel a little differently after we were forced to work together for awhile."

"I sense a but-"

"But," I interrupted him, "I didn't realize how low you could actually go. Kidnapping a seven-year-old. I can't believe you. Go back to Faerie where I don't have to see you again."

Wade's weak smile had totally disappeared. He looked beaten down, far more exhausted than I'd ever seen him. It did make my heart twinge, but I wasn't falling for it again. I turned to back out of the alley the way I'd came. I could find another way home.

"I'm not here to get you back or anything like that, Trish," he called after me. "I need your help. Bad."

A groan slipped out and I ground to a stop. What could he possibly need from me that he couldn't get from someone more qualified, Starren for example?

"It's Starren. She's in trouble."

I whirled around so my glare could melt his face off. It didn't work, but it was a good effort. "If there is anyone in the world I'd be less likely to help than you- which is shocking, I do admit- it would be Starren. I can't believe you'd even ask me that after what happened. It's only been like two months!"

I was starting to shout. That needed to stop before someone looked down this alley to see what was going on.

"I know. Trust me, you don't understand how badly neither of us wanted to do that. But what we both have at stake... Please, Trish, just hear me out."

Since the glare wasn't working, I crossed my arms in front of my chest and glanced away, like he wasn't even worth looking at. My head was spinning so hard from seeing him that I could hardly process. Bile worked its way up my throat, and I swallowed it down along with the terrible memories seeing him had brought up.

Storm seemed to know how I was feeling. He'd stopped growling and followed me when I'd moved back up the alley, but he shoved himself against my leg now, bumping my hip with his head until I dropped my hand and gave his dirty head a little scratch.

All of the good feelings from the last month of spending time at the gym and hanging out with real friends, then going home to Dan and Nina happy to see me, were gone. I was back in the woods, lying on the ground, terrified, wondering what had happened. This jerk had done that to me, good reason or not.

"This is really serious. Really serious. She might die."

Okay, so did I dislike Starren more than I'd even thought possible? Yeah, when she'd taken Jaime and turned on me I had. It had faded a little since then, because I did know how the Council worked, and she had probably been forced to do stuff she didn't like, just like I had been with Jaden. But did that mean I wanted her to die? No way.

"She stuck up for you, Trish. She saved your life when you were helping that family escape, when Vilan tried to stop you all leaving Chicago."

"Fine," I pulled my hand away from Storm and crossed my arms in front of me again, knowing it was defensive posture but feeling better anyway. "Talk."

"The Council is acting like she let you all go on purpose. They won't ask her for the truth, even knowing she can't lie. She's locked up now, and they scheduled her execution for next week. I don't have anyone to turn to. Please..."

Well this wasn't great. Could I really just stand by and let Starren be killed? We'd been on opposite sides of an issue at the end, but she'd treated me pretty well when I'd been on her team.

Leave Dan and Nina again? Risk dying? Go to Faerie, after I'd just compromised everything a good person should believe in to stay away from that place? Starren was amazing. Surely if there was any way for her to escape, she'd have done it by now. And what help could I really be? I had no practical knowledge of Faerie, just what my mom had taught me.

"I can't, Wade. I'm sorry."

"So you'll just leave her to die, then." He sounded disappointed, almost disgusted. "You're the best person I know, the only one I thought would be willing to go against the Council. You've done it before."

That made me snort. "I'm the best person you know? I think you need new friends."

"Starren is my only friend." It came out in almost a broken whisper, and my heart wrenched in my chest. But there really wasn't anything I could do.

"At least help me get back into Faerie," Wade said when I turned to walk away again. "They're watching all the known tunnels, and I can't get back without them tracking me."

"How am I going to help you do that? I don't know anything about Faerie tunnels."

"You don't. But someone that listens to you does. He got here somehow, didn't he?"

Jaden. Wade didn't want to say his name, but he was talking about Jaden. Somehow he'd escaped Faerie and come to Earth to care for his family. He obviously knew of a tunnel somewhere, but we hadn't talked about it.

My shoulders slumped. I really didn't want to talk to Jaden, but it seemed kind of extreme to let Starren die because I felt too guilty to talk to a guy. "Fine. I'll find out where it is, but then you're on your own."

Wade smiled. It was nowhere near the old smile, but the closest thing I'd seen since we'd 'bumped' into each other.

"Meet me here tomorrow morning. I'll see what I can find out."

"I have to wait that long? Time is important right now."

"Trust me, you don't want Dan finding out you're in the city. He'd probably kill you. Just wait until tomorrow morning."

Wade nodded and pulled his scarf back up, then watched me leave. I wasn't hanging around to talk. I could still hardly look at the guy without a pang of betrayal twinging in my gut.

Storm stuck close as we left the alley, watching Wade over his shoulder. I wound my fingers through the long hair on his back. I loved that he hated Wade.

Now for the interesting part. How did I always get myself into these situations? I'd done so well ignoring Jaden since we'd moved here. We had a good thing going. He'd know the second I asked to talk to him that something was up.

I trudged around an extra block to avoid the alley with Wade in it. Thankfully the city blocks were laid out well enough I didn't have to worry about getting lost. Storm slowly relaxed beside me.

"Jaden, I know we haven't really been talking..." Nah, why bring up the fact that I'd been ignoring him? "Jaden, I have a favor to ask..." Nope, that was wrong too. "Jaden, you know how you said if I ever needed anything just ask, since I helped you with your family and everything?" Better, but maybe leave the whole 'I saved your family' thing off the end.

I shifted my backpack. Storm looked up at me. "I know, it's not great, but it's all I've got. You got any better ideas?"

No answer.

"That's what I thought. This should be wonderful."

CHAPTER TWO

Nina was waiting for me in the parking lot when I got to our apartment complex. I ran up to the SUV and knocked on her window. "Can I drive, please?" I put on my best begging face. I'd finally gotten my permit, and I still needed a ton of hours. Plus, I could drive. How awesome was that? And I could use a little distraction right now.

"Not if you want to make it on time," Nina answered. "And you know how Mr. Nelson feels about people being late."

Shoot. She was right. I totally didn't want annoy Mr. Nelson. He'd put me up against one of the huge guys and I'd be too sore to make it to basketball practice tomorrow.

"Fine," I drew out, jogging around to the passenger side and jumping in.

Nina did a quick traffic check and pulled out, speeding a little.

"You're pretty late today. I had time to change and get back down before you even got here," Nina said, looking at me out of the corner of her eye.

Why did she always have to be so observant when it came to me?

"Yeah, sorry about that," I answered without offering an explanation.

I bounced in my seat, pretending to be excited about tonight when

I couldn't even begin to feel anything. Starren, about to be executed? My stomach rolled and I leaned my face against the cool window. Executed because I'd won that last fight, because she had failed. And it wasn't even like it was a fair fight. For some reason nature had stepped in, and it would have taken a whole lot more than Starren and Wade to stop me.

I forced my thoughts away from all that. Maybe Mr. Nelson would let us do sword work tonight. I was totally his best student when it came to that. So many years working with my mom had drilled all kinds of moves into my head, even ones he didn't have names for and didn't let me use. Ha. I knew they worked. They'd kept me alive against Starren and Wade. Would I have won? Absolutely not. But I'd been able to keep them off me until I came up with a different plan. Kind of.

The plants had been really quiet lately. No unusual plant activity. Ever since they had saved Jaden, Jaime, and me, I'd been keeping watch out of the corner of my eye, waiting for them to do something weird. Nothing strange had happened. But then, I hadn't really needed help either. I didn't mind the break. They still kind of creeped me out. Maybe they had some kind of rule about Sanctuary too.

"So, how was your day?" Nina asked, eyes on the road.

"Good. You?" I was actually starting to do polite stuff, like ask another person about their day. Sanctuary was doing weird things to me. Or maybe that part was from caring about people, it was a toss-up.

"Fine. No kidnappings or anything, so that's good." She smiled at me and I rolled my eyes.

The kidnapping thing had only happened once, and it was more than two months ago. She didn't need to keep bringing it back up.

We got to the dojo a minute ahead of schedule. Good thing too. Here in Sanctuary without my powers, pushups actually felt like punishment.

Splitting to go to our separate classes with a wave, I rushed down the hallway to my room. Mondays we separated according to ability. I didn't mind, since Wednesday and Friday we got to do class together. It gave Mr. Nelson the chance to do weapons training instead of just hand to hand. Maybe we'd use nunchucks today. I didn't care, it was all awesome. And I could use an outlet at the moment.

Three more crazy options for talking to Jaden went through my mind. Yeah, having a drone drop him a note probably wouldn't work well.

I slipped into the small changing room in the dojo and slid out of my school clothes and into my shorts and tank top. I shoved all the extra clothes into my bag and dropped it by the one other gym bag in the girl's changing room.

People were stretching when I pushed open the door and slipped inside. Rosie, the one other girl in my class, gave me a little wave. I moved over to stand by her. She was a couple years older than me, but still cool. It was too bad we lived on opposite sides of town, it would have been great to go to school together.

And I never would have thought I'd be saying that about anyone until the last month. Oh how life had changed, and in such a short time period.

"Hey! How was school today?" Rosie asked, leaning down in a stretch to touch her toes.

"Not bad." I shrugged. "Just school. How about you?" Here in Sanctuary, I could have these random chats with people. I could go to a self-defense class and get knocked around, and no one would know I was fae. Here, I was normal. And I was starting to love it. Just that short thought made up my mind on something I hadn't even known I was considering. I couldn't help Wade. Couldn't help Starren. Too much risk, not enough reward. I'd talk to Jaden, and that was it.

"Eh, just school. But some friends and I are going to a movie tonight, think your mom would let you come?"

I stopped mid-stretch and stared. Movie? With her and her friends? Like, I was actually invited to go to the movies with a group? Of seniors? Was she pranking me? She didn't seem like the type, but still, what other explanation could there be? A small smile escaped. That would totally help with where my mind was right now. I'd have plenty of time to talk with Jaden later.

"Ah, sure, I'll ask my... mom after class." Yeah, I hadn't gotten to the point where I was actually calling Nina mom. I had a mom out there somewhere, and it just felt weird. But I also didn't really want to explain the whole foster family thing and have it snowball from there to what had happened to my 'real' parents, et cetera, et cetera, forever and ever. Not something I liked getting into.

Nina would totally let me go though. She'd probably be super excited. She knew Rosie from class and really liked her. The three of us women had to stick together. We were the only females that hardcore came to classes.

We didn't get the chance to discuss anything further. Mr. Nelson stepped into the room and everything went quiet. He wasn't your typical movie dojo leader where everyone had to bow and all that stuff, but he did demand respect at all times and didn't have a hard time keeping it.

Just glancing at him you wouldn't think much. Especially when I'd seen him out and about in his street clothes. He looked so normal. Yeah, he was kind of built, but not in a body builder way or anything. But then, most people wouldn't expect much out of a sixteen year old girl either. They'd be surprised.

I was the youngest in the class, with Rosie being the closest in age. At first I hadn't even been allowed to meet Mr. Nelson, the lady at the desk had laughed when Nina had told her that we wanted in his class. We'd been thrown in the beginner class, but it wasn't long before we'd moved our way up.

Nina worked super hard, and we practiced together at home. Dan was all for it because he wanted to know we were safe, but he still gave us odd looks occasionally. At first I'd thought Nina just wanted to do it to have something to do with me, but since then I'd picked up on some of the things she'd said. I'd realized she was afraid we'd end up in the same situation we had back in November somehow, and she'd be no help again. I hadn't brought up the fact that no matter how many classes, if we were attacked by fae again, she wouldn't be able to do much. No one liked feeling helpless.

But that totally wasn't going to happen again. I was done with all things fae in my life, thankfully. Though the quick healing muscles would have been nice to have after class.

Class went by quickly. No nunchucks, but throwing stars were a pretty cool second.

"Ugh, maybe I shouldn't have scheduled that movie for tonight," Rosie said, throwing her gym bag with her sweaty clothes in it over her shoulder. We'd both taken five minutes to change. "You'd think I'd know better by now."

I wanted to laugh, but that would take nonexistent energy. "At least it's just sitting."

"True."

We made our way out into the hall. Nina was already there, waiting on me. "Hey, Rosie." She gave Rosie a huge smile. "How are you today?"

"I'm good, Mrs. Inza. I was wondering if Trish could come to a movie with me and some friends tonight. I know it's a school night, but I won't keep her out too late." Rosie beamed an irresistible smile at Nina.

Nina paused and looked my way. It took me a second to realize she was asking if I wanted to go or not, discreetly. We still hadn't worked all these signals out yet. "Please?" I asked. "I don't have any homework that has to be done tonight."

"You have your phone? And the movie is rated PG-13 or under?"

I rolled my eyes. She'd seen me take an arrow in the gut. Surely she couldn't worry about me going to see a movie with some human teenagers. "Yes, I have my phone."

"And the movie is PG, Mrs. Inza, I promise." There went Rosie's smile again. She was super convincing when she wanted to be.

"Okay, but be home by ten-thirty."

I jumped forward and gave Nina a hug, something else that was still a little foreign.

She grinned and hugged me back. After letting go, she slipped her purse off her shoulder and pulled out a twenty. "See you later. Have a good time."

After she left I turned to Rosie. "So. Do we have time to get something to eat?"

"We're actually grabbing something before the movie. How do you feel about pizza?"

"Doesn't everyone love pizza? Bring it on!"

Meeting Rosie's friends made my stomach hurt so bad I felt like I could puke. I was pretty much human now, but I was still really nervous with new people. Actually, maybe it was because I was human now. Now I cared more about having some friends, but talking to people other than Dan, Nina, Cray, and once in awhile Jaden still wasn't normal.

Thinking about Jaden just made my stomach turn more. Things were still really awkward between us. I didn't know how to act around him. He for sure knew I would have turned him in to save my own skin if I could have done it and figured out a way to keep Jaime safe.

But he'd never said anything.

He'd been the perfect gentleman about everything, acting like I hadn't tried to stab him in the back.

That just made being around him even harder for me. I avoided him as much as I could, and his family if possible. Okay, Jaime was too cute to be avoided, and I had to see Lucy every day, unfortunately, but I had a hard time looking Rebecca in the eye.

It had all worked out in the end great. But I'd seen what kind of person I was through the whole thing, and I didn't like it. On a good day I could convince myself that I wasn't so bad, I had helped get Jaime, Lucy, and Rebecca moved, and that had ruined a lot of stuff for me. But Jaden and I still both knew what I would have done to stay with Dan and Nina, and it wasn't pretty.

And now I had to ask him for a favor.

"Right?" Rosie bumped me.

Crap. Somehow I was still not paying attention and getting myself into situations. I hadn't even noticed that we'd pulled into a parking spot and she'd shut off the car.

"What?" I asked. I knew better now than to just go along with whatever she was saying.

Rosie rolled her eyes at me. "Movie theater popcorn is the best, right?"

"Oh, yeah," I could totally get on board with that. It was pretty great. "What are we going to see?"

"Some superhero movie. Mason picked it out."

Cue the hyperventilating. Actually caring what people thought of you really wasn't cool. Not that I'd ever completely not cared, but I'd been able to convince myself I didn't.

"So who all are we meeting again?" I asked for the tenth time. I wanted to have their names down.

Rosie rolled her eyes yet again. Hopefully she didn't regret asking a lowly sophomore along. She opened her car door and hopped out. "Mason, Les, and Grant."

I knew that. But I'd had to check. I jumped out behind her and hurried to catch up, running their names through my head one last time.

"Oh, there they are." Rosie waved to two guys and a girl over on the other sidewalk.

Okay, this was it, I could totally do this. I'd fought trolls, a hyran - well kind of on that one- goblins, and fae warriors. Nothing to worry about here.

One of the guys pushed off the wall and stuffed his hands into his pockets. "Hey, we were just talking, we should split up and you girls go get the pizza ordered. We'll get the tickets to make sure they don't sell out and meet you over there."

Then they noticed me.

"Who's your friend?" the other guy asked.

"Mason." Rosie nodded at the first guy, "Grant." She gestured toward the second guy, who was in ripped jeans and wearing his hat backward. "And Les."

"Hey," she said, and smiled. "You're from Rosie's fighting or what-ever class, right?"

I smiled back. "Yep. Three nights a week."

"That's awesome. I'd be there with you guys, but it's hard with varsity basketball all winter and track in the spring."

"I'd just kick your butt anyway," Rosie said, laughing.

One of the guys snorted and the other laughed loudly.

"She's got you there, Les." Grant said. "You guys ready to eat? I'm starving."

I was totally ready to eat. It didn't get as bad as it used to, back when I was out in the real world, but I was still a teenager and I'd still been working out for the last two hours. "I am definitely ready to eat."

"Nice. Meet you there in a few."

They broke off from our little group and headed toward the theater. It was pretty close to the apartment Dan, Nina, Cray, and I were staying in until they finished closing on the house they were trying to buy, so I'd been here a few times.

The three of us girls chatted while we got a table, and Rosie knew exactly what to order for the guys. It was odd, being a part of a group like this. My palms were still sweating, but I was starting to relax. A little. And this was totally the distraction I needed. I hadn't thought about Wade in... shoot. Scratch that.

"Hey, check out that guy by the counter," Les said, elbowing Rosie. "He's super hot."

I should have known right then and there who it was. I kind of did, but I was so hoping I was wrong. A quick peek over my shoulder confirmed my fears. Jaden, in all his ripped jean, faded t-shirt, black-haired, dark-eyed glory. I sunk down in my seat.

Their apartment was in the building next to ours. And they got pizza all the time. I should have guessed that this could happen. I sunk down in the seat a little more, willing him to not notice me. And for the guys to take longer getting the tickets. I didn't know why it mattered so much, but it did. It'd be okay. He'd only be here like a minute.

At least with Leslie along this didn't look like a double date, me and Mason or Grant and whichever one with Rosie. It totally wasn't. It wasn't a date at all. But why did that matter?

Of course, he pulled out his wallet to pay and looked straight in my direction. He lifted a hand in a kind of wave thing. Both girls whipped their gaze toward me.

"You know that guy?" Les whisper/shouted.

I nodded.

"How?" Rosie asked.

I didn't get to answer, because Jaden started our way, slipping in between the crowded tables.

Great. Just great.

"Hey Trish, how's it going?" He nodded a hello at the other two girls. And I felt like a jerk for not wanting to see him. I'd been avoiding him for the last two months since we'd moved here, and he definitely knew it.

"Uh, it's going good," I said, not really knowing what to add.

"Just picking up pizza for Mom and the girls," he put in, when the silence got awkward. "You know how much Jaime loves pizza."

The girls were still just staring. I kicked Rosie under the table and she mock glared at me. I hope it was just a mock glare. This better not ruin my chance of making some friends.

I smiled at him but I felt like it came off more as a grimace. "She sure does." Was that my voice? Going all weird?

"Catch you later, then," Jaden said. He didn't make a move to leave though, until I met his eyes and he smiled at me.

"Yeah, catch you later."

He got two steps away before I remembered I needed him.

"Hey, Jaden?"

He turned back, a smile on his face.

"Can I talk with you later?"

His smile widened a little. "Of course. Just text me." Then he nodded at us and left.

As he walked off back toward the counter. Rosie elbowed me in the ribs. Hard. "Who was that?" she practically squealed.

"Yeah, Trish, dish. He's hot," Leslie added.

I was really glad the boys weren't here. That would make this even more embarrassing than it already was. Though maybe the girls wouldn't be making a big deal out of things if the guys were here. Nah. They probably wouldn't care.

"He's the son of one of my mom's friends." Keep it short and sweet.

"Really," Les said, twisting around in her seat to watch him walk out. "Is he single?"

I shrugged. "I guess. We don't talk much."

Rosie laughed. "You're crazy. I'd talk to him all the time."

Just then the waiter walked up with our pizza, slid it on the table, and asked about refills. The boys were right behind him with the movie tickets.

Jaden was grabbing his pizza at the counter, and watched the boys slide into the booth with us girls. When he caught me looking, he nodded one more time, his face expressionless. Finally he finished at the counter and walked out the door.

Crap.

"Who was that?" Mason asked, grabbing a slice of pizza and plopping it down on his plate.

"Oh just some guy Trish knows," Rosie answered, giving me a look.

"Can I talk with you later?" Les said in a high voice, fluttering her eyelashes.

I could feel my face start to flush. "It isn't like that. Can we talk about something else? Please?"

Rosie raised an eyebrow, but dropped the conversation.

The guys started in about how excited they were about the movie, and I got a reprieve from talking about Jaden. Why didn't I want to talk about him so bad? It wasn't like I was just going to bring up how I'd tried to capture him and turn him over to his enemies or anything. We could be friends. Totally.

Pizza and the movie went really well. It did feel weird watching a superhero movie now though, especially with other teens. I had weird powers like that, what would they think if they knew? I'd never find out, and I was totally okay with that. It was one thing for people to think it was cool on the big screen, another thing entirely when it came to real life.

On the ride home I somehow managed to dodge Rosie's questions about Jaden. I didn't have anything figured out myself, I definitely wasn't ready to share.

Someday I'd have the courage to sit down and go through all those emotions. Someday. But not today.

Since I had until the next day to get back with Wade, naturally I procrastinated talking with Jaden. I got home from the movie far earlier than I would have liked. Homework suddenly didn't seem like such a terrible thing. Unfortunately I didn't have any.

It took Nina all of five minutes of me being home to notice something was off. "You're pretty quiet today, Trish, something happen at school?"

"No," I answered, glad that Wade had caught me off the school grounds since I couldn't lie. No fae could. Which none of us appreciated.

She glanced at Cray like maybe he'd be a little more forth-coming. He shrugged.

"Is today the anniversary of something I don't know about?"

"No, nothing like that." They had waited to have supper, not knowing if I'd eaten or not. I dug at my food, not really hungry even though Nina had made awesome mashed potatoes.

"So that's not it, but something is wrong?" Dan asked from the other end of the table.

I sighed. This was one of the bad things about getting closer to my foster parents. They always wanted to talk feelings and stuff. I didn't have an answer, so I just kept quiet. How terrible of a person was I, that I couldn't face my guilt enough to talk with Jaden, even to save someone's life? I had to do this. Might as well get it over with.

"May I be excused? I need to run over to the Martan's for a few minutes."

Dan cocked his head, considering me for a second. I met his eyes and willed my face to relax. He glanced over at Nina, but she didn't seem to notice because she was studying me intently. Cray just looked confused.

"Sure, honey, but don't stay late. School tomorrow."

"Thanks," I mumbled, shoving my chair back from the table. I should have just gotten this done earlier, stopped by after school and not raised suspicion, then just skipped the gym. But he probably would have been at work, and if I was more than five minutes late from anything, Nina freaked out. Not that I could blame her, with past history and all that.

I shrugged on my coat and buried my hands in my pockets, trudging down the stairs from the apartment. Part of me hoped Storm had waited around, but like usual, as soon as I went in, he was gone until the next time I was going to feed him.

The short walk to the Martan's went faster than it ever had before, even with me dragging my feet. Maybe Jaden wouldn't be home. Maybe he was out with friends or something.

Yeah, right.

They were on the sixth floor, but I didn't take the elevator. All too soon I was at their front door. Somehow this seemed more difficult than fighting a troll at the moment. No matter how strong the urge to run the other way kept hitting me, I couldn't just let Starren die.

I took a deep breath and knocked on the door, only a slight pause with my hand hanging in the air.

There was some yelling inside while people decided who had to go answer it, and then the door popped open. Lucy. Of course.

"Hey," I said. It came out rather stiffly.

"Hey," she said back, her voice betraying her surprise.

"I need to talk to Jaden."

Her face got all suspicious then, and even more grumpy than normal. "Why?"

"Wouldn't you like to know. Just tell him I'm here."

She narrowed her eyes at me, staring me down for a second. I made sure I didn't flinch.

"Jade, Trish is here," she yelled, not taking her eyes off me.

Seriously, what did she think I was going to do, push past her and murder her family? As far as she knew, all I'd ever done was help.

"Trish, hey." Jaden shouldered Lucy out of the way. His smile made the butterflies in my stomach erupt into a molten volcano. Poor butterflies.

"Hey," I answered. Super brilliant. "Can we talk for a minute?" I pointedly looked over his shoulder at the little sister who had not moved. "In private?"

He smiled again. "Sure, let me grab my coat."

The smiling would be over as soon as he found out why I was here. Understandably, he was not a fan of Wade or Starren. I didn't actually know which one he disliked more, but he definitely would not want to help them under normal circumstances. But with a life at stake? Hopefully. He was a good guy, after all.

He was only gone a couple seconds before coming back with his coat and hat. I moved out of the way to let him pass. He headed for the stairs.

"It won't take long," I called after him, staying right where I was.

"That's okay, we can just take a quick walk."

Right, that's exactly what I wanted to happen.

He nodded toward the still open door, with Lucy leaning against the frame. "You said you wanted privacy."

Ugh. Privacy was a must. I so didn't want Lucy finding out about this. But I so didn't want to go on a walk with Jaden either. "Fine."

I followed him and he fell in step beside me. I heard Lucy harrumph and shut the door rather forcefully behind us as we made for the stairwell in silence.

Downstairs, Jaden held the door for me, and we were outside. He put his hands in his pockets right away and gave me a sheepish smile. "California boy."

I didn't know how to answer. I didn't want to chit-chat, I just wanted this over with. Jaden was kind and sweet, and always made the right decisions. Being around him just made me feel the twist of guilt over and over. I'd been willing to ruin his family to get what I needed. How could he forgive that when I couldn't?

We went a block with me checking behind us now and then to make sure we weren't being followed. By Lucy or, worse, Wade.

"So, I have something to ask you," I said, as casually as I could.

"Shoot," Jaden answered, studying his worn tennis shoes.

"How did you get here from Faerie, back in the fall?"

His head shot up and he studied my face. "Why?"

"Eh, long story," I evaded.

He stopped and I looked away to avoid his intense gaze.

"Trish."

I ignored him.

"Why?"

So he obviously wasn't going to tell me without a reason. And lying didn't work. I'd just have to rely on the fact that he was a really good guy and hope that he didn't blow me off.

"Starren got herself into some trouble, and Wade wants to save her. But he can't get back in any of the normal channels."

"What!" Jaden yelled.

I looked around us. No one in sight. "Keep your voice down," I snapped. "It didn't help us any to come down here if Lucy can hear you all the way from the apartment."

"What?" He growled it this time.

I liked the yelling better.

"You've been in contact with him? Do you know how dangerous that is? He's crazy, Trish. You should know that better than anyone. He killed you while you were dating."

"Tried to," I corrected. "We don't really know if I died or not."

"Oh, because that makes such a big difference." He jerked away from me, his body rigid. "You know what they tried to do to my family. Now you want me to help them?"

"You don't have to help them," I answered, my voice rising to meet his. "Just tell Wade how to get there to help her. They're going to execute her, Jaden, and part of it is because she helped us at that gas station!"

He raked his hand through his hair, obviously still angry.

"You don't have to do anything except tell me where the breach is so he can get through. Then we're done."

He narrowed his eyes at me, looking surprisingly like Lucy. "Then 'we' are done? You'll be totally out of this situation too?"

I nodded. I wasn't going to Faerie. No way.

He moved in close to me, leaning over enough that I had to lean back a little. "Fine. But I'm with you when you talk with Wade from now on. I don't think you should be alone with him."

"But—"

"No buts." The growling had gone down to a rumble, but he obviously still wasn't very happy with me. "It's me, or I tell Nina about the meeting so she can go."

I gulped. "No Nina," I got out. She'd never let me out of her sight again if she knew Wade had been in town.

"When's the meeting?" Now Jaden just sounded sad.

It made me feel bad. He'd been so happy to see me. "Tomorrow morning, in an alley close to my school."

"I'll pick you up in the morning and take you to school. And I'll only tell Wade to his face where the tunnel is."

"But—"

"Nope. I said no buts. I'm only telling Wade. I'm not telling you and having you change the time or place and cut me out. You shouldn't be around him. He's dangerous. And I know you. You have a good heart. He might convince you to go help."

"I'm not going. Me being there wouldn't change the outcome. And I can take care of myself," I muttered the last part, not sure if I should be happy he wanted to take care of me or terrified that he was going to actually meet Wade for the first time on somewhat good terms, instead of fighting with him or being captured by him. Oh yes, this could get interesting.

"I know," Jaden said. "Not only did you take care of yourself, but you took care of my family, and Nina too. But you shouldn't have to. Everyone needs someone in their corner."

"I have Dan and Nina." And I did. But I could always use more, and I wasn't sure why I was being so contrary other than the fact that I had a hard time believing he could have forgiven me, and I was waiting for him to figure out he should be mad.

Jaden's face closed off. "True. But you don't want them involved in this, so I'm stepping in. End of story."

I huffed, but he was right. Absolutely no Dan and Nina.

Jaden quietly walked me back to my apartment building. We didn't say a word until we got there, and then it was just goodbye. Even here in this new place, the fae were managing to mess up my life.

CHAPTER THREE

Per usual, Nina was making breakfast when I got out of bed. Not per usual, I had no problem waking up. I badly wanted to just skip over the next hour of my life. That would be really wonderful.

I ate my breakfast quickly.

"What's the hurry there, kid?" Dan asked from behind whatever book he was reading now.

I ignored the question. I so did not want him to know what the problem was.

I was past thinking he'd try to turn me in to get experimented on, because of the obvious reason that he hadn't done it, even if he hadn't seen me do anything out of the ordinary yet. But I didn't trust him to not go after Wade. Wade who he'd disliked when he thought he was just a normal guy I was dating. Wade who he'd disliked a whole lot more when they'd come to pick me up in the wilderness. Wade who he'd wanted to kill when Nina told him the whole story about what had happened on our trip from Chicago to Fort Wayne and the fiasco the day after.

Yeah, probably better to keep this meeting to myself.

"Jaden offered to give me a ride to school today," I said, changing the subject. "Is that okay?"

Dan took a swig of his coffee, raising his eyebrows at Nina across the table. She looked so excited she could burst. Why was she so happy?

"That's great, honey! Jaden's a really good guy."

Oh no, I could see where this was going. They still didn't know about the whole me-turning-Jaden-in-to-save-my-own-skin thing, and they sure weren't finding out now just when things were really settling into a normal life.

"Don't get your hopes up," I muttered.

Nina dialed back the excitement, but it still seeped out at a pretty hefty rate.

"Couldn't possibly be worse than your last boyfriend," Dan grunted. "Every father's worst nightmare come to life. Good thing that guy won't be showing his face around here again."

Well that just emphasized how badly I needed to keep this whole thing from them.

I loved how he just said father without having to think about it. We hadn't had the bonding that Nina and I had, but Dan was a good guy. I was starting to like having a father.

And it was easier to think of him as my father than it had been to start thinking of Nina as a mother figure. I'd had a mother, but never met my deadbeat dad. My mom had literally never mentioned him, and that was enough for me. I didn't care if I ever met the guy. Though I was a little curious. Couldn't help it.

I finished the last swig of orange juice, shoveled in my last bite of eggs, triple checked that my sword was still hanging on my back, and jumped up to grab my coat. I headed out the door before remembering that Nina had taken the time to cook for me. I rolled my eyes at myself. Look what I was becoming.

"Thanks for breakfast," I yelled back into the apartment, then bolted for the stairs. Suddenly I just wanted this to be over. To be done. Every time I thought I was done with all of that life, something came up again.

Jaden was sitting in his little junker downstairs. His family couldn't afford any better. Though that would change soon, hopefully, with both Jaden and Rebecca working. He'd been so excited to get a pickup.

I'd been expecting something a little more... more when I'd first seen it.

"Hey," he said when I opened the door.

"Hey," I answered, not really sure where to go from there.

We rode in silence. I felt bad about fighting yesterday, but I didn't know what his problem was.

The alley wasn't far. Which was good. And bad.

"Park out here," I told Jaden. Wade would spook easily at this point. "I'll go in first and talk to him, then you can come in."

"Nope." Jaden unclipped his seatbelt and opened his truck door.

I sighed and got out of the truck.

"Just remember I'm doing this to help you, Trish, not him, and not Starren."

"Thanks." I huddled into my coat as we made for the alley. The wind ripped through my clothes. Not unusual around here, but hopefully not some kind of omen or anything.

Speaking of omens... Had Jaden seen something? Was that why he was being so weird? His visions were still few and far between, but always accurate when they did come. But he couldn't have a vision inside Sanctuary, right? I actually didn't know how that worked, and it would be weird to ask him now.

I walked awkwardly, unsure how close I should be to Jaden as we moved into the alley.

And then there was Storm, jogging toward us without even seeming to notice the cold.

"Stormy!" I bent down and scratched behind his ears. "What are you doing here?"

"You know this... thing?" Jaden asked, his voice not normal.

"Hey! Don't insult him!" I whacked Jaden on the shoulder. "He can't help it. He doesn't have anyone looking out for him but me."

"You?" Jaden asked, lifting an eyebrow.

"Yeah, so? What's wrong with that?"

"You just don't seem like the type." He knelt down. "Here, boy." He reached out a hand and tried to pet Storm, but Storm snapped at his fingers and started growling.

I laughed so hard I nearly peed my pants. "I don't think he likes you," I got out between breaths.

"Ah, yeah, I got that." Jaden stuffed his hands in his pockets and stood, moving out of Storm's reach. "Where'd you find that thing anyway?"

"He found me, actually." I fluffed up some of his matted hair and picked at a tangle. "We're best friends now," I said in a sing songy kid's voice.

"Yeah. Your best friend doesn't like me much."

"That's okay. He didn't like Wade either." The thought made me grin.

"Good dog," Jaden said. "I forgive you trying to bite me."

We smiled at each other and it felt like the first good moment we'd had since we got to Fort Wayne.

"Am I interrupting something?" Wade asked from the shadows, definitely interrupting something. What, I didn't know, but something.

Jaden's face instantly changed. I couldn't really blame him. If I hadn't known Starren and Wade before they'd taken Jaime, I'd probably hate them too. As it was I just had really mixed emotions. I knew what the Council had held over my head to get me to cooperate. Being torn away from one's family was good incentive. But what had they threatened Wade and Starren with?

I reached out and squeezed Jaden's arm instinctively. Bad move, because Wade noticed and his eyes narrowed.

"What is he doing here?" Wade asked, body going defensive.

"He wouldn't just tell me. He wanted to come in person."

"Yeah? So you can get revenge for your family?" Wade asked.

Well I hadn't even thought of that. Jaden was mad about Wade's involvement with his sister's kidnapping, but he was a good guy. He wouldn't just attack another person unprovoked. Right?

"Not unless you get too close," Jaden ground out. Okay, I'd seen him sad before, and elated, but this angry was different than any emotion he'd let show in the past. When they'd taken Jaime, he'd been resigned. Now he was just plain furious.

"Let's get this over with then." Wade ignored Jaden, looking straight at me. "How do I find the portal you used to get back to Earth from Faerie?"

"Is this some kind of trap?" Jaden asked.

Wade eyed Jaden for a second, his posture loosening a little. "No."

"Are you truly using this tunnel to get back to help Starren?"

"Yes."

Okay, Jaden was using the no lying thing to his advantage, instead of just trusting my instincts. I couldn't blame him. The last time I'd trusted Wade I'd ended up dead in the woods. It wouldn't happen again.

"It's at the Red Rocks Amphitheatre, in Colorado. You'd best get a move on it. It's a long trip and you don't have a portal to just jump you there."

Wade eyed him for a second, like he was thinking something over. "How'd you make it to Chicago from there?"

Well that was interesting. I'd never really thought about how he'd gotten to Chicago from the tunnel before. But then, I hadn't known where it was either.

"I was invisible. I checked people's license plates and hoped they were going toward home and not going on vacation."

"Is that all you need?" I asked Wade. It felt weird, being the calm one in a conversation involving him. But if he was going on a suicide mission...

He stared at me for a second, like he was trying to decide something. "Can we talk alone for a second?"

I didn't really want to talk with him alone. But I didn't really know if what he wanted to say was in front of Jaden appropriate. What if he wanted to talk about when we were dating or something?

"Jaden?" I said.

He considered Wade for a second. "I'll do what you want, but I'd rather stay right here." He didn't take his eyes off Wade. I couldn't blame him. "Go ahead," I told Wade, crossing my arms. I couldn't think of anything I didn't want him to say in front of Jaden. Jaden already knew the things I'd done. Knew that deep down, no matter what Nina thought, I wasn't a good person. I was selfish.

"There's something you need to know, Trish."

I rolled my eyes. "If you're going to tell me again that you actually loved me, or that you had to kill me and didn't have a choice, I'm going to barf."

He looked sad then, even more sad than before, which was saying a lot. "Nothing like that. There's just something you should know. In case this doesn't go well." Wade sounded serious. But he had since we ran into each other yesterday. That wasn't normal. I really didn't want to have this conversation though, because I was starting to feel a little guilty about letting him do this by himself. They were probably both going to die. I just reminded myself once again, that going along wouldn't change that. Maybe I could try to convince Wade to not throw his life away.

I stared at him for a second. Nope. He was as stubborn as they came.

"Stop trying to manipulate her," Jaden growled, inching between us.

I shoved him back. "Say what you need to say Wade. I have to get to school."

"Chances are good we won't make it out of this."

Here we went with the whole he didn't want to kill me thing. My spine stiffened and I felt my face tense up.

"So I want you to know, even though she didn't."

Wait, Starren didn't want me to know?

"She's your sister, Trish. Your full-blooded sister."

CHAPTER FOUR

"We didn't know for sure at first."

My head reeled as I struggled to keep up with what he was saying. A sister? An actual, real sister? I had live family? Jaden put a strong hand on my shoulder, giving me his support.

"That's why she petitioned so hard to have you put on our team. The Council just wanted to have you collected after trying to send you to the school didn't work."

I didn't even have the emotional energy to be mad when he mentioned trying to kill me so casually. A sister? I had an older sister? And it was Starren? What?

"She convinced them to let you work with us so she could keep an eye on you and learn more about you, without telling them who she suspected you were. She'd been looking for signs of you or your mom for years. And she gave herself as collateral."

My sister had been trying to find me. For years. Even if my mom hadn't wanted me, my sister had.

Part of me didn't believe him. It just didn't seem real. But deep in my gut, I somehow knew it was true. And Wade wouldn't be letting all this spill unless he had a reason. He couldn't be lying, and he was telling me too much to be hiding an ulterior motive.

"The Council agreed. She was their top agent, their golden girl. But now that she used her position to find you and then failed to bring you in…"

Starren was my sister, and she was about to die because of me. All of the weird questions she'd asked when we were working together made sense now. All of the times she'd asked about my parents and all that.

"Trish?" Wade asked. "Are you listening?"

"Yes," I croaked out. Starren was in trouble. "Did she ever find my mom?"

Wade glanced away, not meeting my eyes. "No. No trace so far."

I couldn't even let that disappoint me. She'd left me. But my sister had been looking for me. "Does she know our dad?"

"We didn't talk about that much," Wade answered. It was vague enough to be an evasion, but I could only focus on one family member at a time.

"I'm going with you," I said. Then panicked internally. Faerie was a terrible place. The few fae I'd met were horrible, willing to stab a friend in the back, just for amusement. Or even worse, they were creatures that enjoyed death and pain. What was I thinking?

"What?" Jaden asked from behind me. "Just like that? What about your new family?"

Dan and Nina. Obviously Faerie was no place for them, especially when I was a criminal going to help break out another criminal. I waffled for a second. Dan and Nina were my family now too. How could I just leave them and probably not come back? It took me another few seconds. I loved them, that went without saying, but I needed answers.

"They'll understand." They probably wouldn't. But I could hope. "How are we going to get there?"

Jaden put his hands on my shoulders and leaned over, staring me down. "Are you sure about this?"

"Wouldn't you do it for Jaime? Or even Lucy?"

"That's different and you know it. We grew up as a family."

"So you're saying because I didn't grow up with Dan and Nina they aren't my family?" I was twisting things around, but I didn't care at the moment. I had a real sister, and the only way she'd ever die was if I was already dead. Or of old age, but I wasn't going to go there until it was about to happen. I looked around Jaden to Wade. "What's your plan for getting there?"

Wade shrugged. "You're the one that's good with Earth."

I looked to Jaden, who was still staring me down. "You're going to go, no matter what, aren't you," he said. It didn't come out as a question. He let go of my shoulders and stepped back. "We can take my pickup. But I'm only going as far as the tunnel." He shuddered. "I'm not going back to Faerie."

"Are you sure?" I asked. It was a lot. Putting himself in danger for me was one thing. Stuck in a vehicle with Wade forever was another.

He nodded, giving me the ghost of a smirk. "I owe you one, remember? Probably two, actually."

I smiled back. Awkwardness aside, I'd feel much better if he was along.

"Okay then. Skipping school today, I guess. I'll run home and grab some stuff. Dan will be at work and Nina will have left for Hope and Haven. She volunteers there in the mornings." So yes, there were a couple things I wanted to get. But mostly, I wanted to walk through our apartment one more time. Just in case.

"Let's go then. I'll drop you off and make a quick trip to my place," Jaden said.

The ride back to the apartment was silent. Quiet enough that my internal freak out meter skyrocketed before we'd even made it half way.

Jaden pulled up to the curb at the apartment. I hopped out. Wade's door opened, but he closed it again after Jaden glared at him. Probably better anyway, just in case Dan or Nina was home for some reason.

I'd hate to see what Dan would do to Wade, given the chance. Dan was a great guy. He'd done so much for me. He had taken me in, along with Nina of course, and always treated me like I was actually his daughter. And he was pretty forgiving. At least when it came to my multiple screw-ups. But be okay with Wade after he'd shot me? Yeah, that would probably never happen.

Coast was clear. No one was home. I shoved down a twinge of

disappointment even though getting my stuff without them here would be so much easier. I grabbed my phone charger, a couple changes of clothes, flashlights, and a kitchen knife. You never knew when a sword wouldn't be enough. What else did one take on a quest? I should know by now. Oh, a sleeping bag!

And now I had to decide what to do about Dana and Nina. Great. I couldn't exactly call and tell them I was running off to a mystical land on a suicide mission to save my long lost sister because they totally wouldn't go for that.

Which meant I'd be leaving a note. Writing said note was more difficult than I'd thought it would be. Trying to give the facts, not be mushy, and make them understand there was a good chance I wouldn't be coming back? And doing it without making Nina freak out. Who was I kidding. Of course Nina was going to freak out.

Nina-

Nope, that wouldn't work. I crumpled up the paper and started over.

Dan and Nina-

Great start, but now what? The truth, though I still wasn't really good at that.

Sorry that I'm running off on you again, and that I didn't tell you about this in person. I trust you both completely, but I was kinda afraid you wouldn't let me go. Okay, I know you wouldn't let me go, if it was up to you. But I have to. Oh, I haven't told you where yet! I found out Starren is my sister. Who knew? Not me! She's in trouble and I have to try to help. To be honest, I'm not sure this is going to go well. I've never been to Faerie, but you know how I feel about the place. Oh yeah, she's in trouble in Faerie. Anyway, I'm not sure how this will go, so I just wanted to say that I-

Okay, what exactly did I want to say? This whole completely honest thing wasn't cool.

...appreciate all that you've done for me. I couldn't have asked for better parents.

Love, Trish

Did I really just sign that letter with love? Okay, I totally did. No time to redo it now. That's why I was leaving it on there. Of course that was the reason.

Jaden and Wade were already sitting at the curb in sullen silence when I came downstairs. Jaden must have buzzed through grabbing stuff at his place. It wasn't because it had taken forever for me to figure out what to write in that stupid note. Nope, not that at all.

Angry male vibes filled the truck. It was going to be a lovely ride to Denver.

I jumped in the front seat and pulled out my phone. Have a nice day! I typed to send to Nina. Then I figured out that was way out of character and deleted it. But even if it was out of character, so what? It wasn't like she could stop me now. I typed it in again and hit send before I could change my mind, then flipped over my phone and took out the battery. I'd seen enough TV to know what could be done with a phone, and Dan did work in the government somewhere.

It would be lunch before Cray knew I wasn't at school. Plenty of time to get away. He'd probably call Nina, but she would have already found the note by then.

I swiped at my nose.

"What?" I asked Wade, who was staring at me. "It's running from the cold." We both knew that wasn't completely true, but he let it slide. We needed to go before I burst into tears over the fact that I was leaving.

I settled in to ignore the boys as Jaden eased out onto the road and started toward the highway.

We zipped along for a few minutes before Jaden dared to break the silence. "Sorry Trish, but you're going to have to drive once we get close to the Sanctuary border."

Crap. I hadn't even thought of that. He was going to be invisible.

"You want to let her drive?" Wade asked.

"I trust her more than I trust you," Jaden fired back.

"Ah, might be better to let him have this one," I said. "Wade was here for years and driving, and I just started driver's ed."

Jaden's shoulders were rigid as he processed. "Fine," he said eventually. He gave Wade the side-eye as if to say he'd be watching him.

We stopped a mile out from the line and switched drivers. Crossing the border both freaked me out and made me feel whole again. The second we passed it, my body went back to full strength. I felt myself grinning like an idiot, but I didn't care. Then I looked over my shoulder at Jaden. He didn't look any different to me, but his whole demeanor was different. Being a ghost couldn't be fun. Dying on Earth meant he was only here in spirit, unless he was inside Sanctuary.

"We only have so long before bounty hunters figure out you aren't in Sanctuary anymore, and start looking," Wade said from the driver's seat. "We need to make this trip as quickly as possible."

"Fine then. Drive."

"How long is this going to take?" Wade asked.

Jaden shoved some papers through the seats without saying anything. I took them. Directions. Kind of important.

"Good thinking, Jaden."

He gave me a half smile but didn't say anything.

"Looks like it will take us about eighteen hours, just in drive time," I said. "Add what, another two hours for gas and bathroom breaks?"

"Sounds about right," Jaden said.

"How big is the time difference?" Something I'd learned to worry about with the last fiasco we'd been a part of.

"Two hours. That should put us there in the really early morning, like three am. Which is good. No one will be around."

The trip was, in a word, boring. The guys didn't want to talk to each other, and I didn't feel like playing peacemaker. That definitely was not in my skill set. So we drove. And drove. And then we hit huge open road and Wade made me drive. I wasn't happy, but it was better than stopping to let him sleep. I stayed well under the speed limit to make sure I didn't get pulled over.

Thankfully Jaden had thought ahead and brought cash for the gas stations. I had an emergency card that Nina let me carry, but we obviously couldn't use that. As much as I kept expecting something to go wrong, like a biker gang of goblins or a super hot bounty hunter, the trip went really smoothly.

We switched off napping and driving several times. Eventually Wade was lightly snoring in the back, and Jaden and I were in the front. I'd finally relaxed about this whole driving thing, and decided I wasn't going to accidentally kill us all.

"You look much happier," Jaden said from where he was slumped against the passenger side door.

"Give me a break. I'd never drove without Nina before. I wasn't sure how it would go."

"I wasn't worried." He closed his eyes and settled in even deeper.

"Thanks," I said, and meant it.

He opened one eye and smirked. "I already died here once. Can't happen again, so I wasn't worried at all."

I took my eyes off the road for a second to slug him. He laughed and closed his eyes again.

"Jade?" I asked after a second, using the name Jaime always called him.

"Yeah?"

"You've been to Faerie before. You made it out. What do you think the chances are of us getting Starren free?"

His face went grim, and he opened his eyes to look at me. "Not good, Trish. Really not good."

I slumped a little against the wheel. I knew that. I'd known it since the second I'd decided to come, or even before that when Wade was going to come without me. But it made it worse to hear it from him. He was normally pretty optimistic.

"Thanks," I whispered, not really knowing what else to say.

He grunted and settled in to sleep.

Jaden, as usual, was spot on. We pulled into the parking lot for the Red Rocks Amphitheatre at 3:12 am.

"This it?" Wade mumbled from the back when the truck creaked to a stop.

"Yep, this is it." I unbuckled my seat belt but didn't make a move for the door yet. This really was it. The point of no return. If I got to Faerie and changed my mind, it'd be a whole lot harder to get home than it was if I just turned around right now.

Faerie. My stomach churned in my gut. Until now I'd just been thinking about Starren being my sister and everything that meant. But Faerie... I was going there for the first time ever. That I could remember, anyway. What was it really like? Did it hold all the horrors my mom seemed to think it did? Weird monsters, evil fae that liked to pretend they were your friend and then eat you. Even the ones that looked like kids couldn't be trusted, because they usually weren't, according to Mom's stories.

I'd find out soon enough if they were true or not.

"Well. No time like the present, right? We don't want someone catching us here while the place is closed."

"Trish, you should stay here," Wade said.

Jaden looked like he was about to argue, then figured out what Wade had said and snapped his mouth closed.

"I don't want you to actually come to Faerie with me. I just want you to show me the entrance to the tunnel and let me go. I got this."

I cocked my head and squinted at him. "Then why did you tell me about Starren?"

A weird look came across his face. "I just thought you should know. And it was probably your last chance of finding out."

"Do you know what it was like, growing up with no sense of belonging at all?"

Wade just blinked at me, like he didn't follow where I was going with this.

"Of course you don't. You grew up in Faerie, with all your little fae friends. I grew up on Earth, drug around by my mom and then dropped off at a human children's home. Do you know how out of place that makes a person feel? Like there no one out there that wants them? No one that cares? Fae or human."

He just blinked faster, more confused.

"If I'd have known I had a sister, maybe things would have been different. And now that I know I have one, do you really think I'm just going to let her die before I can ask her things? Things like how well did she know our mom? When was the last time she's seen her? Why did our mom go on the run in the first place? This is my only chance to get answers to the first ten years of my life. And I want to know."

Wade reached back and rubbed his neck. "Okay, I can get that. I just don't know that you're going to get any answers, even if we get to Starren."

I just lifted an eyebrow.

"Okay. Your choice. You ready then?"

"What about your family now, Trish?" Jaden broke his silence. "You belong now. Isn't that enough?"

"Don't try to make me feel guilty, Jaden. You have no idea what it's like to grow up unloved. You had an entire family. I had no one. I need to know why." Did Mom abandon Starren too? Was it a choice she made, or had it been the only option? I was suddenly desperate to know. "Get us to the entrance, Jaden, then you can leave."

He crossed his arms. "And how am I supposed to do that?"

Crap, Jaden couldn't drive. It was a long trip and at some point it was inevitable that another person would notice the truck looked like it was driving itself. I didn't think this part through. "Uh, good question." I looked back and forth between the boys. "Suggestions?"

"It doesn't matter." Jaden scrubbed his face with his hands. "I'm coming with you."

"Ah, no. The Council wants you. You're really not safe there."

He snorted and started walking up the path. Wade looked at me, then went after him, leaving me to throw my hands up in the air and jog to catch up.

"Jaden, I'm serious," I called, trying not to be too loud.

"Yeah, I got that. But I'm not letting you go to Faerie alone. The Council wants you now, about as much as they want me, and that's partially my fault." He wheeled around. "Can we have a minute?" he asked Wade.

Wade cocked his head. "Trish?"

I nodded and he moved farther up the trail, keeping an eye on us.

"In a way it's my fault you're stuck in Sanctuary."

He couldn't mean that, could he? I opened my mouth to argue, but he held up his hand.

"If I'd turned myself in the first time, like we had agreed, you wouldn't be in all this mess."

"But the girls-"

"Would probably be dead right now, so I made the right choice. But that doesn't change the fact that I kind of ruined your life. I'm going."

I glared at him a second, to see if he would change his mind. He raised an eyebrow, but didn't budge.

"Fine." I softened a little. "Thank you. But your family already lost you once, when we get to where it's too dangerous, you're going back."

"Once I get to where I deem it too dangerous, I'll go back."

I squinted at him. "Ah no, not good enough. When I think it's too dangerous, you'll go back."

He laughed, the sound echoing in the Amphitheatre. "No. You could send me back right now. And you have no way of stopping me from going with you, so there's no reason for me to make that kind of promise."

Shoot. He was right. It wasn't like I could tie him up or anything. Even if I got Wade to help me get the drop on him and trap him some-where, Jaden could die because no one would find him and untie him, with the whole humans couldn't see him thing. And the fae would love to find him giftwrapped like that.

"Ugh," I said, throwing my phone in the car, and taking off after Wade.

Too much walking later, we got to the top of the stairs and looked down over all the seats. Even with just the light of the full moon, it was an amazing sight. The sky looked huge here, the starlight shining down on the stone just right. No wonder it was such a popular place.

"We have to go around back," Jaden said, taking the lead from Wade.

Wade gave me a funny look, then eyed Jaden, like he was trying to say something without words.

I ignored him and followed Jaden.

Regenerating was really helpful right now. It was a nice hike, distance wise. And it would have been a great hike atmosphere wise, under different circumstances.

We got around back and headed for a huge pile of the red rocks.

"The cave is back there?" Wade asked.

"Yeah," Jaden answered, sounding annoyed.

Inching around a boulder on a tiny path that wasn't meant to be a path made me rethink this whole thing. Okay, it wasn't really because of that. I'd been rethinking it since I'd decided to come. When I'd found out what was going on with Starren, I'd wanted to do something, but known I couldn't do anything. Once I'd found out she was my sister...

We got around the boulders and started across a small open area, littered with chunks of rock. What was with this place and rocks. Sheesh.

"There it is." Jaden nodded toward a dark spot in the rocks.

Here we were. About to step into Faerie. It hadn't felt real until now. Freaky, yes. Slightly nauseating, absolutely. But real? Not so much. Was I totally bonkers for doing this? Yeah, probably.

A grinding noise caught my attention. Jaden froze so quickly in front of me that I nearly ran into his back.

"What was that?" Wade hissed.

"I don't know," Jaden hissed back.

We stood there for a moment before trying to go on. The sound started again. This time it didn't stop when we did.

As a trio, we slowly spun to face the sound. Something huge enough to look like a wall ground up into the sky, blocking out the moonlight. The fact that it wasn't actually a wall made my palms sweat.

"What is that?" I squeaked.

"I don't know. That totally didn't happen last time I was here," Jaden said. He'd gone white under the light of the full moon. No doubt my face matched. Was that thing made of stone? Would our swords even do anything to it? How were we supposed to take on something like that? Our rescue mission may have been doomed before it had really started.

CHAPTER FIVE

"What do you want, fae?" a voice rasped out of the top of the thing, where I assumed its head sat.

It still did a great job blocking out the moonlight. The blackness where there weren't any stars revealed a vaguely humanoid shape. A humanoid shape was the best description I could come up with, because it very much was not human. Did I even reach its knee? I wasn't going to get close enough to find out.

"Only passage," Wade said, moving in front of me.

I stepped around in front of him. He glared and tried slip past me again. I moved before he could. If these two guys were going to try to stop me in fights this whole trip, things were going to get interesting. I might be on that thing's side if I was going to be treated like I was breakable. I wasn't.

"I was asked to guard this entrance. You do not have permission to pass." Its voice rumbled through the ground, deep enough I could feel my eardrums rattle in my head.

"Who assigned you this task? Surely not the Council," Wade asked.

"Not the Council. But that is all I will stay. Turn back."

"Wait a second," Jaden called. "You let me out last time! Were you not here?"

The thing squinted down at us. "I'm not to keep those who wish to leave Faerie, only those that try to enter."

"Now what?" I asked Wade in a whisper. "Think we can change its mind?"

"No," he answered, just as quietly. "Golems are extremely loyal. If its master told it to guard this entrance, it will do that to its dying breath. Unless the thing has some type of order that supersedes that one."

"No way we're bringing that thing down," Jaden threw in. "We'll have to lure it away, then make a break for it."

They both looked at me.

"What?"

Wade scratched at his neck. "I'm not particularly happy with this solution, but you are good at…"

I sighed. "Being bait."

"Wait a second," Jaden interrupted. "I'm not particularly happy with that solution either."

"You'll get used to it," I said, pulled my sword out of its sheath, took a breath and ran at the thing.

"Trish, wait!" Jaden yelled from behind me.

I ignored him. At the moment I liked Wade better. He knew that I could handle situations like this. Or he didn't mind sacrificing me so he could get to Starren which was totally believable, but I was just going to assume the best for now.

Out of the corner of my eye, I saw Wade grab Jaden and drag him toward the small cave Jaden had pointed out earlier.

"Take that!" I screamed at the golem, hacking at its leg. I didn't actually want to hurt the thing, so my first blow wasn't hard. It literally bounced back.

The golem tipped over to look down at me. "Do you wish to die today, fae? Leave, before I'm forced to harm you."

Well great. At least it didn't seem like it wanted to hurt me anymore than I wanted to hurt it. Him? Her? It would have to do. I swung again, this time with just a little more force. A few pebbles bounced down the leg. Nope, absolutely no way we were taking this thing down.

A quick glance showed the guys were getting close to the cave entrance. Even if I had no other skills, I was the master of being bait.

"Halt," the golem's voice grumbled across the ground. Both Wade and Jaden froze in place. "You cannot enter here." It took only one step, and it was in their way.

"We have to," Wade said. "Someone in Faerie needs our help. We're going whether you like it or not."

"I don't like or dislike it. I only do as my master says. And I will crush you if it is necessary to follow her commands."

Her commands. Interesting. But a thought for another time.

The golem raised a foot, looking like a building had just decided to float away.

"Run!" I yelled, jumping forward to hack at the foot still on the ground.

The guys scattered, running in opposite directions, clearly confusing the poor thing. Wait, scratch the poor thing part. It was trying to kill us.

The golem put its foot down, right in front of the cave, completely blocking the entrance. Jaden had better not have been under that foot. I'd kill him if he was.

Wade ran up, startling me. He was panting, his sword drawn.

"What now?" I asked him.

Wade shook his head, bent down, and gulped for air.

"Jaden?" The rocks picked up my call and echoed it all around us. "Jade, you okay?" I watched the golem, but now that it had stopped us from entering the tunnel, it seemed fairly content.

"Here," Jaden said, coughing. He wiped at his face with his shoulder as he stepped around some rocks. I whacked him, and he just took it. I didn't tell him why, but he knew. I didn't like to be the one worrying.

"Now what?" Jaden asked.

I rolled my eyes. "I don't know, genius. Got any ideas?"

The three of us turned to stare at the mountain of stone guarding the cave.

"Bait again?" I asked.

"I don't think it will go for that," Jaden answered.

"I can hear you," the golem ground out. "You will not be passing through this entrance, now, or ever, unless I get permission from my master to allow you through."

"And how do we get ahold of your master to ask permission?" Jaden asked.

"We don't have time for that," Wade hissed. "Starren doesn't have time for that."

"You cannot," the golem answered.

"Well this is just great." I stabbed the end of my sword into the ground and leaned on it. "Is there another way we can get through?"

"No," Wade answered. "Or I would have taken it without involving you in this at all. I didn't want you to come, remember?"

I squinted at him but didn't have anything to say to that.

"HUMANS!" the golem suddenly thundered. The tip of my sword popped straight out of the ground and faced in its direction. No need. The golem fell over, then froze, right where it landed. With just the light of the moon, it kind of looked like a landslide.

"Apparently it doesn't want to get caught," Jaden whispered. I didn't know why he was bothering with whispering at this point. "Maybe its number one order is to not be seen by humans."

"Good for us, I guess, but we don't want any humans seeing us either," Wade whispered.

"We can go invisible," I said.

"Even worse than them seeing us would be them seeing us do disappear." Wade answered. "Think we can squeeze past that thing?"

"Worth a try," I answered. We all bolted forward. Humans out here this early in the morning probably wasn't a good thing. It wasn't like a park employee would be here before sunrise, right?

"Oh no you don't, young lady," a voice yelled from behind me.

Oh crap. I knew that voice. Oh crap. I slowly turned to look over my shoulder and sure enough, there was Nina, marching across the rocky area without slowing or looking down at all. How did she do that?

"Hide me," I told Jaden. He just shrugged. I whacked him again. "Did you do this?" That was the only explanation. If I survived whatever Nina was going to do to me, I was going to kill him.

"Hey," Jaden held his hands out, "It wasn't me. I promise I had nothing to do with this."

Should I make a break for it? Roll over and pretend I was dead? Wait, what was I thinking, I could turn invisible!

Instantly I willed myself to disappear.

Nina lunged forward and grabbed me by the arm before I could make a break for it.

"Trisha Penchant, I'm going to-"

"Oh wow, you really can turn invisible!" Dan interrupted from somewhere behind Nina. "Nina warned me about that!"

I'd been so focused on Nina I hadn't even noticed him. I struggled for a second, but gave up, not wanting to hurt her. Man that woman had a surprisingly strong grip.

Nina shook my arm. I took that as a 'you better change back,' so I did.

"Trisha."

Oh man, had I ever heard her sound that angry before?

"So help me, I'm going to-" she stuttered to a stop, apparently unable to decide my fate

"Wait a second, honey. We talked about this," Dan interjected. Who'd have ever thought there would be a day when he was calming Nina down instead of the other way around?

"We did talk about this, Dan, but now that we're here I just can't stop myself." She leaned into me, making her feel like she towered over me even though we were practically the same height.

Dan looked at me and mouthed 'sorry,' but he didn't look that apologetic.

"Uh, hey Nina," I said.

"Hey, Nina?" Her voice started to rise. "That's it, just a 'hey, Nina?'"

In hindsight, I should have figured out what I'd say when I saw her again. But then, I'd been pretty sure I wouldn't be making it back from this, so I hadn't really thought I'd have to.

"You are literally going to be the death of me, Trisha." She was still using Trisha. Not good. "You.. you..." she ran a hand through her hair. "You scared me." Then the tears started rolling down her face.

Okay, mad I didn't like one bit. But crying? Shoot. Nina didn't use tears as a weapon intentionally, but she might as well have.

"Sorry." I reached out and patted her on the back. "I really am. I just didn't have a choice."

Oh boy, wrong thing to say. The tears turned off, and she glared at me, her red rimmed eyes glittering dangerously in the moonlight. "Didn't have a choice?"

"I have to go. I told you, she's my sister. And it's not like there's anyone else that can help."

Nina gestured to Dan and back to herself. "No one? Seriously? No way you're going to Faerie without help." She turned her angry glare on Wade. "Especially not with him along."

"You shouldn't be going at all," Dan added.

Nina gave him a look.

"You know it's true," Dan said, hands up. From those looks they were giving each other, this was an old discussion. But they had been in the car together for hours, so it probably was.

"I'm sorry, I'm going." For once I actually felt bad about disobeying, and for once I had a really good reason to be doing it. "I don't want any hard feelings, but at this point you don't have any way of stopping me."

"Speaking of go, we need to, before something stops us from entering the tunnel," Wade said, the first time he'd been brave enough to speak in a while. He got a glare from both Dan and Nina. He probably knew to keep his mouth shut after that.

"He's right. We need to go," I said. "One question though, how did you find us?"

Cray stepped out from behind Dan.

What? That little... "Cray, you traitor," I hissed. If Dan or Nina got hurt because he'd helped them find me... I'd never hated his ability to track anyone, anywhere, more than I did at this moment. As long as they were in the same area as we were, they were in danger. Jaden and I were targets as soon as we'd left Sanctuary, which meant they had instantly become targets as well. And we hadn't even stepped foot in the tunnel yet.

"I was worried. About you. And about Starren," Cray whispered.

I crossed my arms in front of my chest. I'd deal with him later. "You can't stop us. I'm going after Starren."

Nina crossed her arms right back at me. "I know there is no possible way for us to stop you this close to the tunnel. That's why we're going with you."

I opened my mouth to argue that yes, I was going, when my brain caught up with my mouth. "Wait, what?"

Nina lifted an eyebrow at Dan, then eyed Wade. "If you're going, we're going."

What? Dan and Nina in Faerie? Like that wasn't a disaster waiting to happen. "You can't go to Faerie! Do you know the kind of things that are there?" My voice was rising, and I didn't even care.

"No, not really, but if there is stuff there that you're worried about us being around, then that's all the more reason for us to go," Dan said. "Just to be clear, my vote was to hold you down until you changed your mind."

"We know you're excited about your sister," Nina said. "And I can't take that away from you. But there is no way on this earth that you'll be going anywhere without us."

"You don't think we'd let you do this alone, do you, Trish?" Dan asked.

"This is crazy. You don't know what you're getting into."

"Neither do you," Nina said. "You've never been there either."

"Yeah, but I heal," I argued. This was such a bad idea. So bad. Like, seriously bad.

"I'm so torn about that," Dan mused out loud. "I really want to actually see it, but I really don't want you to get hurt."

"Focus, Dan," Nina said. "If you're going, we're going with you."

"Humans are forbidden in Faerie," Wade said.

"Yeah, yeah, and Jaden and Trish have a bounty on their heads. It looks like we should probably not be seen," Nina answered.

"Could we just tie them up?" I asked Wade.

"Hey!" Cray interjected. "That's not nice!"

Wade shrugged. "I don't know. It probably wouldn't be very effective since they know where the tunnel entrance is now. They'd probably try to follow us and get killed right away instead of later."

Wow, super optimistic.

"Okay then, you can come at first, but you might have to go back. Jaden might be going back too, so he can take you."

I looked at him. He stared back. Jerk.

"Jaden is here then?" Nina looked around, like she should be able to see some evidence he was here. She couldn't, of course.

"Yes, he's here."

"I need to let Rebecca know. She wanted to come but had to stay with the girls." She pulled her phone out of her pocket and started furiously typing.

"Shall we go then?" Wade asked. He kicked at a rock. "Before this thing wakes back up?"

"What thing?" Dan asked, moving up to walk by Wade.

Wade sighed. "Never mind. We just need to get on our way before any humans find us."

Dan's eyes narrowed.

"Uh, other humans," Wade added, like that totally made it better. "If either of you need to continue yelling at Trisha, it can happen while we're traveling."

I tried to whack him with the dull side of my sword, but he dodged out of the way too quickly. Nina watched the whole thing, lips tight, disapproving.

Jaden went first, followed by Wade and Dan, who was keeping a close eye on Wade. I couldn't really blame him. He didn't understand all the dynamics of why Wade had made the decision to shoot me. To him Wade was a murderer. I didn't feel quite that strongly about it anymore, but I still wasn't completely sure where I stood.

I poked at the stones with the end of my sword as we made our way to the tunnel entrance. The golem giving up that quickly made me suspicious, but it made sense if its master didn't want humans to find out about it. Thankfully Nina and Dan had somehow missed it.

And then there was Cray. I glared in his direction. I wasn't going to talk to him for a week, at least. I couldn't remember ever being this frustrated with him. He knew how much Dan and Nina meant to me, but here he was, letting them throw themselves into danger. After I was done giving him the silent treatment, we were going to have words.

Getting into the tunnel was tight. The golem had almost managed to fall close enough that we wouldn't be able to fit through, but not quite. In my mind, I could see it opening an eye with me right beside it like it always happened in the movies, but it didn't. I kept my sword ready just in case.

"We would have never beat that thing," I said.

"Absolutely no way," Jaden answered.

This tunnel was entirely different than the one that I had met Starren in. More like a cave, it stretched on and on in the dark. I pulled two flashlights out of my backpack and handed one to Dan. Wade didn't look happy. He could have brought his own.

The walls didn't give us room to walk together, so things were pretty quiet for a little while. I didn't mind. Nina had let me off light compared to what I'd expected, which led me to believe she was stewing. Stewing was bad. Very bad.

Eventually Dan, who was in front stopped. "It's blocked," he called back to us.

No, that couldn't be right. We had no other way to get into Faerie, no other way to save Starren. I wiggled up around him, trying to get a look myself. It all looked clear to me, just open tunnel. What was he talking about?

"It's like a portal, Trish," Jaden said. "Humans can't see through it. Faerie is just on the other side, though we still have a ton more tunnel left before we get out."

"Can they get through it without us?" I asked.

"I'd say they can get through from Faerie to Earth, but I'm not sure about the other way."

"Awesome." The perfect opportunity to leave them behind. Not that I didn't want them with us, I really did. They were the only family I had. I just didn't want them dead. My mom leaving me behind and being missing hurt enough, but dead? Dead was so much worse.

I sidled up to Wade, who got the evil eye from Dan when he saw us together. Considering how long it had taken me to even get this close to being okay with him, I didn't blame the guy. I would never be able to truly forgive Wade for shooting me, but at least I'd learned to work with him when Starren had been our buffer.

A pang hit me. I hadn't really had time to go through the whole thought process of having a sister, let alone that sister being a crazy awesome fae leader of some kind. Time for that later.

"Make a break through the portal," I whispered to Wade. He gave me a slight nod in acknowledgement, but if I hadn't been looking for it I wouldn't have seen it. The guy was good at this stuff.

I took one last look at Dan and Nina. "Love you guys." Then I jumped through the portal.

Wade followed right away, and then Jaden.

"Are you solid now?" I asked Jaden.

He patted himself. "I can't tell."

We didn't get five feet away before the portal thing shimmered and spit out people. Specifically, Dan and Nina, sandwiching Cray.

"Awww, come on, Cray," I whined. He shrugged.

"Trisha, if this continues I'm going to tie you to myself." Nina stormed my way and I cringed. "I told you we'd help, you can't just keeping trying to run off."

I huffed and crossed my arms in front of my chest. "It's not like I'm some stupid teenager, Nina, I'm not just trying to leave you behind because you're my parents. A lot of stuff could go wrong on this trip, and I don't want you to get hurt."

Nina smiled.

"What?" I asked. That was a completely illogical reaction to my statement.

Dan slung his arm around Nina's shoulders. "You called us your parents."

I huffed again. They were missing the point. "Yeah? So? What about the second part? You don't know anything about Faerie, it isn't a safe place. You really don't want to be here."

Dan cocked his head, considering. "You're right. I don't really want to be here."

My internal self died a little. So I couldn't make up my mind, I'm a teenager. I wanted him to want to be here for me, but I didn't actually want him here because I didn't want him to die.

"But when you're in a family, sometimes what you want is irrelevant. If you're throwing yourself into danger, we're going to be there beside you. Though my original plan was to stop you somehow and get some friends involved, I can see that with that stupid portal, that isn't going to happen. Are you sure we can't just go back?"

He sounded like he was actually asking me, like he wasn't trying to force my decision, but he really didn't want to go. If only I could tell him that all I wanted was to go back too.

My silence was answer enough.

Dan eyed Wade, like he was trying to decide if he could take him in a fight. Wouldn't that be just wonderful. But he didn't do anything. He seemed to know that Wade wouldn't let them force me back, even if they decided that would be the best thing to do.

Wade casually stretched, showing his sword.

Dan casually stretched, showing his gun holster.

I didn't think Dan would really shoot him. Probably not.

Could Dan take him in a fight? Maybe. I didn't know, I'd never seen Dan fight. But I doubted it. And Dan seemed to also. Other than just shooting Wade, Dan didn't stand much of a chance.

"How much danger are we actually in?"

I looked back and forth between Dan and Nina.

"A lot," Wade answered for me. "A serious lot."

"And there's nothing I can say to get you to just go back?" he asked me.

I just crossed my arms in front of me and let that stubborn look that always tried to come out have free rein.

"I had to try, one last time." Dan narrowed his eyes at Nina. "You said you'd go back if things got out of hand."

She waved her hand at him. "You know I'd never leave you. Or Trish."

Dan sighed. "Worth a try. Ever onward, I guess."

"You can't take the gun, though," Wade said. "Faerie doesn't like guns. They become unpredictable, and dangerous."

Dan snorted. "Yeah, right. And your sword isn't very safe either."

I hadn't heard about this before. But Wade couldn't lie.

"Dan," I said. "He's telling the truth."

"We aren't going on while you have it," Wade said.

I cringed, waiting for it to be a thing.

Nina put her hand on his arm. "We don't know anything about this place." She glared at Wade. "As much as we don't trust him, he has to tell us the truth. You should probably leave it here."

Muttering under his breath, Dan stashed his holster behind a rock. "But someone has to get me a sword now."

"Guys?"

Cray did not sound good. I glanced over at him. Even in the dark I could make out his sick expression.

"You okay?" I asked.

He did this weird little nod/shake at the same time, like he couldn't decide if to say yes or no. "I don't think I can go any farther than this."

Poor guy, always getting involved in stuff that had nothing to do with him. He didn't handle stress well, and this was about as stressful as it could get.

Nina reached over and gave him a hug. "That's okay. You've done more than anyone could have expected. Thank you for helping me find my wayward daughter."

Wayward daughter, seriously? Like I'd run off to a party or something. Sigh.

Cray gave her a small smile. "You're welcome. I'll be waiting nearby, for when you come back."

"No," Jaden said, tossing him the keys to his truck. "We have another vehicle. If we aren't back in forty-eight hours, head home. Take care of my mom and sisters."

"Can you throw our phones in the car?" Dan asked. "It's not like we'll have service, and it's one less thing to worry about losing."

Cray nodded. He took the phones, gave Nina a short hug, stared the rest of us down for a second, and then left.

It would feel weird, Cray not being along. He'd been part of all my other questing. But part of me was glad. He wasn't the hardy type, by any sense of the word. He watched us walk away, and I gave him a small wave before adjusting my backpack and going after Wade, who hadn't stopped.

Nina hurried to catch up. I threw one last look over my shoulder.

Cray had stopped and looked forlorn enough standing there by himself that I almost felt bad for him. Then I remembered Dan and Nina were here because of him and got over it.

The tunnel widened and the air cooled as we moved toward Faerie. Would I know when we passed the border? Would I feel it? I shivered. Was all of this really worth it? Starren and I hadn't left each other on good terms. She probably still hated me for ruining her life. Did she care that we were sisters? She'd never said anything. But then, Wade had said she had been trying to make sure she hadn't made a mistake, that I was who she thought I was.

"Whoa!" Dan said, skidding to a stop.

I spun his direction, sword flying from its sheath.

Nothing.

"What?" I asked.

"You get used to it," Nina said.

I glanced over to where they were looking. Jaden.

"Hey Nina, Dan," Jaden said, giving them a little wave.

"Hi," Dan said, not sounding like himself at all. I almost snorted. If he thought that was bad, this trip would blow his mind. I hadn't ever been to Faerie, so it'd probably blow mine too, but I wasn't going to let anyone see that. This at least answered the question about if Faerie felt different. No.

Wade humphed and started marching forward again. I followed.

We hadn't made it very far before Nina sidled her way up to me.

"Trish-"

"I know, I'm sorry. You don't have to say it."

Nina's narrowed. "Apparently I do. This is dangerous. We are a family. No leaving without talking with us first, that's how this whole family thing works."

It also worked by all of us trying to protect each other, but I didn't add that. Somehow I didn't think it would go over well.

"How are you doing?" Nina asked.

"Fine?" I answered, thrown by the quick change of conversation.

She looked at me funny, like she didn't believe me. "So you find out you have an older sister you didn't know anything about, she's about to die without you getting answers, and that's it, you're just fine?"

"Okay, maybe not fine, exactly..." I trailed off, not knowing where to go from there. Nina was my mom now, just as much as my real mom, but normal kids didn't really share emotions with their real moms either, right? I didn't know how this worked, I hadn't been around enough healthy relationships to figure it all out.

Nina grabbed me and pulled me into a tight hug, right there in the middle of the tunnel, making the guys all stop to wait. "It's okay to be upset." She squeezed me even tighter.

I closed my eyes and snuggled into her warmth for just a second. Then I remembered Wade and the fact that I didn't really want him to see me like this and stepped back. "Thank you," I said quietly.

As usual, Nina seemed to read the things I wasn't saying out loud. She gave me a smile and a nod, then walked past me like she wasn't the reason we'd stopped walking.

Wade jumped forward to keep ahead of her, and I jogged for a second to catch up with him and Jaden. Dan brought up the rear.

"What's this tunnel like?" Wade asked Jaden.

What did that mean?

"Not great," Jaden answered. Wonderful.

"The wild ones usually aren't," Wade said, voice grim.

I glanced back at Dan and Nina, who were holding hands now. We might not even make it to the surface in Faerie, if the boys were worried with reason. I couldn't lose those two fragile humans.

"Is there somewhere we can lock them up?" I asked Wade.

He looked confused. "Who?"

I jerked my head back at the lovebirds following us.

Wade blinked at me.

"Don't fry your brains trying to figure it out, Wade, I just don't want them to get hurt."

"Oh!" he said. "That makes sense. Nowhere that they would be able to free themselves if we don't make it back. It would be more of a risk than letting them come with us, and trying to protect them."

"But this is pretty much a suicide mission."

He looked grim. "Which tells you how bad of an idea leaving them behind would be. Human flesh is a delicacy to some here, they would be hunted down within a day."

Well that really wasn't great. "How bad is it here, really?"

"Not-"

"Horrible-"

Jaden and Wade answered at the same time.

I raised an eyebrow.

"Everything has an agenda, and anyone will stab you in the back," Jaden clarified.

"Yes, but everything is gorgeous, magical, and there are no humans," Wade added.

Uh, yeah, I was going to go with Jaden on this one. Not that it really mattered. Soon I would see the place and be able to decide for myself.

CHAPTER SIX

With the big deal that Wade and Jaden had made about this being a wild tunnel, I'd been super uptight for the first hour of walking. At this point, I was just bored.

"We should stop and get some rest," Wade said.

Nina lagged behind, obviously exhausted, Dan looking almost as weary. Jaden and Wade were both doing their best to not look it, but they were tired too. I wouldn't mind stopping, walking this much was enough to kill anyone, especially in the almost dark with nothing to see. So much for it being dangerous here, other than tripping and killing yourself. I wouldn't complain about the no danger thing though.

"Are you sure?" Jaden asked. "This doesn't seem like the best place to camp."

Good thing he was a few steps away, otherwise I would have kicked him.

"Faerie is going to be where it's dangerous," Wade answered. "We should be rested when we leave the tunnel. That way we will only need to stop and rest once before we reach where Starren is being held."

"Just sit our stuff anywhere?" Nina asked, obviously fully on board with stopping for a while.

"Close to a wall. You first, then Dan, then Trisha and I'll be on the outside. That way everyone is as safe as possible. Jaden can take first watch."

Dan's eyes narrowed. "I'll be between you and Trish."

Wade held his hands up. "She regenerates. You don't. I really should have put her all the way on the outside."

He was right. It would have been the logical thing to do. If there was a surprise in the night, I'd be the one to survive. A shiver went through me. That was a terrible thought. If we were attacked, I would lie in here until I healed, waking up to find everyone dead.

"I think we need two people on watch," I said.

"Good idea," Jaden said.

"Fine with me," Wade answered. "You can-"

"Take a turn with me," Dan interrupted. "You boys can share a watch."

I rolled my eyes. There was a good chance we were going to die on this trip. Boys were about the last thing on my mind. But Dan meant well. And I got the feeling that if he wasn't here to do that, Nina would be the one butting in.

Dan and Wade stared at each other for a second, then moved off to discuss where to post watch.

I sidled over to the wall. "So... Jaden."

"Hmm?" He looked up from where he was setting up a bedroll.

"Did you bring anything to snack on?"

He rolled his eyes, but there was a smile in there. "Yes, actually, I knew you wouldn't be able to make it a whole day without something to eat." He picked his backpack up off the tunnel floor and unzipped it, then dug around for a second before a chocolate chip granola bar came whizzing at me.

I smiled at him and unwrapped it, taking a huge bite. "My favorite," I mumbled.

"I noticed," Jaden answered, his voice going all funny. I froze, staring at him.

Dan looked over from where he was talking with Wade, eyed him for a second, then me.

"What?" I asked, a little more rude than I'd aimed for.

He shrugged but kept staring.

"What?" I asked Jaden.

He shrugged like he had no idea either, and went back to setting up his stuff. "I want this ready when I get to go to bed. It's been a long couple of days." He got up and brushed off his pants before going over to Wade and Dan.

I pulled my sleeping bag out of my knapsack and tossed it on the hard floor of the cave.

"Soooo...." Nina said, nudging me with her shoulder.

"Yeah?" I asked, like I didn't know what she meant.

"What's going on with that?" Right to the point.

"I have no idea," I groaned.

She crossed her arms in front of her chest. "That's fine, you've got plenty of time. But we are going to talk about you sneaking out again. About you not trusting us. You should have told us what was going on, Trisha. I thought we were past all this."

Jaden stepped in. "That's what I said." No doubt he thought he would get points for that. How wrong he was.

"I'll get to you later," Nina's voice had dropped dangerously low. "You're almost as bad, going along with this whole thing. I thought I could at least trust you."

Jaden wilted. I knew how he felt.

I stuffed my hands in my pockets and went into a defensive slump.

"After everything we've been through, how could you not keep us in the loop? Especially me."

Ugh, this was Chicago all over again. Okay, not as bad, but bad enough.

"Are you not going to answer?" Nina's voice had a hard edge. She'd kept it together until now, but she didn't like being ignored.

I wasn't ignoring her. Really. I just didn't know what to say. "I didn't want you to get hurt!" The words burst from me. Okay, consciously I hadn't known what to say.

Nina's face instantly softened, and she came over to give me a squeeze. "We're the adults here. Let us worry about that."

Yeah, like age had anything to do with why I worried about them getting hurt and not so much about me.

"You thought the fae we went up against last time were bad. Just wait until we get to Faerie!" Not that I knew first hand, but you didn't need to swim in the ocean to know somewhere out there, there were sharks.

There went Nina's face again. "It's too late. We're going. You can't stop us."

I groaned. She was right. I might as well shoot them myself if I left them here. "Fine," I whispered. I was too tired for this fight.

"Jaden and Wade are taking the first watch," Dan said, walking over to Nina and me. "I would have taken the shift with Wade so I could keep an eye on him, but then you'd be up with Jaden. Think he can handle Wade?"

Nina slapped Dan's arm lightly. "Jaden is a good kid."

I groaned again. "I'm going to get some sleep." I sat down and snuggled into my sleeping bag. And here I'd thought it was awkward enough traveling with my ex-boyfriend and my... whatever Jaden was. Now I had to add my parents into the mix. This trip was going to be miserable, even if we did survive.

Surprisingly, we made it almost until my shift for watch before something happened. Unsurprisingly, it wasn't a good something.

A gentle hand on my shoulder jerked me out of some seriously deep sleep. "What?" I mumbled. And not very nicely, which I would have maybe felt bad about except for the fact that someone woke me up.

"You need to get up," Jaden whispered, his voice harsh. That caught my attention. Jaden didn't do harsh. "Wake up Dan and Nina, then gather your stuff slowly."

"Wha-"

"No talking." Then the hand was gone.

I opened my eye a slit, afraid of what I might find. Nothing. But Jaden wasn't one to get upset for no reason. Maybe he'd 'seen' something. That thought sent me into overdrive.

"Dan," I hissed as I shook his arm. "Dan!"

"Our turn for watch?" he asked, somehow sounding like he hadn't even been asleep. But he had to have been, or he would have had a comment about what Jaden had said. We were all too close together for him to have missed the conversation if he'd been awake.

"Something's going on. I don't know what. Get Nina up and pack your stuff," I answered.

Without commenting, he rolled over to wake Nina.

I pulled my sword and sat it within easy grabbing distance, then slowly started stuffing my blanket into my knapsack, keeping watch for Jaden or Wade. Where were they? If he'd freaked me out for no reason...

"Whaaa.. what's going on?" Nina's garbled voice came from over where Dan was trying to wake her. She was not a morning person.

I couldn't hear Dan's reply, but Nina kept quiet after that. They rolled their stuff up quickly, grabbing Wade and Jaden's packs as well.

Backpack thrown over one shoulder, I picked up my sword and strained to hear something. Anything. A few little scuffles of sound, and then Jaden and Wade burst around a corner, flashlights swinging wildly.

"Run!" Wade yelled, apparently giving up on the whole quiet thing.

Crap. If he was running instead of fighting, this was really, really bad. Fighting was his favorite thing.

Dan grabbed Nina and flicked his lantern on in one swift movement, jerking her along the tunnel in the direction of Faerie. Or so I assumed. It was too easy to get turned around in the dark.

I dashed after them. The boys could take care of themselves just fine, the parents not so much.

I had to run full out to catch up with Dan and Nina. Normally I had no problems keeping up with humans, but they were moving seriously fast. Nina glanced over her shoulder, probably making sure I was coming. "Just run!" I yelled. What did they not get about me healing and them not?

A flurry of noise chased me down the tunnel. Like, wings maybe? Not that I'd really heard wings anywhere but in the movies. We had better not be running from bats. I peeked over my shoulder. Jaden and

Wade were gaining ground on us. I stumbled in the dark and Wade was there to grab my arm. He jerked me forward, not saying anything, his breath coming in controlled bursts.

"What's going on?" I asked, able to breathe and run without much difficulty. Yay for no Sanctuary.

He glared at me and pulled on my arm harder.

I glanced back again, to make sure Jaden was keeping up. He was close, taking up the rear, sword unsheathed, with the flat of the blade resting on his shoulder as he ran. That didn't seem very safe. The fact that these two were kind of freaking out made me want to freak out, but that wasn't going to happen. Nope, I'd faced Starren. Seriously, what could be worse than my sister?

Shrieking started up behind us, growing louder way too quickly and nearly covering the sound of wings. I jerked my arm from Wade and covered my ears.

"They can't survive in light!" Jaden yelled from behind. "Get to the end of the tunnel!"

The end of the tunnel? My gut churned, acid clawing its way up my throat. How far was the end of the tunnel?

Nina stumbled ahead of me, and I sprung forward to grab her other arm. She'd kept running at home after all the stuff had happened with Jaime, said she had a better reason to stay in shape now. Never had I been so glad. Dan had some physical for work he always complained about, so he usually ran with her. I'd bet they were just as glad as I was at the moment that they did.

Nina regained her footing, letting go of my arm to clamp her hands over her ears too. She looked back over my shoulder, and her face went white.

I looked wildly behind us. A black mass moved in our direction, incredibly fast, pulling in the small amount of light left from our lanterns and flashlights.

"What is that?" I asked again, this time a little frantic.

No one answered, sucking in air as we ran.

Several small specks of darkness were beating the rest, nearly catching up to Jaden. He swatted at them with his sword.

"Don't stop!" Wade panted out.

"Not planning on it!" Jaden yelled back, swinging wildly as he ran.

Something slammed me from behind, knocking me off balance.

"Trish!" Nina screeched, but Dan didn't let her turn around.

Another little monster bounced off of me, then another. I pulled my sword while running, imitating Jaden and whacking at the little shadows as I went.

Each little... thing I managed to make contact with twirled to the ground, blood curdling death sounds making me wish I had another arm so I could cover both ears and wield a sword at the same time. The little death machines began to hurtle themselves at us more and more quickly, Wade, Jaden, and I strained, trying to keep them from getting to us, or past us to the humans running in the lead.

Dan and Nina both stumbled more often as we fought our way in what I hoped was the direction of the exit. They wouldn't make it much longer, and I wouldn't leave them behind. The question was, would Jaden and Wade?

Then finally, there, a tiny bit of light!

Dan and Nina sprang forward ahead of me, apparently encouraged by the chance that we were actually going to survive.

The racket behind us grew exponentially. I dropped my sword to cover my ears, going to the ground in pain. Even with my hands clamped tightly over my ears, the sound was overwhelming.

Two small hands grabbed me under my arms, dragging me toward the light.

As soon as the light touched the ground, the blackness paused. A couple little shapes didn't get stopped in time and fizzled as they twirled to the ground. The rest of them must have decided that we were out of reach, because the sound instantly stopped.

"You okay?" Nina asked. I could hardly hear her over the ringing in my ears.

"Yeah. You?"

She nodded that she was fine, and moved over to check on Dan. Jaden and Wade seemed fine, even if they did look like they were about to fall over from exhaustion.

I walked over to the closest of the shapes that had fallen to the ground. "This is what we were running from?" I squatted over it, trying to get a better look. It almost repelled light. The spot where it laid on the dirt of the tunnel pulled shadows in from nowhere. "So we were never in any real danger? I mean, look at the thing."

It was tiny. Like a little flying teddy bear. No big ugly teeth or anything weird like that.

Wade looked at me like I was insane. "Why do you ask stuff like that? You didn't think the hyran was dangerous either."

"You met a hyran?" Jaden's eyebrows hit his hairline. "When did that happen? And where? And how are you still alive?"

"What's a hyran?" Dan asked. He looked like he'd just ran a marathon. Well, he kinda had. But he didn't look great.

I waved my hand. "Long story." He didn't need to know about the whole I tried to trade Jaden's life for mine thing. Dan and I were just starting to really get along, no reason to ruin that by letting him know what a backstabber I was. Am. Still working that part out.

"These little beasts are like flying piranha," Wade said. "They can strip a person's flesh in a few seconds."

I kicked at the dead one on the ground. "But they're so cute."

Wade groaned, Jaden started rubbing the back of his neck, and Dan sighed.

"How do you know about piranha?" Nina asked.

Wade shrugged, not looking at me. "I had a lot of time to kill while Trish was at school. There were some really interesting programs on Animal Planet."

"Seriously?" I grouched.

Wade just shrugged again.

I looked back into the darkness. "I don't think piranha give up that easy."

"What makes you think they gave up?" Jaden asked.

I shivered. What indeed. Were they just chilling in there, waiting for us to come back? We really needed to find a different way home after this was over. If we were alive and all that. And maybe getting the rest of the way out of this tunnel would be a good idea.

"Do those things leave here to hunt at night?" Dan asked.

"If the moon isn't out," Wade answered.

"On that cheery note, are we ready to move on then?" Nina asked.

"I'd really like to get as far away from this tunnel as possible. As quickly as possible. Definitely far away before dark."

Not a bad plan. Except… I'd dropped my sword. "Ah, guys. Slight problem."

Everyone looked at me at once.

"I dropped my sword, just inside the dark area. It isn't far."

Wade groaned. "You have got to be kidding me. Do you know how difficult it was to get you that sword?"

I flapped my hand at him. "I know, I know, but it was so loud. I'd love to see you go through that with extra great hearing."

"You have extra great hearing?" Dan asked. He glanced at Nina, an unspoken 'we'll have to be more careful when talking behind Trish's back' passing between them.

"I'm not leaving without that sword."

Wade studied the tunnel for a second. "Enough of them died that they should be pretty cautious about now. How far back did you drop it?"

"Not far, I already told you that." Wade was the one going to help me out? Weird. "Like ten feet, at the most." I moved back up the tunnel.

"Wait," Nina yelled.

"She should be fine." There was Wade, defending me again. "We took out quite a few of them. They probably headed back to their den to regroup."

"Probably?" Dan asked.

"Probably isn't good enough," Jaden said.

I rolled my eyes and took off up the tunnel while they argued. It took me like thirty seconds of near terror, the light rustle of wings in the dark nearly giving me my own wings, but I found the sword and took off at full speed back out, sliding the last couple feet into the light like I was going for home plate. That worked, right? Watching baseball was not on my to do list.

All conversation had stopped when I took off, and everyone's body language had gone super tense.

I jumped to my feet and held my sword up, waving it in the air. "Got it."

Nina just shook her head, like she was giving up on me. Probably wise, at least in this area of my life.

"Are we ready to move on, then?" Wade asked.

I shoved a wave of fear back down to where it belonged. Ready as I'd ever be. Faerie, long lost country of mine, here I come.

CHAPTER SEVEN

I stepped out into the sunlight behind Wade. Sunlight might not be the right word. Light, yes, but I didn't see any sun. And the light itself looked odd, almost muted. It came from the sky like there was a sun, so maybe it was just out of sight.

After blinking several times, I got my first real look at Faerie. Or this section of it, at least. Did it have its own name?

Foliage stretched on in both directions. Foliage, because I didn't know what else to call it. The plants were unlike anything I'd ever seen at home, ranging in color from purples to yellows and back, even the stems. The only color not strongly represented was green. Trees that I could only describe as magnificent stretched above us, their branches full and leaves different shades of red, some with flowers hanging from long stems.

"Like it?" Wade asked, giving me a small smile. I nodded. "I've been waiting to share it with you for so long," he added, making my stomach flip. He was acting like what we'd had was real, like the Council hadn't made him date me. Of course we had almost died together like five minutes ago, that did tend to change a person's perspective. At least he seemed to have caught his breath by now.

I didn't get a chance to answer his comment before Dan came

stumbling out of the tunnel. He took a second to check on Wade and me, very dad like, then reached back to help Nina out. Jaden brought up the rear.

For once Nina had nothing to say as she took in the scenery, mouth open.

"Wow," Dan finally said. "This is... wow."

Jaden grunted and pushed past Dan. Apparently his hatred of Faerie extended to the plants.

I walked over to a flowery stalk and held a hand out. Were these plants like the ones at home in the most important way? Would they help me if I needed it? With living in Sanctuary, I hadn't had the chance to use that ability since that night Starren and Wade had taken Jaime. Oh how things had changed.

Hard to know if they were on my side or not. Or even if they were alive, or whatever. Harder to trust anything from Faerie. I glanced at Wade. Hardest to trust him. If this was some kind of trick...

Not knowing my thoughts, Wade gave me a small smile when he caught me looking. I flushed and looked away, glad he couldn't tell I was trying to decide if he planned to stab me in the back or not.

Maybe I should be past that by now, but I wasn't. Not by a long shot. Surprisingly, and without noticing, I had forgiven him. But forgiveness and trust were entirely different things.

"We shouldn't stay here long," Wade interrupted my thoughts. "If anyone finds us here, the tunnel will be discovered, then collapsed or guarded. The humans wouldn't be able to return home."

"And Trish," Nina added.

Wade looked at me for a moment. "And Trish. Getting her home is the most important thing to me."

Why did it sound weird coming from him? Had he really changed enough that he wanted what was best for me, wanted me to be happy, instead of just insisting I go to Faerie with him?

"By all means then, let's move," Dan said. Thank you father figure for breaking up an awkward moment.

"You mean we're going to have to go back through that thing?" I heard Nina squeak behind me. I couldn't blame her. If there was literally any other way to get back, we were taking it.

Wade started right off, somehow confident in the direction he'd chosen. I couldn't see any way of knowing which way to go, but he seemed to have it figured out.

I let Dan and Nina go ahead of me, assuming Wade didn't want me to hate him again, so hopefully he would keep them safe from any threats up front. He'd seemed protective in the cave, which had surprised me. I reached back and slid my sword an inch out of its sheath, just to make sure it was easily accessible, then let it slip back in. Protecting the rear would be up to me. No way I would let anything happen to Dan or Nina, not after they had put themselves in danger to come here, just for me.

"We should have tried harder to leave them behind," Jaden said, moving to walk beside me. "They could have died back there. We all could have, but they would have first. And that wasn't even the worst of what's to come."

Part of me agreed. The other part jumped up and down in joy about the fact that I had parents that would put themselves at risk to help me. Then I was back to sweaty palms freaking out because we'd almost died back there. The parents that cared about me had almost died.

"Wait." My stomach clenched. I turned and gripped Jaden's forearm, squeezing hard. "You're just saying that, right? You didn't..." I glanced ahead to make sure no one was listening. "see... anything, did you?"

"No." He ducked his head in close. "I just know what this place is like. Even out here with no specific person trying to kill us, we could easily wind up dead. Almost did, before we even made it to Faerie. Just wait until we start running into people that aren't really interested in allowing you to spring your sister out of prison."

I loosened my death grip on his arm and blew out a breath. Jaden's foresight couldn't be controlled, but I still trusted it. If he'd have said something would happen to Dan or Nina, I'd have had to tie them up and make Jaden drag them home. The long way, wherever that was.

"Well yeah, it's a horrible idea, but what did you want me to do?" I asked.

"Um, I don't know, tie them up or something!"

"Then they would have died for sure." I marched past him, following the little group. He was right, and that's why I was being rude about this. We both knew it, but that didn't mean I had to admit it. For once I had people in my corner, and it felt better than words could even say. "Hey, Wade," I called as I trotted to catch up with him. Or, more honestly, leave Jaden behind, but semantics.

"Yeah?" he asked, keeping up his pace. The way he was studiously trying to act normal told he'd been listening in to my conversation with Jaden. Human ears wouldn't have been able to pick up us whispering back there, but his fae ears probably had.

"How far is it to the prison?"

"And do you have a plan yet?" Dan chimed in.

"A day's walk, depending on how the forest feels about us."

How the forest feels about us? Did that mean the plants were alive like back at home? I couldn't stop the side of my mouth curling up. I had backup. Hopefully.

"Well that sounds weird. But the plan?" Dan asked again.

"Same as always. Trisha goes in as a distraction, I go in and get the job done."

What he really meant was I would go in as bait.

"Oh no you-"

"Just a second here-"

"Not happening." Dan, Nina, and Jaden all interrupted each other.

I stopped dead, crossing my arms in front of my chest. "Hey, you can't all make decisions for me. I can be bait if I want to."

"Right?" Wade said. "If you wanna do something, you should do it."

I raised my eyebrow, staring him down.

"I was just trying to help," he mumbled.

"We can work on a plan when we camp tonight," Dan interjected.

Camp sounded good, and we hadn't even gone far since the last camp. But running and almost dying had taken its toll. Plus we hadn't gotten to rest long last time anyway. Dan looked fine, which made me wonder what kind of situations he'd been in before. Wade and Jaden were good of course, but Nina looked a little sick. I moved up beside her and bumped her with my shoulder, like she did for me when I was lost after something going down.

"Hey." She smiled at me, but it wasn't her normal bright smile.

I frowned back. "You okay? You didn't get hurt anywhere, did you?" Somehow we'd switched roles, because at the moment I wanted to frisk her for injuries.

"No, no, I didn't get hurt anywhere. Guess I'm just a little out of my league. I wanted you to have help so badly I didn't stop to consider Dan and I might not actually be any help." She smiled at Dan's back. "Well, me at least. But if you'd left and never came back, I'd have never stopped hoping it was you every time someone was at the door, looking for your face when I was getting groceries."

It was no pang of guilt that hit me this time. More like a tsunami. Okay, that was so not fair. I hadn't asked for them to love me, I'd been just fine on my own, I... was going into defense mode again. "Thank you for caring about me, Nina." The words had to be beaten down and dragged out of my mouth, but the smile I got was worth it.

Wade went super quiet and kept us at a forced march. I tried to ask him questions about the area we were in, but he would hardly answer. I'd never been interested in Faerie, avoided all contact or even thoughts about it, but now I didn't have a choice. Now I needed to know everything I could. If something happened to Wade while we were rescuing Starren, or if we got split up, we would be in trouble.

Dan let Wade pull us along at that grueling pace for a while before grabbing him. "We should slow down. Get some rest." He nodded at the little clearing we'd just made our way into. "It's dangerous letting everyone get too tired. Mistakes can be made, and if we were attacked by something we wouldn't be able to defend ourselves." He was right, of course. The group looked like we'd been through a major battle, not just chased by little light sucking bat things.

Wade grunted and we all took that as an agreement, because Dan and I dropped our bags to the ground at the same time. He stretched his arms out, rolled his shoulders, and then moved his neck.

"Not as young as I used to be," Dan said, then grinned at me. How old was he? I'd never even thought about it. Every once in a while a thought like that would hit me, and then I'd feel bad because I didn't know. There were so many details about their lives that I hadn't even thought to ask about. Did that make them think I didn't care? Hopefully not, because I seriously did, I just didn't really know how to be in a family yet. We were working on that.

I had asked Nina about her parents though. But she'd gone all vague, so I'd dropped it. Something she'd said about raising Aunt Wren had sent the gears turning, but she'd never told me why. Had her parents died? Or worse, were they alive and just didn't want her, like mine? How did she turn into such a nice person if that was the case? My money was on dead.

"Will it get cold tonight?" Dan's question broke me out of my thoughts. "Is it safe to get a fire going?"

"Get a fire going? Burn plants?" Wade sounded horrified. "In Faerie? Do you want a tree to reach out and crush you? Or vines to strangle you in your sleep? Moss to smother you? That's what's going to happen if you start burning their family members."

"I just meant dead stuff, Wade," Dan sounded really confused. "Things that fell off the trees."

I looked around. Now that I thought about it, we hadn't had to knock down one piece of brush, or step over a single fallen log. "Do plants not die here?"

"Not unless someone kills them," Wade answered, his voice grumpy.

Okay, that was weird. And scary. And how was the entire place not overrun? And if these plants were as vengeful as Wade had just made it sound, that meant they had feelings. If they had feelings, then they had thoughts, right? Which meant they were at least as alive as the plants back home. Question was, were they as helpful?

"What did you think I meant about the length of our trip being dependent on the feelings of the forest? So far it seems to be willing to let us pass. We haven't come upon any obstacles."

"It doesn't get cold here," Jaden answered the question Wade had ignored. "Everything stays the perfect temperature."

"Well that must be nice," Nina said, dropping her bag to the ground next to Dan's.

"It is," Wade said.

"No it's not," Jaden countered. "No fall, no snow."

"But always the beauty of spring," Wade disagreed.

"To each their own. Neither is necessarily better," Nina said, no doubt trying to keep the peace.

"I lived in California," Jaden said. "No changing seasons gets old fast."

"We don't travel at night here," Wade changed the subject. "So rest for a little while if you need to, but then we push on. We need to travel at least another five of your human miles before sundown."

I groaned. Five more miles, seriously? Just tonight?

Nina dumped her bag out, then Dan's next to hers, and laid down on top of it. I copied her, not needing the warmth but not wanting to lay straight on the ground. I shouldn't have worried about it though, because the ground was soft, the moss under my blanket almost like an air mattress. Funny, it hadn't felt this squishy when we were walking.

Wade raised an eyebrow at me like he knew what I was thinking, then sat down beside me. "What did I tell you about Faerie? It's the best place there is. Anywhere."

Jaden snorted from over where he was standing. "Sure it is, if you're part of the in club, if this has always been your home. If you're one of the higher class, and don't have to worry about things happening to you just because of who you are."

Wade rolled his eyes and settled back.

"I'll keep watch," Jaden muttered, then took off into the trees.

"Jaden," I called after him. This had to be rough for him, coming back here when he hated this place so much. I knew he owed me, but still, this was more than I ever would have asked of him. He was risking a lot just being here.

"I'm going to help him keep watch." I jumped up and ran after him before any of the other three could protest. It was only fair, I didn't even really get tired, so if anything I should be taking watch by myself. Except for the fact that I didn't know what I was doing and there was a good chance I'd get everyone killed.

I stepped into the trees exactly where I'd seen Jaden go in, but he was gone already. "Jaden?" I called quietly. "Jade?" No answer. I placed my hand on a tree. "Know where he went?" I asked it.

Was that a slight shiver? Maybe, maybe not, but no real answer. "Thanks anyway." Might as well keep things polite, just in case. I wouldn't want them to not respond when I needed them because I'd been rude. The other times I'd been helped, my life had been in danger. Hopefully that would never happen again. Ha.

"Jaden?" I whisper yelled again. I didn't know what was out here, I really didn't want to call more attention to myself than was absolutely necessary.

"What?" he asked, stepping out from behind a tree and almost getting punched.

"Don't do that! I almost hurt you." I punched him in the shoulder, just to show him.

"Uh huh." He cocked his head, his lips going into a straight line. "What do you want, Trish?"

Now I knew something was wrong. He'd never really been this short with me, even when I'd been about to turn him over to Starren, and therefore the Council. "Just checking in. You seemed kind of tense." Was I really asking for someone to tell me their feelings? Maybe this was a bad idea. I didn't know what to do with feelings. I avoided feelings at all costs.

Jaden's eyebrows went up and his body relaxed. "You mean you're trying to see how I'm doing?"

Okay, yeah, totally bad idea. "Never mind," I mumbled, and turned to leave.

He grabbed my arm with a loose grip. "No, I think it's nice. Thanks." He dropped my arm once I stopped trying to make my escape and leaned back against a tree, pinching the bridge of his nose. "I just really, really, don't like being here. I'd thought it'd been long enough, that I'd be fine. I'm not as fine as I'd thought."

That was not great. At all. He was here for me, and here was really not a good place for him. "You can go back. If you want."

"And get eaten by firnen?" He gave me a weak smile.

"Firnen?"

"Those things. The flying piranha."

I frowned. "How did you get past them on the way out the first time? On your way home after escaping the school?"

He frowned back. "Now that you mention it, there weren't any."

So no flesh-eating flying teddy bears one way, and like a million of them going the other way. That wasn't weird at all.

"Do you think they'll be after us when we try to leave?"

He shrugged. "I hope not. Maybe it has something to do with which direction you're going. Like, if you're trying to get into Faerie, or out. The golem was the same way."

That made sense. And I was just going to believe it was true for now. Believe that we had an escape plan, for after we'd rescued Starren. Because I had to believe we were going to get her.

"You going to be okay, then?" We hadn't really talked, but he seemed better. Yeah, I was going to go with that, then I'd be able to avoid a conversation that involved emotions.

"Yeah, I'll be fine. Go hang out with your parents. I'm going to stay here for a bit."

My parents. It still felt weird. And not quite right. But so good at the same time. At least I wasn't accidentally correcting people and saying fosters anymore.

"Okay. Don't stay out here too long though. I don't want to have to come find you when Wade is ready to go."

Jaden nodded and ambled off. I watched him go, still worried, and still not liking the fact that I cared.

Wade didn't let us rest long. I wasn't surprised, but wasn't happy either. I'd wandered around checking things out until I Nina yelled for me. Wisely she hadn't left the little clearing. Good thinking, hopefully she kept that up.

She'd settled down quickly after I popped out of the trees. Well, after her heart rate went down after I popped out of the trees. Seriously, I hadn't meant to startle her. That much.

Jaden must have heard all the shouting for me, because he meandered out of the trees soon after I did. They'd already packed up all of our stuff, so we were on our way quickly.

Even the wonder of Faerie began to wear off after about a mile. Man, I really did hate walking. So much. But it was still better than any other hike I'd had in the woods. The last one I'd been too mad at Wade to talk and it had just been the two of us, and the one before that I'd ended up dead. Also Wade. I eyed him sideways, so he wouldn't know I was looking at him. A lot had changed since then. He wasn't after me anymore, but I still didn't know exactly where we stood. We weren't really friends. Definitely weren't boyfriend and girlfriend. Not just acquaintances, and not really teammates.

But I didn't need to figure it out. Tomorrow we'd either have rescued Starren and split up, or we'd be dead. Either way was a great reason to not have to think about what our relationship was now. And an even better reason to not have the awkward conversation to figure out where he stood on things.

"Anyone getting hungry?" Nina asked from behind us. "I brought snacks."

My stomach rumbled at the thought. Nina giggled. I rolled my eyes.

"We should conserve the food. We'll need it tomorrow," Wade said. He plucked a piece of fruit off of a tree and handed it to Dan. "We should make use of what's available."

"Wait!" I smacked the fruit out of his hand. "Don't eat that!"

Dan and Wade both looked confused.

"Why not?" Wade reached down and picked it up, putting the fruit to his mouth and taking a bite, like he was proving a point. "It's perfectly safe."

"But if a human eats something here, doesn't it mean they have to stay?"

Wade just looked more confused. "Ah, no. Where did you hear that?"

Where had I heard that? Not from my mom. Just from human legends, probably. But how was I supposed to know which ones were true and which ones weren't? Some had been pretty spot on up to this point.

"Uh, just around I guess. But how many humans have you brought here? Have you tested it?"

Wade shrugged. "I've never brought a human to Faerie before. It could be true, I suppose, but I've never even heard a rumor of something like that."

Well then. What now? "Jaden, Wade, and I will eat the stuff here." I pointed at Dan, then Nina. "You two just eat what you brought. I don't want to take any chances."

"No chances sounds good to me," Dan said.

Nina dropped her backpack and pulled out a can of Pringles. Okay, now I was jealous of the humans. Who'd a thought that would ever be a thing.

Wade tried to hand me the piece of fruit he'd taken a bite of, but I shoved his hand away and moved over to pick a piece myself. We weren't together anymore, I wasn't eating after him.

The fruit was a weird purplish color, about as big as an apple, but so soft it bruised as I pulled it off the tree. Juice dripped to the ground from the imprints my fingers made, but it wasn't sticky, more like water.

Hesitantly I put it up to my lips. I took a bite and sweetness made my mouth start watering.

"Don't eat too much at once," Wade warned.

I ignored him and took another large bite. This thing was really good. After one more bite, a slow fire built in the back of my mouth, like I'd taken a spoonful of the hottest salsa ever made. "Uh, what's it doing?" I asked Wade.

"It's fire fruit," Jaden answered for Wade. "It heats up after it sits for a few seconds. That's why you're supposed to eat it slowly. The more you eat at a time, the more it reacts to itself and the hotter it feels."

"You couldn't have warned me?" I gasped out, tears leaking from my eyes.

"Wade warned you." He grinned at me. "Would me saying anything have made a difference?"

Probably not, but he could have tried. I coughed, not even able to yell at him.

Nina came up behind me and patted me on the back. "Are you okay?"

I waved her off. I'd survived broken bones, penetrating wounds, and a gunshot. This fruit was not going to best me.

Oh ouch. It was getting to the point I almost couldn't see. "Water," I mumbled, it barely sounding like a word. My tongue and the back of my throat were going numb. Numb was better than the burning.

Jaden's grin went to a lop-sided, sympathetic smile. "It will go away in a few seconds. That much fruit at a time probably left real burns, but you won't feel it long before you heal."

I glared up at him, snot dripping out of my nose, my face letting off so much heat I could tell it was bright red without even looking in a mirror. "Jerk."

He just laughed and grabbed a piece of fruit off the tree. He took a small delicate bite and chewed, still smiling.

Grrr. But he was right. The pain was fading by the time Nina got a water bottle pulled out of her bag, got the cap off, and handed it to me. I took a swig, and by the time it trickled down my throat I was nearly back to normal.

I looked over at Wade, who was grinning even bigger than Jaden. Two jerks.

"Maybe you should think about listening to a person that knows the area," Dan said.

Like I hadn't embarrassed myself enough already. "Yeah, got that," I answered.

Nina handed me a Kleenex and patted my shoulder. Seriously, Kleenex? What all did she have in that bag? She couldn't have had long to pack, they'd only gotten to the tunnel area like twenty minutes after we had. Of course, Dan probably felt a whole lot more comfortable speeding, and I'd been trying to not get picked up.

Jaden continued to nibble on his piece of fruit and looked totally fine.

"It's really good Trish, if you take it slow," Wade said, taking a small bite of his piece.

I glared his way, picked a new piece of fruit since I'd dropped my other one when I'd grabbed at my throat in pain, and took a medium, I'll show them, bite.

Wade rolled his eyes at me, Jaden sighed, and Nina gave me the look.

Okay, yeah, it was dumb. One medium sized bite though wasn't bad. Hot yes, but nothing like the three huge bites I'd taken a few minutes before.

Yeah, I could totally get behind having this fruit, now that I knew the trick to eating it. Some Pringles for variety would be nice though. I eyed Nina's Pringles. She eyed me back, no doubt knowing what I was thinking, then laughed and handed me a couple.

"I packed enough food for all of us, so with the three of you having other food sources, we should have plenty. Dan has the jerky, I packed a ton of that since we need protein and it's going to be hard to get it anywhere else. There are some nuts in there too."

I fist-pumped into the air and headed for Dan's bag. Even when I wasn't healing, I needed a ton of extra food. Nina knew me so well. She'd probably packed like three portions just for me.

"How did you get all this?" I asked as I rifled through the bag.

"She cleaned out every gas station we stopped at," Dan answered for her.

I smiled at her as I unwrapped a granola bar.

We munched on the go, Wade introducing me to all kinds of new berries and fruits. When he handed me a new type, I'd only nibbled it, sending him into a fit of laughter. How was I supposed to know it was completely safe to eat as fast as I wanted? None had any weird secrets like the fire fruit, making me wonder if he'd picked that one first on purpose.

The last couple miles dragged by so slowly I was about to give up on Starren and just leave her sitting in prison. It wasn't like she'd come save me if I needed it. Right? Right. Of course she wouldn't. I was the reason she was in prison in the first place. She was probably not going to be happy to see me, even if I was here to rescue her. Her whole life had changed when she failed to bring me in.

Not that I felt guilty about that or anything. It wasn't like I was going to just let her take me and have them lock me up.

We made camp as it was getting dark. I couldn't say as the sun set, because I assumed it was the same as at home, but I couldn't see it and this was Faerie, so who knew. Weirder things happened here, or so I'd heard.

Being here did make me feel close to my mom. Which was strange, since I'd never been here with her, at least that I remembered. But this was her world. Where she felt most at home. Even with all the bad things she'd told me about the place, I always got the feeling she loved it. Now that I was older, it almost seemed like the stories I was told were meant to keep me from wondering about here, from wanting to see what it was like. Who really wanted to go somewhere that the wildlife was likely to kill you, and the other fae were even more eager? My mom had wanted to keep me away from Faerie for sure, but why? Wade's passionate stories were almost enough to sway me into believing that maybe it wasn't as bad here as Mom had thought. But then, Wade wasn't very reliable when it came to decisions and opinions.

Without the need to cook or set up tents, settling in for the night only took about two minutes. I rolled my sleeping bag out. Nina took one side, and Dan moved over to take the other. I rolled my eyes, but not where they could see.

There wasn't much talking. Wade took the first watch, which I would have been uncomfortable with even a few days ago, but somehow was okay with now. He was different now, softer. If soft could ever be used to describe him.

For once I was perfectly happy going to bed. I thought I'd sleep well after all the excitement, and then all the boring walking. But sleep didn't want to come.

"Nina?" I whispered in the dark. I was met with her soft snore. Not wanting to bother her, I snuggled deeper into my bag even though it wasn't cold at all. "Dan?" No answer there, either.

"Need something?" Jaden asked.

Dan and Nina had taken both my sides, so the top of Jaden's head rested almost against the top of mine.

"Just can't really sleep." We laid in silence for a second. "What's it like, having sisters?"

Jaden chuckled. "Depends on the day."

I snorted. "And it isn't like Lucy is an easy sister to have. But seriously. You guys seem to care about each other." That was a total under-statement. They would do anything for each other, even if they did grumble about it the entire time.

"We do care. We more than care, we love each other. That's what being a part of a family is."

That made me go quiet again. I cared about Dan and Nina. A lot. Maybe even loved them. Okay, I totally did. Ugh, that was even more scary than those stupid bat things. Dying didn't hurt as bad as a broken heart. I had experience with both.

But what did the fact that I loved them even mean? What did I do with that? Whatever, I didn't want to think about it right now. Did I love Starren? That took a little more thought. Could you love someone just because you were related to them? We hadn't exactly left on the best of terms. And she'd even known we were sisters at that point. Why hadn't she said something?

"There is something special about siblings, Trish. A connection that you don't really get with any other type of relationship. You can dislike each other, you can think the other one is an idiot, but in the end, you both know you'd be there for each other, no matter what happens. I didn't want you to come to Faerie, I admit it. But just because it isn't a good place. It looks beautiful on the surface, but underneath..." he trailed off.

I reached above my head and awkwardly patted his shoulder, attempting to give comfort in the same way Nina always made me feel better. I didn't know if it worked or not, but he took a breath and continued.

"But I'm glad we're here now. Whatever else has gone on between you two, you're family, and that's what counts."

He went quiet again. I didn't really know what to say. I'd always been on the outside, looking in at families, wishing I was a part of something. Now I was. I didn't always know what I was doing, but I was getting there. A whole new aspect had been added the second Wade told me about Starren, one that I'd have to figure out. I had no idea how to be a sister. But I'd had no idea how to be a daughter either, and that was starting to go pretty well.

CHAPTER EIGHT

Once I'd fallen asleep, I slept like the dead. And I did not want to get up at all.

"C'mon, kid, we have to go," a familiar voice disturbed my sleep. Ugh, Dan. I heard him move over and start on Nina. She was just as hard to get out of bed in the mornings as I was, so my subconscious wished him luck as I rolled over. Oh wait, sleeping bag, soft ground, Faerie! I sat up quickly.

"Who took my watch?" I asked.

"Jaden and I split the watch last night," Wade answered.

"You all looked tired," Jaden added, nodding at Nina, who Dan was still failing to get up.

That was really sweet. Who'd had the idea was pretty obvious. Wade didn't do sweet.

I may, possibly, have stalled a little while packing. Sure, getting to Starren was our goal, but getting to Starren meant I had to see Starren. I wasn't quite ready for that. As a friend, like I'd thought we'd been, or a sister, which I'd found out we were. Boy was she going to be surprised to see me. And even more surprised to see Dan and Nina. Which reminded me.

"We never went over a plan last night," I said, to no one in particular.

"We didn't." Wade swung his pack over his shoulder and moved toward the tree line. "But I thought about what we were going to do all night while on watch."

The rest of us finished throwing our stuff together.

Wade started off.

"So let's hear it then," Dan said. "I have some experience with planning."

Some experience with planning? Planning this kind of thing? Um, that was weird. Like, really weird.

"What's this prison like? What's the perimeter like? Is it in a town?" Dan asked.

Wade looked back over his shoulder, head cocked, calculating. "Stone, metal cells. It's in a clearing but fae don't have towns like humans do."

Hmm. I'd never really thought about that, never had a reason to. But it made sense. Fae were hard to get along with in general, even when it was getting along with each other.

"Guards?" Dan asked.

"Many guards," Jaden answered.

"How did you escape?" Wade asked.

Jaden adjusted his backpack. "I'd rather not say."

Wade stopped to glare. "Why not? It could be the key to us getting Starren out."

Jaden just kept walking, passed Wade and took up the lead. "I'd rather not say."

Wade marched behind for a second. I could see the wheels turning in his head as he went. "That means someone else was involved. Someone helped you and you don't want them to be discovered."

That would explain it. But that meant Jaden had friends here. Or more than friends? A pang of jealousy hit me, followed by a pang of guilt. I had absolutely no right to be jealous of anything with Jaden, he'd been super nice to me since we'd all moved to Fort Wayne, and I'd just kept blowing him off. But still.

"Like a girl helped you, or a guy?" I asked as casually as I could.

I heard Nina catch a giggle as it tried to escape. I shot her a look and she mimed locking her lips and throwing away the key. This was stupid. I didn't even like Jaden. I totally didn't like Jaden. I didn't like anyone like that right now. I was still getting over Wade, or more likely, getting over his betrayal. Nope nothing there, nothing at all. It wasn't like Jaden was super cute or anything, not like he was crazy nice, even when I didn't deserve it, not like he treated his family well or anything.

Crap. I did kind of like Jaden. I looked up to where he was marching next to Wade, both of them tight lipped and grumpy. And my feelings for Wade were incredibly confusing now, as frustrating and complicated as that was. Feelings like what we'd had didn't just go away. Even if he had shot me, his reasons made sense once I found out why he'd done it. Sure, I still hated that he'd done it. But he seemed to hate it even more than I did.

Ugh, like I'd needed any other confusing things in my life right now. Time to push it away until after we found out if we were going to live through the day or not.

"So," Dan said, breaking the awkward silence. "The plan?"

"It would be best if no one finds out Trisha is here. She is an even bigger prize than Starren, and we would be hunted even more strongly if anyone discovers her. I will go in, get her and Jaden disguises, we'll wait until evening and go into the prison together. Trisha will use her ability to cause a distraction while I break Starren free. Jaden will stay with her in case she needs help." He looked at me. "I know, I know, you can take care of yourself. But just in case."

"How is Trish being able to regenerate going to be a good distraction?" Nina narrowed her eyes. "You'd better not be planning on her getting hurt."

Good point. How was that going to help?

"Not that ability. The other one."

Now Nina's narrowed eyes were on me. "The other one?"

"Uh," I let out a nervous giggle. "I need to talk to Wade for a second." I glared at him and he went wide-eyed. He had no idea he'd just gotten me in trouble, and therefore, gotten himself in trouble.

"Uh, no," Nina said. "Anything you have to say can be said in front of all of us." She crossed her arms in front of her and stopped dead. "Explain."

"You never…" Wade pointed at Dan, then Nina, then back to Dan.

I ground my teeth. "No."

"There aren't supposed to be any secrets between us, Trisha." Nina's disappointed voice made me feel worse than her angry voice ever could. If she was angry, I could just get angry back. Disappointed? That I was not equipped to deal with.

"Sorry," I mumbled.

"So what exactly have you not been telling us?" Dan asked.

"I thought it was a one-time thing!" I protested. "It hasn't happened since I got in that fight with Starren and Wade."

"Yeah, thanks for reminding them of that," Wade said quietly enough only Jaden and I could hear him.

"It's your fault," I whispered back. "You chose the wrong side to fight on." Plus, if I threw him under the bus maybe Dan and Nina would be reminded to be mad at him and forget about me.

"Oh, we still aren't happy about that. That's one of the reasons we're here." Now Dan's arms were crossed in front of his chest too. Shoot, I was in a lot of trouble. "But that's all water under the bridge. What haven't you been telling us?"

So much for getting them to focus on Wade. I shoulda known better.

"Sometimes, when I'm in a lot of trouble, plants help me. I don't do it on purpose so I didn't see any reason to bring it up." And I was already weird enough with super powers and weird family and friends. I didn't need anything else wrong with me.

"Plants help you?" Nina stepped closer, dipping her head to look me in the eyes as I stared at the ground. "How exactly? Like more healing properties or what?"

"Not exactly."

"She goes all Poison Ivy and controls the trees," Jaden said. "That's how she beat Starren and Wade, she wrapped them up and squeezed until they surrendered."

"Thanks a lot, Jaden," I hissed. Not that there was really a great way to break it to your foster parents that you were even more of a freak than they thought, but surely he could have come up with some-thing better than that.

"Well that's... handy," Dan got out.

"Anything that keeps you safe is a good thing in my book." Nina pulled me into a loose hug. "After we get this whole plan thing sorted out, I'm going to need to hear that whole story."

I shifted my arms around to hug her back. I should have known it wouldn't change their minds about me, but I still didn't get why they loved a mouthy, weirdo teen like me. I knew they did, I just couldn't understand why they did. There had to be something that would tip the scale in the wrong direction. One small thing that was too much, that would make them see I wasn't really worth all of the heartache and tears I put them through. The thought made me sick. Hopefully whatever the breaking point was, I never found it.

"Sure, the whole story is yours as soon as we get an idea on how to get Starren out."

Dan waved his hand at the closest tree. "So you can just tell this to do whatever you want?"

"No, not really. Like I said, it only works when I'm in trouble."

Nina squeezed me tighter before letting me go. "Then I hope we never get to see it."

"Amen," Dan added. "Though it does sound pretty cool."

"More than cool," Jaden said. "Kind of epic, actually."

Wade huffed and marched off, which made me grin. Of course he didn't think it was that epic. He'd been on the receiving end of what-ever it was.

"The plan must be revised, then," Wade said. "Jaden will cause a distraction, Trish will be with me. We will get to Starren, get her out of her cell, and meet in the woods."

"This isn't a very detailed plan," Dan said, frowning. "What do you want Nina and me to do?"

"It wouldn't take the fae long to figure out you two are humans. You will wait outside."

"Wait outside?" Nina didn't sound very happy about that. I was though. Less chance for them to get killed. But what happened if we got caught while inside and they were left alone in the woods? No good choices here.

"Can you find your way back to the tunnel if we get separated?" I asked. Everyone knew the unspoken or killed was in there also.

Dan held up something in his hand. "My compass works here. I've been taking notes while we traveled."

Wow, I should have thought of that. Just in case something happened to Jaden and Wade. Or that this ended up being some kind of weird trap and Wade was still after Jaden, but let me go. Or any number of scenarios. But even if both Dan and Nina made it back to the tunnel, how would they survive the firnen?

"But it doesn't matter," Nina said, giving Dan the stink eye. "We aren't leaving without you."

"I just meant we need somewhere to meet, just in case we can't get to each other at some point," I said, doing my best to sound sincere. Somewhere inside I didn't want them to leave me, otherwise I wouldn't be able to say that. But the bigger part of me screamed to keep them safe. I gave Dan the eye.

He nodded. I hoped he knew what I meant. Get Nina out, if it came down to it. He would do anything to keep her safe. I hoped that included leaving me to face whatever consequences there were if I got caught. This whole thing had been my choice, after all.

"Besides, how are we supposed to get past those things without all of you?" Nina asked. She had a valid point.

"I don't think the firnen will attack on the way out," Jaden said.

"Don't think?" Dan sounded skeptical. I had to be with him on this one.

"We won't know for sure until we try to go back, but they weren't there when I went home. And it hasn't been long enough for a colony of that size to develop in such a short time. So either they are there to guard the entrance to Faerie, and anyone is allowed to leave, or..." he winced.

"Or?" I asked.

"Or they are attracted to humans, and that's why they chased us this time and not last. I don't know much about them, but those seem like the two most logical solutions."

"Let's just get a plan for getting Starren out, then we'll work on getting back to Earth," Wade said. "Once she's free, she'll have all kinds of ideas. Strong ideas."

"Are you planning on coming to Earth with us?" I asked Wade. I hadn't really thought about it until now, but him and Starren were from here. Loved it here. Would they try to stay, to find somewhere in Faerie to hide out?

"I won't know until we talk with Starren," Wade answered. "Either way, we'll see the three of you safely back to the tunnel."

Whoa, he must be serious if he could say that out loud. Well, he'd better be serious about keeping us safe, but still. That really did make me feel better. Not that he wouldn't trade any of us, especially Dan or Nina, for Starren, but at least he was planning on helping us back.

"Without a floorplan of the prison, it makes it pretty hard to figure out an entrance and exit," Dan said. "Is there only a ground level, or is it bigger than that?"

"There is only one level, but the inside of the prison shifts around."

"Shifts around?" Dan asked. "That's new."

"Doorways move, to help prevent escapes," Jaden added. "But I know the patterns."

Wade gave Jaden a hard look. "Eventually you'll tell me who helped you escape."

Jaden's face didn't change expressions at all. "No, I won't."

"So that means Wade should be doing the distraction, and Jaden and I will be doing the rescue part," I interrupted, before Wade could get mad. This was actually good. I'd feel safer with Jaden anyway. He had never done anything but looked out for me.

"That won't work," Wade said. "Starren isn't going to trust you. I'll need to be there, or she might not leave her cell." He started walking again, more of a march. Poor Dan and Nina. This was probably more walking than they normally did in a week, even if they did try to jog every day.

"Well Trish isn't getting out of my sight," Jaden said, voice heated.

Wade turned and poked him in the chest. "Trish isn't getting out of my sight," he answered.

"Hey!" I yelled. "Trish is just going to do her normal job! I'm good at being bait. I'll cause the distraction, you boys can get Starren out. Got it?"

They both looked at me, then glared at each other like it was the other one's fault that I had a mind of my own.

"Sounds like a plan to me," Dan said. "Nina and I can help with the distraction." He narrowed his eyes and stared down Wade, then Jaden. "Then Trish doesn't have to leave my sight."

I sighed. I should have come by myself.

I glanced over at Nina. She was giving me a look, laughter in her eyes. I rolled mine. "Fine then, plan is made. Let's just keep moving."

After that things were pretty quiet as we trudged through the forest. Somehow the temperature was just right. The ground was soft, easy underfoot, and the trees beautiful. I could see how a nature person would love it here. I wasn't a nature person, and I still wasn't immune to its charms. Was it possible Faerie wasn't as bad as Mom had made it out to be? Why had she hated it here so much?

Wade pointed out a deer as we walked. It had no fear, just kept grazing in a patch of grass. Was the other grass mad at the deer? Wade had made it sound like the plants were alive here. Somehow this deer seemed different too, even with many similarities to the ones at home. Not that I had a lot of experience with deer, but this one seemed larger, more majestic, its movements flowing and controlled. Maybe it was just my imagination.

Wade stopped us, finally. "We're here."

"Here, as in here, here?" I asked. Maybe hiking wasn't so bad. Yeah, we could totally do some more of that.

"What other kind of here is there?" Wade asked, shrugging off his backpack and dropping it to the ground. "The humans can keep watch over our stuff."

"Dan and Nina," I managed behind gritted teeth, "Will be with me, so I can make sure nothing happens to them."

"You'll be intentionally calling the guards out to cause a distraction. I think they would be safer here. But do what you want." He shrugged. "They aren't my humans."

"Well that's a bit racist," I heard Nina mutter behind me.

It totally was, but he was probably right. I would be throwing myself out there, did I really want Dan and Nina to be a part of that?

"I guess you should stay here," I mumbled.

"I don't think so," Dan said. "You aren't doing anything like that alone. I wish you weren't doing it at all."

I gave Nina a quick hug. "Sorry, Dan, but I am. Don't worry about me. I'll be back A.S.A.P." And then I went invisible. Sure, any fae that walked by would totally see me, but Dan and Nina couldn't, and that was what counted at the moment.

"Trish?" Nina's voice was well over an octave higher than it normally was.

"Sorry, Mrs. Inza," Jaden said, then followed my lead and disappeared as well.

Wade of course didn't even pretend to be polite. He just popped into thin air.

I gestured to the guys to follow and moved off through the trees in the direction I hoped the prison was in. I pointed and cocked my head, asking Wade. He nodded and took the lead.

"Trish? Trisha?" Nina was calling softly after me. She sounded a little frantic, but I had to turn off the part of me that cared, for now. She was safer staying here, and I had a job to do. My sister needed me. Sister still felt so weird. How long would it take until that felt normal?

Hopefully I got a chance to find out.

Nina's calls got louder, but faded away as we moved on. Dan had better put a stop to that. I was leaving them behind so they stayed safe, not so they accidentally became the distraction.

Once we were for sure out of sight, I dropped the invisibility. I didn't know what was normal in Faerie, but seeing a fae trying to be invisible when other fae could still see them and there were no humans around seemed like a good indicator that we weren't from around here. We didn't need any extra help in that area.

We walked for a bit, but never came to any clearing or anything that could hold a prison. "Where is this place?" I finally asked Wade, under my breath.

He crooked a finger and moved a tree limb out of the way.

There, a portal, the edges formed with tree branches. Of course.

Another stupid portal. I hated portals. "That's just great," I moaned. "How am I supposed to cause a distraction? I thought there would be some big door or gate or something I could throw rocks at."

Wade looked at me like I was an idiot. "Why would you think that?"

"You visited Alcatraz! That's the only example of a prison I know."

"Oh, okay." Wade said. "Fae prisons aren't like that."

"I think she figured that out, Wade," Jaden said.

"Oh yeah?" Wade asked. "You think?"

"Okay, boys." I shoved my way between them, a hand on both their chests, forcing them apart. "Either one of you geniuses have an idea on what I should do for this distraction?"

"Jump through the portal, hit one of the guards, jump back and run." Yep, about the type of plan I would expect out of Wade.

"Got anything better, Jaden?" I asked. I didn't want to ask him about his ability in front of Wade. As far as I knew, Wade, and by extension, the Council, still didn't know what Jaden could do. And I bet he wanted to keep it that way.

Jaden shook his head.

I sighed.

"Okay then. Punch a guard it is. You're one hundred percent sure she's in there?"

Wade nodded.

"Out loud, please." Best to get it straight from his mouth, so there was no way he was lying.

"I am one hundred percent sure that is where she was when I left to find you, and they have had no reason to move her that I know of. She is imprisoned and not being treated well, and needs to get out of there as soon as possible."

Okay, that was pretty sure. "Be ready, boys." I pulled away from both of them and jogged over to the portal, pausing just on this side. I could do this. I totally had this. Being bait was my normal job. Nothing unusual here, just like the good old times. Except in the good old times I knew Starren would bail me out, whether she wanted to or not. My safety blanket. I didn't have that here. Do something wrong and I was probably dead. Oh well. This was what family did to a person.

I jumped up and down, rolling my neck and shoulders like I was some football player or something. Okay, yeah, at this point I was just stalling.

Taking a deep breath, I jumped through the portal.

CHAPTER NINE

The portal rush barely bothered me this time. It almost felt nostalgic, actually. If only this was just some quest where I'd run into a troll. I was probably an idiot for giving the Council even more reason to hate me and want me caught, but what choice did I have? No good ones, that was for sure.

I popped out on the other side of the portal and blinked. Wait a sec. This was the same white material as the Fae Distribution Center. There was no way I'd ended up there, right?

There were the doors, stretching on into infinity. There wasn't anyone around. This was stupid. I stuck my head back out the portal. "Are you sure this is right?" I hissed in Wade's direction.

"Yes," he whispered back.

"There's no one in here," I said.

He looked confused, then jogged over and went through the portal right beside my head. I jerked back and turned to catch him staring. "Something is off," he said.

"No kidding."

The words were barely out of my mouth before the white walls flickered. Not like the lights or anything, but the actual walls, showing cave like walls behind them.

"It's just a glamour," Wade said, sounding relieved.

Jaden popped through the portal behind us.

"A glamour," I explained, like I'd been the one to figure that out. "So these doors aren't real?"

"The doors themselves are, just not the layer over them. Look under what you would normally see."

Oh yeah, cause that really explained everything so well. I squinted and tried to do what he'd said. The white walls flickered more, until I was nearly reeling from the walls coming down all around me, until I could see where we actually were.

"But what about the guards?" I asked.

"Good question," Wade answered. "Just a second." He turned and walked back out the portal.

I leaned up against the wall. "So." I said to Jaden. "What you got to eat?"

He grinned, but reached into his pocket and pulled out a granola bar.

I was popping the first piece into my mouth when Wade's disembodied head came back through the portal. "Come on out here," he said.

I crammed the last piece of the chocolate chippy goodness into my mouth before going after him. Wade didn't say anything when I came out, just walked around to the other side.

"Try this side," he said, after Jaden had joined us.

"Okay," I said, and started to jump through.

"Wait," Jaden grabbed my arm.

I paused.

He pulled his scarf off his neck and put it around mine. I expected him to say something weird, like for luck, but he just pulled the bottom of it up so it covered the lower half of my face. That was actually a really good idea.

But enough of that. I turned from Jaden and slipped into the portal.

Okay, yep, much more prison like on this side. Walls carved out of rock, tall ceiling, dark with flickering torches, check, check, check. Didn't the fae have better lighting options? Even humans did and the fae were supposedly so much superior.

"Hey," a voice said. "You aren't authorized to be here."

I stopped staring at the ceiling and looked ahead of me. A desk, with two male fae, one standing by it, the other sitting behind it. Hopefully they didn't recognize me. The fae weren't big on technology, so they probably hadn't been passing pictures around or anything.

I turned and bolted back through the portal, running toward the trees. I paused after about ten feet, not wanting to lose the guards when they came through. Wow, they were really slow. And still nothing. I looked over to where I knew Jaden and Wade were hiding in some other plants. Wade's head came up out of the bush and he gestured toward the portal.

"Okay, okay, no reason to get in a hurry," I mumbled.

The guards had better not be waiting right on the other side to grab me. I went through the portal again. Both of the guards had gone back to whatever they were doing before I'd interrupted them the first time.

"Hey, kid, what did I tell you?" the first guard said. "Get out of here."

So they thought they'd run me off last time. I took a few steps closer. Close enough to get a good look at the armor the guards were wearing. It was pretty amazing, right out of some epic fantasy movie, with all the metal flashing and whorled inlays.

"Did you not hear what I said?" the guard said, standing up from behind the desk. His armor was a dark blue, and the other guy's a light grey. Were the colors significant, or just random? Whatever, this wasn't getting me anywhere.

I marched forward and stopped right in front of the second guard, who shoved off the desk and stood at full height, looking down at me. He was huge. Super tall. Maybe this hadn't been a great idea.

I didn't want to say anything. I didn't want them to be able to recognize my voice. So I leaned in, and the guard leaned down like I was about to tell him a secret. Then I popped him in the nose.

He bellowed.

I ran.

I dove through the portal, both guards hot on my heels. "Here they come!" I yelled before the guard in the light armor barreled out of the portal behind me. The one in the dark armor was close on his heels.

Out of the corner of my eye, I could see Jaden and Wade slip into the portal as I took off into the trees. Hopefully I could find my way back. And hopefully I didn't run into Dan and Nina wandering around looking for me.

I'd expected a lot more guards. Or for them to be ogres or something. Why hadn't Wade just taken these guys out? He fought like some sword master, why did he need help getting Starren free?

Then the one guard in the dark blue armor split into two guards in dark blue armor. And then the two morphed into four.

Seriously? How was that fair?

I hadn't been putting a ton of effort into running up until this point. That changed quickly. I tore off as fast as I could, checking to make sure I wasn't losing the guards. Not. Opposite, actually.

"Come on, Trish, you got this," I panted out. "Bait is always your job. You know what you're doing."

Yeah, except usually the enemy couldn't quadruple themselves.

A fireball whizzed by over my head, sending me slamming into a tree. Well that was new. I didn't even take the time to dust off, just jumped to my feet and ran.

Dan and Nina were out here somewhere. I needed to make sure that I kept these guys going in the opposite direction we'd left my fosters, otherwise who knew what would happen. Dan may be some super spy or something, but he definitely couldn't stand up to a fireball. And I couldn't even think about something happening to Nina.

I dodged left. Left again. Right. Left. Keeping them guessing only worked for a couple minutes. I checked over my shoulder. They were making progress, fast.

"Shoot. Shoot. Now what?" I asked myself, diving to miss a fireball and rolling to land on my feet. Dang it, how did I keep ending up in places like this? Why had I ever said yes to coming to Faerie? And why in the world had I insisted I'd be great as bait?

A vine from one of the trees shot down, wrapped around my torso just under my armpits and slingshotted me up into the trees. I literally clamped my teeth, only allowing a small whimper to escape. Impressive considering a scream was trying its hardest to get out.

The vine tossed me into the air, and just as I started to plummet to my death another snatched me out of the sky.

I flipped through the heavens for a couple moments, switching vines multiple times before I was set gently down on the limb of a huge tree. I swayed, the world rushing around me as I did my best not to puke. The branch that had set me down came back instantly to steady me.

"Thanks," I managed to croak out, keeping my eyes tightly closed and leaning heavily on the trunk of the tree. "Maybe not quite so fast next time."

Indistinct shouting sounded from below, and I shrunk even tighter into the tree trunk. Vines flowed around me, completely obscuring me from view from the ground.

I bumped one with my finger, and it seemed to feel my intent. It wiggled slightly over and I had a small peephole to the forest floor. There was the guard in the dark blue armor. Well, one of him. And then that one split into two, and then four more. Jeez, how many of himself could that guy make? No wonder Wade hadn't wanted to take him on. He could have warned me.

"We need to get back to our post," the guard with the light colored armor said.

"We need to find that girl," all the guards with dark blue armor said at the same time. "No one gets away with hitting an agent of the Council."

Okay, maybe the punch had been a little excessive. But I'd needed them to chase me, and that seemed like the most effective way to get them to do it.

They went into a staring match for a second, but then the dark guard relented.

One by one the extra guards poofed into nothing, until all the ones in sight were gone. I stayed put and sure enough, a minute later the guards turned and walked by together, going toward where I assumed the portal was. I had gotten all turned around while nearly losing my granola bars across the tree tops.

I waited a couple more minutes, which was impressive for me. Patience was definitely not my strong suit. "Are they gone?" I asked the trees. They shivered in response, which I took as a yes. "I need to get back to the portal, please." The trees complied, wrapping branches and vines together to create a bridge for me.

Going straight back to the portal didn't take long. I must have done quite a bit of zig-zagging in my wild run away from the guards.

Once I was within sight of the portal, yet still far enough away to feel safe, I sat down and dangled my legs off either side of a large branch. Vines knit around behind me, forming a small half hammock for me to lay back in. This would be a good break. If I wasn't worried the boys were in trouble, which, of course, I was. They were the boys.

Time ticked by slowly. The sun didn't really show, so it was hard to tell. But the shadows were in different places than before, for sure.

"What's taking so long? Not that you aren't comfortable," I said, patting the tree. "I'm just getting even more worried." Wade and Jaden had been in there a long time. Forever, it felt like. Had they been captured? Wade betrayed Jaden? Fought to the death? Found Jaden's girlfriend, who had freed him last time? Okay, probably not that one, but there were too many options here. "Down, please," I said, and patted the tree. A vine wrapped gently around my waist and floated me to the ground. "Thanks."

It was a relief to know the plants here did care. That made life so much easier. And staying alive.

Last time through the portal, for real. I'd just pop my head in, take a look around, then be done. Unless the boys were in the middle of a fight, then I'd figure it out as I went.

I pushed my head through the portal.

Oh crap.

Not only were both the normal guards there, but also about ten of the copies, and a few extra guards that hadn't been there last time. Two of the dark colored armor guards rushed me.

I flung myself back away from the portal and tore for the trees.

One of the copies jumped through the portal after me, but dissipated as soon as it got through. Did they have to be within a certain distance of their original?

A new guard burst through the portal. He took just a second to get his bearings, then reached for me. I was a good distance away, but it was almost like the space between us shrank. He was able to grab my ankle and jerk me back to the portal entrance.

"Let... go..." I growled as I reached for my sword. I didn't want to hurt anyone, so I just left my hand on the hilt.

"Who are you, and what do you want?" He sounded totally bored. Well that take down had been pretty easy for him. Ha. He had no idea the can of worms he'd just opened.

I whispered to the trees. I could feel their anxiety as they watched the guard drop me to the ground. Vines crawled toward us. I tossed a dirt clod at the guard to keep him occupied and give the vines a chance to get over here.

"None of that, now," the guard said, jerking me to him and clamping a hand over my mouth. It didn't stop the vines.

Two more guards came through the portal, just as a vine grabbed my foot. It started to tug, trying to pull me back to the tree line.

One of the new guards grabbed onto me, adding his weight to the first guard's, making my body groan at the pressure of being pulled so strongly from two directions. The third guard pulled a sword and cut the vine that had snaked its way up to my thigh. It flailed around and slid back toward the trees. Three more replaced it.

I whimpered audibly, my leg pulsing where the vine had tried to hold me back. Bruises healed as they formed.

"Get her through the portal," the third guard yelled.

I did pull my sword then, but the guard pounced on me before I was able to use it, wrestling it out of my grip.

The first hefted me to my feet and drug me toward the portal. I bit and scratched and screamed, but it didn't faze him. I flailed, reaching for my sword on my back. The vines moved toward us as fast as a car, nearly leaping over the ground. The second guard let go of me and pulled his sword, taking on the vines with the third guard.

The weird sensation of too much distance being covered happened again, and we were close enough to the portal for the guard to toss me through.

Ol' Replicator was waiting for me on the other side. I was mobbed by about seven of them. There wasn't any use fighting back at this point. The vines hadn't followed me through the portal, so either they had been chopped to pieces or couldn't feel our connection. I dropped my sword and held up my hands.

One of the men knocked me to the floor and two others helped him pin me to the ground.

The two guards that had stayed behind staggered through the portal and fell at the other guards feet. The one with the sword rolled to his feet and stalked over to me. "You!" he pointed a finger at me.

I squeezed my eyes closed. Don't cry, don't cry. Warriors did not cry. And I was a warrior. Kind of.

With my eyes closed, all I felt was a flow of air before a boot caught me in the side. Pain exploded through my whole body, starting at my ribs.

"Think you can make fools out of us, eh?" he kicked me again.

What kind of man kicked a teenage girl when she was on the ground? So maybe Faerie itself was fine, but mom had been totally right about the fae.

"I didn't need to," I said, opening my eyes and glaring at him. "You did that for yourself."

I didn't get a reaction from the other guards like I'd hoped. They didn't even act like they'd heard me.

I got another kick. This one was hard enough to roll me over. I curled into a tight ball, protecting the injury until it could heal, telling myself again not to cry. Where were Wade and Jaden?

"What was going on out there?" one of the guards that had been out in the clearing with me shoved his face in mine, his terrible breath making my stomach roll. "What were you doing to make those vines help you?"

So Cray had been right. Well, and Wade and Starren too. Plants being your friend was not a normal fae ability.

I set my face and glared stonily at the ground. I couldn't lie, so no answer was better than a true one.

The guard that had taken such pleasure in kicking me raised a hand, but another caught it and shoved it back down. "This isn't our place. Send for Wurt." He nodded toward another guard. "And you, take that sword from her."

A tear dripped out of the side of my eye. I wiped it off on my shirt. Dan and Nina were out in the woods, waiting for us. Why had I given up a life with them for a suicide mission to save a sister that pretty much hated me?

Someone grabbed me and lifted me up by my arms, pinned behind my back. I kicked out, just for spite since I knew there was no escaping. I got cuffed in the head in return.

"Put her in ten until Wurt gets here," the guy in dark armor commanded. "The Council may be interested in this one."

The sword guy and a girl I hadn't noticed before both grabbed me, dragging away from the portal. I drooped intentionally, not wanting them to find out about the healing. Supposedly not all fae had abilities beyond what everyone had, and these people didn't need to know about mine. The vines were going to be enough of a problem.

They jerked me along forever, somehow not getting tired. We passed cell after cell, curious inmates crowding the doors to see what the guards were bringing through until we finally stopped in front of one.

"Step back," the female guard said, slapping the door.

Something hissed inside, but must have moved out of the way because the other guard unlocked the door and pulled it open with a clang.

Without ceremony or any warning, both guards grabbed an arm and with a practiced motion pitched me inside. I took a wild look around, trying to find the source of the hissing. The door clunked shut behind me, and I plastered myself to it, letting my eyes adjust to the dark.

"Hello?" I asked, cursing the fact that my voice sounded so warbly. "Hey?" I asked again, this time with better faked confidence.

No answer.

Something brushed against the back wall. I stepped to the side of the door to let the light trickle in through the bars.

A girl squinted back at me. She didn't look that old. Had she been what was making that horrible hissing? Probably just trying to scare her new cellmate so she could be the one in charge or something. The only knowledge I had about prison was TV, and that probably didn't count for much. Though the human/fae difference didn't seem to matter at this point. All creatures acted about the same when they were trapped.

I moved a little closer to her, keeping my body language as unthreatening as I could.

"Do you know if they brought a couple of guys through here earlier? Both pretty tall, one dark blondish hair, green eyes, the other darker?"

The other fae ignored me.

"Hey." I stepped closer. "I asked you a question. It's important."

She jerked in my direction, baring her teeth and growling. I jumped back, hands in the air. Okay, those weren't normal humanish teeth. She glared at me, her teeth shrinking back down into her mouth, making her look like a normal person.

I raised my hands up, going with the universal 'I don't mean any harm,' move. "If you'd just answer my question, we could totally pretend the other isn't even here. Did you see my guys?"

She cocked her head, making me wonder if she even understood. But then she shook her head no. That was good, right? Hopefully that meant they hadn't been caught. But now I needed to come up with an explanation for my weird behavior. And even weirder ability. Why would someone be stupid enough to go into a jail and punch a guard? No reason that I could think of, other than they were trying to break someone out. I did not want that to be the explanation this Wurt got out of me.

What could I say that wasn't lying? Someone told me I couldn't, and I thought I could? Not exactly lying. Dan had definitely told me I couldn't. But would that really be believed by anyone? And what about the whole vine thing? Would they keep me just for that? The Council might not know about it, I hadn't thought to ask Wade. Fingers crossed they didn't, or I was in serious trouble. It sounded like that would be a pretty identifiable trait.

I slid to the floor and leaned against the wall, dropping my head to rest on my knees. This was it. I'd gotten Dan and Nina killed. Even if they were still alive at the moment, they wouldn't be for long. The tears flowed hot and heavy then. I couldn't even begin to stop them this time. Even if Jaden and Wade had gotten to Starren and gotten her out, the whole place was on high alert now, they would never be able to get to me.

Jaden. If Jaden was free, he would take care of Dan and Nina, even if Wade and Starren didn't want to help.

But they wouldn't leave me here. Jaden, Dan, or Nina. They'd get killed or captured trying to save me. There was no way out of it this time.

I held back the wail trying to escape, my whole body shaking with the effort.

In my near despair, I forgot I had an audience. A hand on my shoulder nearly sent me through the wall. I looked up just as the other girl jumped back away from me. She looked totally freaked out, but if it was because of my crying or I'd startled her, I didn't know.

"What's your problem?" I asked. "Do you think this is funny or something?"

She held up both hands, like she was trying to calm me down, and backed away slowly, until she was at the complete other side of the cell.

I would have felt bad for scaring her, but I didn't have room for anymore guilt.

Time moved oddly here. I sat forever, then I got up and moved around forever, the other girl always keeping the exact same distance away from me.

Finally clanging started up and down the outside aisle. I scrambled to the door to see what was going on. My heart leapt. Maybe Jaden and Wade had come for me.

Crushing fear returned when I got sight of a small cart with a pot on it, and some bowls hanging off the side. Mealtime, apparently. For once I wasn't hungry. Even the thought of eating turned my stomach. I slumped back against the wall, my ribs aching from where I'd hit the floor. Why weren't they healed? I kicked at the wall. Probably some kind of blocker here. It wouldn't do to have prisoners shooting fireballs at other prisoners, or turning into water and sliding under the door.

This was just great. I'd gotten used to no healing while living in

Fort Wayne, but this was different. There I didn't have to worry about getting attacked at any second. I was good with a sword, but without the healing and extra good reflexes, I was no match for any of those guards.

A guard knocked on our door. "Prisoners, come get your meal."

The girl watched me, waiting to see what I'd do. I gestured for her to go ahead. She bolted past me to the door.

Shoving a small bowl of something through a hole, the guard looked around the other girl to me. "So you're the new one, eh?"

I didn't answer.

"No use having an attitude. That doesn't get you far here."

I still didn't answer. I wasn't making any friends here, and we all knew it.

After grabbing her bowl, the other girl rushed to the back of the cell and started slurping. Rude. Was that what I was normally like?

Another bowl of whatever made it through the hole. "Here kid. Take it," the guard said.

I ignored him.

"You'll regret it later. Next meal ain't for a long time."

I looked the guy in the face. I wasn't one hundred percent sure what he was, but definitely not high fae. They probably thought this job too menial for them.

"Thanks, but I'm not hungry."

He was just doing his job. He probably didn't like it, and didn't have a choice.

"Your choice." He started to pull it back, but the other girl jumped up and ran across the cell, snatching it from his hand. She handed him back her empty bowl without looking him in the eye.

"Do you know when I'm going to get out of here?"

"No, do you?" he snarked back, then walked away, headed for the next cell.

I tipped my head back against the wall and closed my eyes. The last couple days hit me like a ton of bricks. I needed a nap so bad. But I didn't want to be asleep if Jaden and Wade showed up to save me. I snorted. Or just as likely, Starren.

Once I heard the guard leave, I'd get up and take stock of everything. Maybe Starren was in a cell nearby.

The guard worked his way down the line of doors, me fidgeting the whole time. Seriously, how long could it take to hand people bowls of food? I didn't even know what kind of food it was, there was no smell.

At last the sound faded away. The main door opened, then thudded closed. It was a completely different sound than the cell doors. I stood and moved over to the door.

"Hey," I called softly through the bars. No one answered. "Hey," I tried again, a little louder.

"What?" a deep voice said from across the aisle way.

"Have you met a prisoner here called Starren?"

A large face pressed against the bars on the other side of the room. "Yeah. What's it to you?"

My heart leapt. Finally, something small was going right. "I need to speak with her. Do you know where she's kept?"

"Here's your phases, girl. One, escape plan. There aren't any good ones. Two, caring about other prisoners and trying to find them, that's where you're at. Three, try another escape plan. Four realize that there is no escaping. Five give up and don't give a care anymore. The faster you get through the phases, the better. Then the rest of us don't have to listen to you."

Was everyone in this place rude? Seriously.

"Anyone else got anything to add?" the woman in the other cell yelled.

No's chorused from all the way down the aisle.

So much for solidarity and all the that. But at least I'd found out she was here. Wade had been right about that. They fed us in our cells, but they had to let us out to get some outside time, and showers and stuff, right? I'd run into her eventually, and we'd figure this out. If she didn't kill me. And even if that didn't work, they'd let me out eventually. All I'd done was annoy a guard. Surely that wasn't a lifetime sentence. They'd just thrown me in here to scare me, I'd be out in no time. Right? That had to be right. Because Dan and Nina were out there.

But what if that wasn't?

I moved back from the door a bit and sat down again, tipping my head back against the wall. What did I know about prison escapes? Nothing. And if Starren couldn't get herself out of here alone even though she was Starren, how in the world did I think I was going to break myself out? I might be reckless, but I wasn't an idiot.

I sat like that in the dark, for what felt like forever, my mind spinning with all of the things that could be happening to Dan and Nina right now. They could have been captured. Had they ran? I tried to shut down the last thought, but it didn't work. Were they even still alive? The only real sounds to distract me were the occasional cough from one of the other inmates. No one even talked. What was wrong with these people?

Eventually my stomach growled.

A hand on my shoulder nearly sent me skyrocketing. I swung wildly, opening my eyes. The other girl in the cell dodged back. I actually didn't even get close. She had fast reflexes.

"Yeah?" Maybe the rudeness was something in the air, something I was catching.

She held out the bowl she'd taken from the guard earlier.

I peeked over the edge. It didn't look like a bite was missing of some white cereal stuff.

"You kept this for me?" She just cocked her head without saying anything. "You sure? Maybe you should eat it." She was way too thin. She could use the extra calories. If there were any in that slop.

She just shoved it at me, spoon and all.

I took it warily. Since when did kindness make me worried? Since everyone else here seemed to be jerks.

I spooned a bite into my mouth, tensing up for the inevitable bile rising to my throat. Prison food was supposed to be even worse than hospital food. According to movies and stuff. But no. Even cold the flavors burst across my tongue, making my eyes go wide.

"What is this?" I asked the girl. Maybe she'd actually talk if I was being nice.

She didn't. She just watched me.

I shoveled the rest of the food into my mouth in record time. Seriously, what was this? I so needed to know. Did everything in Faerie taste good? I couldn't believe they had some kind of chef here, not with how the cells looked.

Unfortunately, I was starting to need to use the restroom.

"How do I get a guard to take me to the bathroom?" I asked.

Typical no response. I was tempted to stop trying, but I wasn't one to back down from a challenge.

A snort came from across the aisle. "Where you from, girl? No guard is coming to take you to use 'the bathroom."

Laughs sounded from the cells around me.

"Ladies, do you think they'd let us take baths?" another voice asked, sending the room into laughter again.

Wait, what? No baths?

A fist thudded on the other side of the main door. "Quiet in there," a guard yelled.

"We aren't even allowed to talk?" I whispered to my cellmate. She at least shrugged this time.

If we didn't get taken to go the restroom, where was I supposed to go? I shoved myself up and took a tour of our tiny cell. The girl stayed opposite of me, moving in sync to stay as far from me as possible. Someone must not have been very good to her in the past.

And then I found it. A small hole in the back, where much of the smell was coming from. "In there?" I whispered in horror. I'd gone in lots of weird places, the woods for example, even an alley once when I was little and no where would let us use the restrooms without a purchase and my mom had no money. But somehow, this just felt worse.

"Buck up, Trish, you don't have a choice." So I went. I wasn't happy about it, but back to the no choice thing.

Turned out there were no beds in this cell. I hadn't noticed until I did the whole tour thing. What was wrong with people here? How could they treat other people like this? My eyes started to well up again, making me really glad for the dark.

As if she could tell what I was thinking, the girl inched forward and picked up a blanket, then held it out to me. Why was she in here? She seemed way too nice.

I threw the blanket over my shoulders, trying to ignore the smell.

It had apparently been in here since they built the prison. "So..." she cocked her head at me again. "What should I call you?"

She blinked, then started waving her hands around in the air. Okay, not waving, making shapes. Signing! She was deaf! That explained so much.

"Uh, sorry, I don't understand any of that."

Her shoulders slumped, and she looked at the ground.

I moved forward slowly, so I didn't startle her, and touched her arm. She flinched, but didn't run. I pointed at myself. "Trisha." I moved my lips slowly, in case she could lip read. I really didn't know how to handle this at all.

She signed something, pointed at me, then signed it again. I mimicked her and pointed to her. She shook her head no, signed it again, and pointed to me. Okay, so she'd named me. I pointed at myself and signed my name, then pointed at her and did my most confused face.

She actually gave me a slight smile and signed something, very slowly. I totally didn't get it. I held up my finger, telling her one second, and patted around on the floor until I found a rock. I moved over to the small section of light the door let in, and scratched out Trish on the wall, then handed it to her.

Taking the rock carefully, she moved around me and scratched at the wall. It took her forever, she must have some perfectionist thing going on. When she moved, I got to actually see what her name was. Nara.

"Like NAra, or like NARa?" I asked, stressing different syllables. I knew she wouldn't be able to answer me, but having this weird conversation was keeping my mind off stuff for a few minutes.

She shrugged and gave me that small smile.

I tried to remember how she'd signed her name to me, but I totally got it wrong.

Her eyes grinned, even if her mouth didn't, and she signed her name to me again.

I copied her and she nodded.

Well there. At least I'd gotten something out of being stuck in this place. I knew how to say some random fae girl's name in sign language. How did a fae go deaf anyway? Was she born like that?

Nara went back to the wall. It took a second for me to realize she was carving the alphabet. Apparently I was about to learn a whole lot more than just her name.

It was good though. A good distraction. We worked on it for quite a while before I got so tired I could barely keep my eyes open. This few days had been such a whirlwind of emotion and activity. The activity I could do non-stop without a problem. The emotion part, not so much. I pulled the foul blanket over me and curled up close to the wall in the dark in the corner opposite the door, but away from the hole in the floor. It didn't take long before I passed out.

CHAPTER TEN

I woke up to the exact same lighting as when I'd gone to sleep. I stretched my neck and it popped. That confirmed the whole blocking theory. Sleeping against a stone wall without powers was so terrible. How did Dan and Nina deal with this stuff all the time?

A pang hit me, like a small warning wave before a tsunami. I started to hyperventilate, my hands going clammy. Dan and Nina were out there somewhere, running around Faerie. Or worse, the fae had them. What would they do to humans caught in Faerie? It wouldn't be good, that was for sure.

The sound of the small food slot doors opening and closing pulled me back from the edge of a panic attack. Food. Food was good. I liked food. There was comfort in food.

I glanced up to find Nara staring at me.

"What?" I snapped.

She wilted, and I felt bad. Even deaf she must have been able to tell what my tone was from looking at my face.

"Sorry," I muttered into my knees, realized she couldn't see that, and did my best to remember how to sign the letters to her.

She waved it off like it didn't matter. Had I really made a friend down here? The fae locked other fae up for weird things, any small trespass a punishable offence, but what if she was a serial killer or something?

The guard shoved our food in without a word, and this time I took it. The same white stuff as... last night? Yesterday? I didn't know. I handed Nara her bowl.

"Hey," I said to the guard as I handed him the empty bowl from my last meal. "I thought I was going to talk to some guy named Wurt."

The guard raised his eyebrows. "That's unfortunate for you." It was a different guard than the last time. Shift change?

"Do you know when that's supposed to happen?" I forced my voice not to change. How bad could a guy named Wurt be? The guard was probably just having fun with me.

"No. You'd better hope it's as long in the future as possible."

I rolled my eyes, doing my best not to let him psych me out, and sat down to eat my food.

"Girl," someone hissed after the guard had finished his rounds. "Girl."

I peeped out between the bars from my seat on the floor. "Me?"

"Yes, you. What did you do bad enough to have Wurt make the trip here to see you?"

Wasn't that a question there was no good answer to. I didn't want to offend anyone here, especially since I wasn't healing right now, but I also didn't want to go around telling everybody who I was.

"You got me, I don't even know who he is," I answered.

"He's the official interrogator for the Council," someone else whispered. "If he is being sent to speak you, you must have done something extreme."

Okay, yeah, the Council did kind of hate me. But they didn't know it was me here, did they? How could they? This whole mess just kept getting worse and worse. Not only were Dan and Nina in trouble, but now it sounded like I was in more trouble than I thought. So much for the guards just wanting to scare a stupid teenager.

"Wade, if I ever see you again, I'm going to kill you." I muttered to myself. "You couldn't just leave me in peace with my new family, could you?"

Nara was still staring at me, which I found weird until I realized she couldn't hear any of the other women. I was literally all she had going on in her world right now. How long had she been in this cell by herself, completely cut off from everything?

Was this empathy? I was spending too much time with Nina.

We spent the day, or night, or whatever, working on sign language. I'd actually graduated from letters to signs by the time we agreed we should get some sleep. Not that I really knew any sign language at home, but I didn't think much of this was the same. It was probably a skill I would never use after I got out of this place, but what better did I have to do? And it gave me something to do other than my imagination going wild on Nina starving to death in the woods, Nina being captured by the fae, Nina getting her flesh chewed off her bones by firnen as they tried to escape through the tunnel. Jaden being captured, Jaden being locked up to rot. Yeah, thinking about sign language wasn't so bad.

Another meal, a little more sign language, and then the big door at the end of the aisle opened. I froze. Somehow I knew, this wasn't going to be good for me. Either they'd caught someone I'd come here with, or Wurt was here. Amazing how just a name could put a knot in the pit of your stomach. And I hadn't even met the guy.

Three guards showed up at our cell door, blocking the light. "Annoying one." The guard from my first meal was back on duty, apparently.

I faked shock. "Me?"

"Yeah, you. Get up. Someone wants to meet you."

I pushed to my feet, doing my best to hold back the tremors so the guards couldn't see how scared I was. I just got stupider and more sassy the more freaked out I got, so this probably wasn't going to go well. Like it would even if I was an angel, but still. At least they might feel bad about being mean to a nice kid, instead of dealing with a snarky teenager.

The door opened. Nara looked at me, panic in her eyes. I waved her off. This didn't have anything to do with her.

Two female guards came in and drug me out the door. I went limp. No use helping them. Besides, I was still achy from the rough treatment when I'd been brought in. This not healing thing was seriously a pain.

We went through the big door and instead of going right which would take us toward the portal, we swung left. I had to close my eyes when we got through the doorway. It was super bright in here compared to the dingy light in the cell room.

We went quite a distance, passing a couple more doors set far apart. Were all of those cell blocks? Was Starren down one of them? Wade and Jaden?

Stopping at a door, one of the guards spritzed me with something.

"Hey!" I protested. "What was that?"

"You smell." She set the small container down on a table outside the room, opened the door and shoved me in.

The room was small, with a table and one chair. I moved toward the chair.

"Oh no, that isn't for you," a voice said.

I looked down.

A dwarf? This was Wurt? This could be Cumat's brother. How was I supposed to take an interrogator like this seriously? "Wurt?" I blurted out.

"Oh no, no, no," the dwarf answered. "I'm his personal assistant. I'm just here to tell you how this will go, get all of the preliminaries out of the way."

Okay, maybe this guy really was Cumat's brother. The fake politeness under weird circumstances was the same. Then what he said hit me. The interrogator had a personal assistant. Weird. Leave it to the fae.

"What took you so long to get here?" I moved over and plopped down in the chair. They were going to torture me already, I might as well have some fun with the guy.

Yep, definitely related to Cumat. That was the same reddish-purple hue he turned when I messed with him.

"That is Mr. Wurt's chair."

"Oh, is it Mr. Wurt? I was wondering if that was his first name or his last."

The dwarf let out a long-suffering sigh. "You won't be so flippant when Mr. Wurt arrives."

I tipped the chair back on two legs. "Oh yeah?"

"Oh yes. Now here are the items we need to cover. Answer every question as soon as possible. You may take a moment to collect your thoughts. No screaming, no crying, no asking questions."

I rolled my eyes. Like I would just start crying. That was pretty stupid.

"Is everything understood?"

"Yeah." Might as well get this over with.

The dwarf went over and rapped on the door. So cloak and dagger.

The door opened and a giant, hairy, beast-man thing ducked to step into the room. I tipped the chair back to be able to see his face, and promptly fell to the floor. I scrambled up and tipped the chair upright, shoving it in his direction.

What was that thing? I'd never seen anything like him. He towered over me, back hunched over like he was used to hitting his head on the ceiling.

"You," the beast said, his voice thundering in the small room. "I know you."

"Me?" I squeaked out. "Are you sure? I'm pretty sure I'd remember meeting you. Sir. Mister. Wurt."

He bent over me, studying my face. "It's her, Medar. Send someone with news to the Council."

"Um, who do you think I am?" I managed to ask.

The thing straightened, the top of his head brushing the ceiling. "I know who you are. It's you who doesn't know. Trisha Penchant. Such a human name."

Oh crap, he did know.

"She's the one the Council has been trying to capture," Wurt said.

I dropped my head, defeated. He knew my face. There was no other explanation, and no reason to keep trying to fool them. He was too sure. So much for an interrogation, though I couldn't stop the relief that flowed through me over the fact that I wouldn't be tortured for information.

"The Council will want her right away. They sent you suspecting it was her, but now that you know they will be most interested in seeing her," the dwarf told his master.

"Have her escorted through the portal," Wurt answered. "As soon as I'm done with her." He held up his massive hands and stretched out his interlaced fingers.

This was it. I'd let that relief hit me too early. What I'd been frantically dreading, it was actually going to happen. Maybe it was better that I couldn't heal right now, that way he couldn't keep hurting me over and over without killing me. The room spun a little and I closed my eyes, trying not to vomit.

Get it together, Trish. Don't let them know you're afraid. Like anyone with any sense at all wouldn't be terrified right now. But I opened my eyes anyway, staring the big guy down.

"What more do you need from her? Maybe it would be best to not antagonize her," the dwarf said quietly. "If this truly is the girl who grew up on Earth, than you know who her father is."

He knew who my father was? That was more than I knew. But I didn't want him to know that, so I just tipped my head and gave him a cocky look. The dwarf. Even I wasn't stupid enough to get the monster angry.

If they were scared of my father, whoever he was, then maybe I could push a little further. "I'll go with you to meet the Council willingly if you let me see Starren first."

Wurt cracked his neck and grinned, baring his fangs. "You'll go either way."

"Yes, I'm sure you can make me go wherever you want, but wouldn't it be easier if I was cooperating? My father isn't going to be happy if I show up with bruises or broken bones." Not that I knew that, but I could assume. No parent wanted their kid to be beat up. At least no decent parent.

A frown took over Wurt's face. I actually liked it better than the smile, surprisingly.

"It seems like a fair bargain," the dwarf said.

My heart leapt, just a little. That meant Starren was here, and alive.

"That depends," Wurt growled. "We haven't taken a side."

Taken a side? What did that mean?

"Will you swear to not mention to the Council that we allowed you to see Starren?" the dwarf asked.

Since I couldn't break my word, that was kind of a big deal. But at the same time, I'd do about anything to see Starren right now, to get some answers. To make sure she was okay. "Fine. I will not say anything to the Council about you allowing me to see Starren."

"Or any agents of the Council. Anyone, really."

"And no agents of the Council."

The dwarf rapped on the door and one of the guards came in.

"Take her to see her sister."

Did everyone know about that but me? The guard nodded and spun around. I scrambled to keep up. We went back toward the door that led to my aisle of cells, but stopped at a different door before we got there.

A guard stood on duty outside of this door. The guard leading me to Starren nodded at the other, and she let us through.

And here I'd thought my section of this place was bad. This wing of the prison was nearly dark, and super damp. Guards in full armor with giant spears were stationed every twentyish feet. This must be where they kept the dangerous criminals.

The air stank like rot and sewage. Moans came out of several cells as I walked by, but no one was talking, at all. What was wrong with the fae that they could do this to people? My blood boiled and I nearly drew blood literally biting my tongue. I'd just make it worse for Starren if I caused a scene and made the guards mad.

We finally stopped in front of a door. The guard unlocked it and pulled it open. It ground as it went, like it hadn't been opened in a while. There was no way I was leaving my sister in this place. I'd go before the Council, escape and come back. No one should live like this, especially when it wasn't even her fault she was here. It was mine. I was the one who had betrayed her trust.

"Starren?" I said quietly. The cell was dark enough I couldn't see much.

A lump on the ground moved over against the far wall.

"Uh, hey, Starren," I managed to get out.

She stood and I had to stop myself from going over to her. Once she moved into the light, she glared at me murderously, the look even more scary than usual with her greasy hair and black bags under her eyes.

"As if you hadn't ruined my life enough, here you are." She didn't give me time to answer. Before I even knew what happened, her arm went back and she popped me in the nose.

"Ow!" I yelped, hand going to my face, blood dripping from between my fingers. "I'm here to rescue you!'

"This is the type of rescue I'd expect from you," she fumed.

So much for her looking all sad and weak when I'd walked in. I officially no longer felt sorry for her. I let go of my nose and wiggled it a little, testing for pain. Not too bad, but I'd be glad when we left here and it had a chance to heal. She still packed a wallop, even after being in prison for a while.

"You okay?" I asked. "They don't hurt you or anything, do they?"

She deflated, the Starren I knew and kind of loved completely gone.

"No. They don't hurt me."

But that only answered one question. She was avoiding the whole are you okay one.

"What are you really doing here, Trisha? How did you even know I'd been placed in prison?"

I eyed the door and moved closer to her, noting her frame had lost all its muscle, and the fact that she had open sores on her face. Whoever did this to her was going to regret it. "Wade came and got me," I whispered. The guards didn't need to know I wasn't working alone. "He's still out there, somewhere." I hoped. I didn't mention Jaden. She probably disliked him even more than she disliked me.

A guard clanged on the door. "Time's almost up."

"I just got here," I yelled back.

"So?"

I grumbled under my breath, then turned back to Starren. "I have to go to the Council for some reason, but as soon as I can I'm going to get away. I'll be back for you." I moved toward the door, but Starren grabbed my hand.

"Don't go to the Council. Don't come back for me. Just get out of Faerie, Trisha. You can't stay here."

"No way-"

She didn't let me continue. "I mean it. You're going to get yourself killed. Get out of here. There is so much going on that you don't understand."

"What about our dad?" I asked. "Maybe I can find him. Maybe he can help you."

Her eyes went wide. "No. Promise me you'll stay away from him. Promise me."

"Let's go," the guard said from outside. "Don't make me come into that cesspool."

I tried to move for the door, but Starren's grip tightened. With desperate strength she held me back. "Promise, you won't look for our father."

"I can't do that, Starren. I'm sorry." Why did she not want our dad to help? She'd rather stay in this place than have help from our father?

The guard yanked me out of the cell and slammed the door closed. I gripped onto the bars, getting a last look at Starren, so pale and miserable.

"Remember what I told you!" I called as the guard dragged me back up the aisle out of the room.

Starren moved to the door and pressed her face into it, watching as I got pulled away. She didn't say anything, but really, what could she at this point. We'd both said what we needed to say. I could wish that I had more information on my dad, but that wouldn't get me anywhere. If I had to find him to save Starren, I would. Whether she liked it or not.

The dwarf was waiting for me on the other side of the big door. "This way." He took off without waiting to see if I would follow or not. He probably knew the guards would see to it.

Thankfully Wurt wasn't in sight.

"You're a lucky one," the dwarf, was it Medar? Yeah, Medar, said. "Wurt recognized you before he got started. You may appreciate his methods, but you wouldn't like them. No, wouldn't like them at all."

I shivered, actually feeling a little lucky even when I really didn't like the idea of going before the Council. That would be terrifying, but it was trouble for another day. Hopefully Jaden and Wade were waiting outside somewhere, and they'd rescue me before I got anywhere close to wherever the Council was. Or the trees. The trees would help me, if I could convey to them that my life was in danger.

We marched along until we were in the main room, where I'd first come in. The guards handed me off to some different guards, these in matching armor with red overlays. Wurt had been wearing that same color, so it must mean something that I didn't understand.

Without even monologuing, we went straight for the portal.

Stepping out into the light and sweet air of Faerie, I nearly teared up. I'd have never guessed that there would be a time in my life where I would be so happy to be outside. Instinctively I searched the trees for someone I knew, hiding and waiting to save me.

"How long will it take us to get to the Council?" I asked Medar.

He looked at me like I was crazy, walked around to the other side of the portal and gestured for the guard to drag me through. Oh no, no. I was supposed to be traveling with them for a couple days. Surely it had been a couple days in the cell when I waited for them to get here. How were Wade and Jaden supposed to find me? How were the trees supposed to attack, tearing these guys to pieces and setting me free to save my sister?

"Wait a sec, I thought this was going to be a journey."

Medar stared at me for a moment, looking bewildered. "Why would you believe that? Didn't you use portals on Earth while attempting to apprehend the escapee?"

"Well, yes, but you guys didn't get here right away after I was caught, so I thought-"

"You thought that we were traveling that whole time." That was very un-Cumat like, interrupting someone. He wouldn't stand for such rudeness. Maybe they weren't related. "No, Mr. Wurt was with another prisoner. You weren't high on the priority list." He gave me a little bow. "If we had known that it was you who had been captured, we would have been here much sooner. The buffoons here didn't recognize you."

Okay, that was scary. People should be able to recognize me here? I knew I'd made the Council pretty mad when I'd disobeyed them, but just how deep did that anger go? I was about to find out, whether I wanted to or not.

"After you... What is it that you prefer to be called?"

"Trish."

"After you, Trish."

CHAPTER ELEVEN

A small gasp escaped when I stepped out on the other side of the second portal. We'd gone into that hallway Jaden, Wade, and I had seen, and then Medar had chosen a door. I'd thought I'd seen beauty on Earth, and a different kind of beauty here when we'd come out of the tunnel, but nothing I'd ever seen compared to this.

We were super high in the air, standing on a platform made of flowering woven vines and branches. Ornate doors were embedded in the massive trunks of the trees that towered above us, going so high I couldn't see the tops. I scooted over to the edge, but I couldn't see beyond the limbs and leaves below us to the ground. Somehow I knew though, we were way up there.

"I thought the Fae Council met in some clearing or glade or whatever," I said to no one in particular, backing away from the edge.

"Not for hundreds of years now." Medar had come through the portal behind me and I hadn't noticed. "That was before the current way we govern. Back then the King of the Faerie Court made all the decisions, with the Council only there to advise him. But there is wisdom in the many over the one, so now the Council makes most of the rulings, with the King carrying them out."

I couldn't really care less about how the fae were ruled.

The guards snapped into formation around me, boxing me in with one on each corner. Talk about uncomfortable. What did they expect me to do, throw myself over the edge?

"This way," Medar said politely. He marched off toward one of the trees, then moved on to a small woven walkway that went around the side.

Okay, this was really poorly designed. No railings? Someone could totally plunge to their death. Wait! Maybe this was my chance to escape. I skootched over and looked down. Lots of branches. Would these trees help me?

Hey, anyone out there?

I waited for a second. That was dumb. It wasn't like they talked to me.

If you're willing to help, give me a sign. Wave a branch or something.

No movement. Could these trees not hear me? Or could they, but they weren't a fan for some reason? If I threw myself over the edge, would they help me?

That seemed like something I should know before I tried it.

We came around the tree and I craned my neck to see beyond the guard. This spot could almost be a clearing on the forest floor. The footing was covered in live leaves, walls formed by interwoven vines with a gorgeous array of flowers, and five thrones set at the other end, made out of living polished branches.

So this was it. No time for processing, no long wait before a trial like back with the humans. They found out who I was and within an hour, I was standing before the Council.

The Faerie Council looked about what I would have expected them to, if I'd stopped to think about it. Two women, three men. All dressed in weird robes that covered pretty much everything. Leafy colors, though it was the leafy pastels of Faerie, not of Earth.

No smiles here. The area was warm, with all the beauty, but not the Court. Their faces were frigid, chiseled from stone. Yet anger radiated off of all of them.

"Bring the accused forward," one of the women said.

Accused? Accused of what?

One of the guards shoved me in front of the whole group.

"You, known to yourself and the humans as Trisha Penchant, stand before the High Council of Faerie. How do you plead?"

"I don't even know the charges!" I said, probably sounding pretty disrespectful, but it wasn't on purpose. I was about to pee my pants. Was there a chair around here somewhere? I might faint.

"Were you not raised on Earth as a human?" one of the men asked.

"Did you not miss the deadline for coming in to be trained?" another said.

"Did you not attack an agent of the Council when told that you must return to Faerie?" the third one added.

Okay, yeah, I'd done all those things. But that didn't mean I was guilty of anything. "Not guilty." Apparently my fae side agreed with me that this was totally bogus, because I could say it, and therefore it wasn't a lie.

"Did you do any of those things?" the woman in the purplish robe asked.

Well yeah, but how did I get out of that question without lying?

One of the guards prodded me from behind when I took too long to answer.

"Yes." Keep it short, keep it concise.

"Did you do all of them?" the other lady asked.

I clenched my hands tight enough to leave cuts in my palms from my fingernails. They healed right away, but it was definitely a good indicator about how I was feeling about these proceedings. "Yes."

"Then by your own admission, you have committed a capital crime. The punishment is death."

"Wait, what?" Death? Because I hadn't gone to school and I'd beat Starren and Wade in a fight? Seriously? "Wait a second!" I tried to protest, but the guard behind me covered my mouth with his foul-smelling hand.

They were going to kill me for a few infractions? No one could be that cruel, could they? Apparently they could. I should have jumped off the walkway when I had the chance. Better to trust the trees than rely on mercy from the Faerie Court. At this point I had nothing to lose. I flailed around wildly, trying to break free, no plan in mind, only terror.

You were right, Mom. The hysterical thought went through my head. I should have stayed away from the fae. I should never have made any emotional connections.

"The sentence will be carried out tomorrow, at the height of the day. Everyone within traveling distance is required to attend." Not only was I going to die, but everyone was coming to watch. No doubt I was supposed to be a lesson to others. This was what happened when you defied the Council. They had to know my ability, right? How did they plan on killing me enough that I stayed dead? I went limp in the guard's arms. There was nothing I could do against this many. Unless...

Help me! I begged the trees. Did you hear what they're going to do? There was no answer.

"Place her in the holding cell meant for such occasions. Spread the word. There will be plenty of time for all to make it here."

With her final proclamation, a wall of willow-like branches fell, separating us lowly fae from the Council. That wasn't dramatic at all, my frantic mind cackled in the background.

If I was going to do anything, now was the time. Once I was locked up, I wouldn't be able to do a thing, and tomorrow there would be too many people around. No, this was it. I side-eyed my guards as they went into formation around me, Medar leading the way to my new cell.

Even though I'd only been locked up for a couple days, the thought of being trapped again made my body feel like a wet noodle. How had Starren made it through all that time there and still be herself? How was Nara fine? But maybe they weren't fine. Maybe they were just better at hiding it than I was.

The opportunity would come. I just had to be patient. As soon as we got close to the edge, I was going for it. If the trees refused to help, I'd still heal, even after destroying everything in my body from falling this far. Hopefully. And if not, it was probably a better execution than whatever they had planned for me. They knew I could heal, so there was no way this was going to be pleasant.

The guards stuck pretty close. I could easily make it over the edge if I rammed one, taking them with me. But did I really want to do that? I'd never killed someone before, and as far as they knew they were escorting a known criminal, evil enough to be sentenced to execution. They were just doing their jobs.

So no. No murder today. Just more waiting, which I could totally do. Not well, but I could force myself.

We reached the edge of the platform and moved onto one of the small walkways that went around the trees. The guards fell into single file, making it Medar, two guards, me, two more guards.

I forced myself not to look over the edge. Not that they would expect anyone to be crazy enough to jump, but I didn't want to give myself away just in case one of them could figure out what I was planning.

I worked on psyching myself up until we got close to the next platform. Now or never. This was really, really, going to hurt if the trees didn't feel like helping a girl out today. Hopefully it didn't just kill me like with Wade, and I woke up the next day in prison again, with a bunch of still healing bones.

But no other options had presented themselves. Time to take my life into my hands and all that.

I looked over my shoulder at the guards. "See you on the other side. Or you know, hopefully not."

Then I turned and fell.

CHAPTER TWELVE

A screech ripped out of my throat as I plunged toward the ground, faster than I could have imagined. The air-flow made my eyes water, and my throat ached from the scream that still spewed out of me as I fell.

"I could use a little help!" I yelled, the words difficult to form.

Slamming through branch after branch panic turned my movements into a frenzy, flailing around, trying to grab something, anything.

Then I was caught around the stomach by something, completely stopping my fall and bungeing me back up a few feet. The air was knocked out of me, and it took me a second to get my breath.

"Thanks," I coughed out.

The vine didn't do any of the happy little things vegetation normally did when I talked to it. It just lifted me higher, and passed me on to another vine.

"Uh, wrong way, guys. I need to go down."

The vine ignored me, then tossed me up into the air. I sucked in a breath, holding in another scream. A branch caught me and launched me up in the air again, moving toward the platform. I was close enough now to hear someone shouting up top.

"Wait a second," I managed to pant out. "I really don't want to go up there. Those people want to kill me. We're friends, aren't we?"

The vine didn't seem to agree. Its hold tightened and it kept moving upward. I struggled, wiggling as hard as I could, thrashing enough that the vine had to fight to continue pulling me toward the platform.

But it made it. It deposited me at Medar's feet.

"Are you quite done, Ms. Penchant?" Medar asked. I was too dizzy to answer. "The trees in this area were enchanted when the King made this place for the Council to meet in over a thousand years ago. They will protect the Council's interests. I assume you believed you could heal once you hit the ground?"

I still didn't answer. Yes, I'd been assuming that, but I'd actually hoped the trees would help me. Medar didn't seem to know that was a possibility. Or he just didn't want the Council to know, with all the weird stuff he'd been talking about with Wurt. Had Starren not told them that plants liked me? If she hadn't that was a huge advantage for me. Other than the fact that these stupid trees didn't listen to me. Traitors.

"Shall we continue to your cell? I do have other things to do with my day."

One of the guards reached down and hauled me to my feet. I stumbled for a second, equilibrium still not back after that whirlwind of a ride.

They marched me forward for a couple of minutes, passing massive trunks with intricately carved doors in them, before stopping in front of one. The front guard opened it with a flourish, and motioned for me to go ahead.

I moved into the small room and took a look around. Definitely a five star hotel compared to my last cell. There was actually a bed here, and everything smelled good, like I was outside in the open air. There were even windows, with a loose almost basketlike weaving over them, spaced widely enough I could see out but tightly enough there was no chance of escape.

Ah, but there was the kicker. There was an actual toilet, of sorts. It had a pull handle, which probably let rainwater in from a basin above or something like that, but it was insanely better than what passed for a toilet at the prison.

"You will be served a meal tonight, one in the morning, and then your last meal before your execution tomorrow. I suggest you spend your time here in meditation, dwelling on the choices you made that brought you here." And with that Medar slammed the door shut.

Instead of locking, the door slowly melted away until I was staring straight at the inside of a tree.

I walked up and placed my hand where the door had been. "What's wrong guys?" I asked. "I know Medar said you're supposed to listen to the Council here, but couldn't you make an exception, just this once? All you have to do is put a hole in the floor, I got the rest."

No response. Not even a shiver. It was like these trees were dead.

I moved over and plopped on the bed, trying to find something to criticize. The thing definitely couldn't be bed quality. And it wasn't. It was way better. This thing was like sitting on air, and I pretty much knew what that felt like now. I pulled my legs up onto the bed and curled up in a ball.

Not even Jaden and Wade were going to be able to save me from this. In fact, fingers crossed they wouldn't try. Hopefully they'd grabbed Dan and Nina and were heading through the tunnel right now, back to their lives. All of their lives had been better before they met me, anyway. Well, all but Jaden. Somehow I'd actually improved his life. It had ended me up here, but here felt inevitable. Like it would have happened no matter what I had chosen when I was standing in that alley, deciding if to help the guy in front of me, or turn him over to Starren.

I pulled a blanket over me and did my best not to do as Medar said. Not to sit and stew in all the things I could have done differently. But I couldn't stop.

Life with Dan and Nina was stable. The first stable I'd had... maybe ever. We were becoming a real family. And Jaden... Nope. Not going there. But there were so many things I'd never gotten to do with Nina. Or I'd had the chance, but I'd shut it down because I was scared. And now those chances were gone. I went through every variable in my mind all night, without any chance of sleep.

The food they brought me for supper, and again for breakfast, was super good, but sat mostly untouched. I didn't have a name for it, but it had an interesting texture. I couldn't eat much, sitting here thinking about dying soon. I found myself wishing for the white gruel back at the prison with Nara.

Some woman had brought my other meals, but it was Medar that brought my last meal. He moved into the room and sat down at the foot of the bed.

"Ms. Trisha. While normally this isn't a part of what I do, I volunteered to bring you your meal."

I just looked at him dully, not really caring.

"I want you to know, I've done everything I can to help you." He leaned in, gesturing for me to lean in too. "I have contacted your father for you. Even Mr. Wurt doesn't know. Please keep that in mind."

"Okay?" It came out more of a question than a statement. What did he expect me to do with that information?

"It's almost time." He actually sounded sympathetic. At least there would be one person watching me die that maybe didn't want me to. He slid the tray toward me over the bed.

I picked at the blankets, not acknowledging the tray of food. Last meals were almost barbaric, in a way. Give the prisoner something nice before you murdered them. Nothing weird about that.

Thankfully they didn't tie my hands or anything like that. I hadn't slept at all, trying to figure some way out of this. I hadn't come up with anything. Not even a single crazy plan. I was going to die today. I didn't really believe otherwise at this point.

That was okay, if Jaden, Dan, and Nina were okay. I would have died fighting for a family I didn't have until a few months ago. Starren was on that list now too, whether she wanted to be or not.

There was no weird fanfare music like in the movies. No drums or people booing. But there were people. A lot of people. Really strange people. At first glance they looked like any other strangely dressed crowd. But when I looked closer, I noticed details that I'd missed on first glance.

Horns here. Eyes a little too big over there. Pointed ears. Pointed ears were actually a thing?

"So nice of you all to come watch me die," I muttered under my breath.

It was eerily quiet. No talking, not even any coughing. The crowd didn't need to shift out of the way, they'd already left plenty of room. If they knew exactly where to stand, how often did these things happen?

There, out of place just in front of the raised dais the Council sat on, was a block, a basket, and an axe. That answered the question on whether or not I'd die if I lost my head. Apparently the Council thought so.

Strangely enough, I was almost past fear. The tears and screaming from last night were gone. It was like I was watching this entire thing from up in the trees somewhere. Well, not these trees. These trees could burn for all I cared.

I almost felt like I should struggle, just because. But what was the point? There were so many guards. The Council, with no doubt amazing powers sitting so close. Even the trees were against me. There was nothing I could do.

One of the people seated at the foot of the dais stood when I got close. "The one known as Trisha Penchant to the humans stands before you guilty of treason to the Council, and of attacking an agent of the Council. Thus happens to all who do so." He nodded to a guy, who came forward and pulled me surprisingly gently toward the block.

This was the executioner? No weird hood?

He looked at me, his eyes almost sad. That would be just like the fae, make someone who hated killing be an executioner.

"Not your fault, man." I shrugged. "If you didn't do it, someone else would."

Whatever his answer would have been was lost when a murmur started from the back of the crowd. I didn't really care at the moment what caused it, it had given me another couple moments to live. Unless it was Jaden and Wade, then yeah, I cared a lot. And they were in serious trouble.

"Hold," a voice shouted from somewhere behind.

Okay, yeah, now I cared. I craned my neck, trying to see.

A group of fairly normal looking fae flowed up the walkway. There was really no difference between them and the crowd, but somehow there was a danger about them, an assuredness that made me think that they were warriors.

They shoved other fae back, making room for a man who stood a full head and shoulders above the rest of them. He was handsome for an older dude, and carried himself with a cockiness that said he was used to being obeyed.

"Since when do executions happen without the King being present?" the man asked. Was he talking about himself? Because I could respect a king that didn't need some poor guy out in front talking for him. And he certainly looked like a king, all regal and used to having everyone obey him.

"You were out of reach, sire," one of the Council said coolly. "We did not wish to drag this out any longer than necessary."

"That, and the fact that you didn't want me to interfere." He moved in closer. When he saw me, he stopped dead. "Mareena," the man breathed out, like he was nearly in shock.

"What does that word mean?" I kept my eyes on him but asked a random guard out of the side of my mouth. I really should know more of the fae language, but to be fair I hadn't had anyone to speak it with since mom.

"It's a name," Medar answered.

A name? I looked around, but no one seemed to be responding to the guy.

The guy came closer, towering over me. He held out his hands, putting one on each of my shoulders. I should have been creeped out, but somehow I wasn't.

"I have searched for you for so long."

Did that mean... could it be possible? His eyes, his smile, even something in his voice. "Dad?"

He reached forward and touched my face. "Yes."

It was him. I'd never met him, but this was him. My missing father, the one I didn't know, King of the Faerie Court. Wait, what? How had this never come up? Obviously my mom had to know about this. Did that mean she was the queen? I didn't know how this worked at all. Would she be queen just because he was king, like the humans did it, or not? And Starren was a princess? What? I nearly giggled at the thought, mostly because of the nerves.

"These proceedings must be postponed until an investigation can be launched." He didn't take his eyes off me as he talked to the Council.

"You can't just come in here and change Council rulings." One of the men stood, flailing his arms around, his robes flowing all over.

"I can, and I have," the king answered, shifting his gaze over to the Council. I realized I had no idea what my own father's name was.

"The case is open and closed. There is nothing to investigate," one of the women said calmly. "It would be best for you to tell your daughter goodbye."

He whirled toward the dais, his long dark hair fanning around him. "Present your evidence."

"Your daughter herself has told us." The Council member that had questioned me the day before said. "Trisha, did you betray and attack an agent of the Council?"

I crossed my arms. "She attacked me first."

"After you betrayed her," one of the men prompted.

I didn't answer.

My father looked over at me. "For what reason did she attack you?"

"I was trying to get a girl back, one she'd kidnapped from Sanctuary. She broke fae law." I didn't want to make this worse for Starren, but she was already in a ton of trouble and I couldn't help her if I was dead.

"That's true," the other woman on the Council, who hadn't spoken before, said. "By her own admission, Starren broke the law by taking a half-fae girl out of Sanctuary. It is one of the reasons she is imprisoned now."

Maybe this was starting to swing my way. If I could just find ways to answer questions without the whole truth, I'd be good. Oh shoot.

I'd also be very fae. Did I really want to live like that after seeing Dan and Nina and their policy of being honest to a fault? I'd do my best to answer with non-answers and see where we went from there.

"Hold!" Someone else shouted.

Everyone's heads whipped around to the back. Again. What was this? Was this normal? If this was normal than they really needed to find a better way of doing things.

Fae dressed in the armor from the prison marched forward, dragging something with them. Two somethings. My heart sank to the pit of my stomach. No way this was a good thing.

"Council, we found these in the woods." The guard shoved a small form forward.

Nina!

She stumbled and nearly fell, a bag over her head. Could she even breathe? Dan was next, shoved to the floor next to where Nina was standing.

"Let them go," I shouted, punching at the guard right in front of me.

"Trish?" Nina asked, her voice muffled from the bag.

"Yeah, I'm here Nina, I'm okay."

Quiet sobs leaked out of the bag, fueling my anger. I punched the guard again, but it didn't seem to be doing anything. He grabbed me and pinned my arms, covering my mouth with a hand.

"So you admit to knowing these two?" One of the Council asked. She had laser focus, like Dan and Nina were just going to vanish. "You brought humans into Faerie?"

A huge outcry broke from all around us. Okay, this was not good. Things had seemed to be going my way, but not so much anymore. The crowd was angry. Super angry.

"Humans? In Faerie? Has that ever happened before?" another Council member asked. His baleful gaze moved between Dan and Nina and me, burning its way back and forth.

One of the guards whipped the bag off Nina's head. Everyone on the entire platform stared her down. She blinked for a couple seconds, then looked around wildly until she found me. Even in the position she was in, as soon as she saw me she relaxed a little. What had I ever done to deserve her and Dan?

"Not that I can recall. And as most of you know, I can recall the last five hundred years," a third member said, his voice high and smooth.

Okay, he totally didn't look five hundred years old. Was he serious?

Now if this went badly, Dan and Nina would get to watch me die along with everyone else. I pleaded for forgiveness with my eyes, my mouth still covered by the guard. I had known this was the most likely ending, known that this was probably what was going to happen, and yet I'd come anyway. I was such a fool.

The guard let go of my mouth after a glare from my father.

"Please," I asked, tears in my eyes, "help them."

He cocked his head, considering me for a second. "The humans have done no wrong. They are under my protection. Release them."

This set off another round of muttering, but the guards listened instantly. That was a good indicator if they were more afraid of the Council, or the King.

"This cements her sentence," the old Council member said. "The humans may have done no wrong, but there are strict rules about bringing humans to Faerie. Even if this was her only infraction, she would be sentenced to death."

"I suggest you re-think your ruling," my dad said, the threat evident in his voice.

"Who's that?" I heard Dan's muffled voice ask Nina.

"I don't know," she answered.

The Council all moved in close, muttering to each other. With everything else going on, I couldn't eavesdrop on them at all.

As one they turned back to the crowd, folding their hands inside of their robes. "Quintin, our ruling stands, though we will allow a one day delay for last goodbyes. The humans will be held until it can be decided what will be done with them."

I nearly deflated in relief. One day wasn't a lot of time, but it was a whole lot more than I'd had a few minutes ago. I could at least make sure Dan and Nina were taken care of, even if no one could do anything for me. My father was the king, surely that meant something. Surely he could get Dan and Nina out.

Quintin. That processed really late. My father's name was Quintin.

I was escorted back to my cell, Dan and Nina close behind. Nina tried to say something, but the guard at her elbow shut it down before she got a full word out.

When we reached my door, a guard shoved me in, and then they started past with Dan and Nina. "No, wait! Can't we share a cell?" I asked.

The guards looked at each other. Then one looked over his shoulder back to the platform where my father was arguing with a Council member.

"If that's what you wish," one of the guards said.

"We do." Nina threw her arm around me.

They looked at each other again, but then put us all into my familiar cell.

I practically fell into Nina's arms while Dan ripped the bag off his head. Nina grabbed my face and skipped her normal body check for injuries to go straight to my emotional health. "Was that your father?"

I grabbed her wrists, squeezing back. "Yes. How did you guys last in the woods? How did you get caught? Have they been treating you okay?"

"Did you literally just meet?" Dan asked, moving in to pull us both into a group hug.

"We hid in the woods forever, then got really worried and started poking around. That's how we got caught," Nina said.

"You should have just left!" I pulled away from the group hug, taking a couple steps back and crossing my arms in front of me. "That was the plan, you were supposed to leave. I'm going to talk to Quintin, but I don't know if I can get you out of this." I hunched over protectively, trying not to cry.

"Get us out of this?" Nina moved in slowly, reaching forward to tip my face up with her index finger. "Honey, we aren't going anywhere without you."

"You don't understand." I stepped away again, not looking her in the eyes. "I'm in serious trouble, Nina."

"Oh, we do understand," Dan said. "We were in the back for most of what was going on. Were they really going to kill a sixteen-year-old kid?"

"The fae aren't as forgiving as humans tend to be," I muttered. I couldn't decide if it was a good thing they knew everything or not. At least I didn't have to tell them I was about to die. That would get really awkward really fast.

"Where are Jaden and Wade?" Nina asked.

"Shhh." I put my finger to my lips. I didn't know if there was someone standing outside the window, or someone with some weird ability to hear long distances, or even just a guard. "I don't think anyone but us even know they're in Faerie."

"Good," Dan said. "That's good. The boys are resourceful."

"Resourceful enough to take on a whole crowd of fae to get me away from a chopping block?" I asked.

"Maybe not that resourceful. I'd hope they would be smart enough to try something before we get to that point."

A knock interrupted our conversation. I should have known someone was going to want to speak with us, the door hadn't disappeared. Of course I was hoping for someone specific.

And for once I got what I wanted. Quintin, my father, poked his head in. "Is this a good time for me to visit?"

He was so polite! Maybe he wasn't actually my father. Polite didn't fit well.

He nodded at each of us, then his eyes went to me. He stared me down for a second, long enough to make me uncomfortable. "May we speak, Mareena?"

Dan moved in front of me and stuck his hand out. "It's a pleasure to meet you. I'm Dan, Trish's foster dad."

I wanted to hug him. I moved in closer to Nina. This was a moment I'd dreamed of for literally as long as I could remember, yet now, here we were, and I couldn't think of a thing to say. So many questions, yet none would come out.

Quintin eyed me, then looked to Dan and shook his hand. "Quintin." Apparently he had some experience with humans, or he wouldn't know what to do with a hand put in front of him.

"Is it okay if we spend a few minutes together?" he asked. "I've been waiting so long for this moment."

"Of course." I gave him a small smile. "I've been waiting too."

"Medar can take your humans somewhere for a few minutes, so we can have the room, or you can come with me somewhere more comfortable."

Okay, his casual use of humans was very normal for fae. But it still rubbed me the wrong way.

"We've been Trisha's parents for a while now," Nina said. "We would like to be involved, if you don't mind."

Quintin gave her a toothy smile. "And if I do mind?"

"It won't matter," Dan said, his voice hard. "We don't know your intentions."

Quintin held his hands up in a placating gesture. "Good, good. I just wanted to know what your relationship with my daughter meant to you."

The door opened behind him and three chairs were passed in. I took the bed, but made sure Nina was sitting close enough that I could feel the peace and love rolling off her.

"Where do we begin?" my father asked. My father. I still couldn't really wrap that around my mind. I'd had my mom as a kid, and then connected with Nina through the whole getting hit by an arrow and being forced to do a true confessions thing, but a dad? Dan was wonderful, but this felt different somehow.

"Why did Mom take me to Earth?"

Nina reached over and squeezed my hand. She could probably feel the emotion in the question, which I hated but loved at the same time.

"Your mother was worried that a very dangerous man wanted you for his own gain. She took you away in a misguided attempt to keep you safe."

"I got that part, that's why we were always moving. What man? Why did he want me?"

Quintin stretched back in his chair a bit. "You'd have to know who it was and ask him specifically. My turn for a question. Do you know where your mother is?"

Why did he want to know? Did he still care about her? Or was there something else? She'd kept us on the run, but from who? "No, I have no idea where she is. I haven't seen her in years." And for the first time, I was grateful for that.

His head fell. "I… miss her."

My insides melted. Of course he did. "I miss her too. You said you've been looking for us?"

"Yes." His face drooped, eyes sad. "Ever since you disappeared, I have searched for you."

So much of the anger, almost hatred I'd had for him dropped away with those words. He hadn't abandoned us. He'd searched for us.

"Why didn't mother find you after we were safe?"

"Things were complicated, and you were the only thing she could think about. I'm sure she was just doing her best to keep you safe."

It made sense, but I still didn't like it. She'd left me in an orphanage when I had someone that would have taken care of me. What was wrong with her?

We talked after that for over an hour. Me learning things about my mom that I never knew, learning things about Quintin, him asking questions about my life. Dan and Nina were a mostly silent, supportive presence, only interjecting occasionally to clarify something.

After the questions had petered out, Quintin stood. "I should go for a bit. I need to see to some things. There are some people that have a lot to answer for." He must have seen me stubbornly holding back a question. "What is it, child?"

"Are you really the king?" I'd been avoiding the question. It was kind of awkward. Him being the king meant what for me?

He smiled. "I am." His brown eyes, so like mine, smiled at me, only at me.

"Does that mean you're going to be able to help Trish?" Nina asked.

His smile went grim. "The Council has been pushing their authority more and more over the last hundred years. They are attempting to take away the power of the king. I have my supporters, but they also have theirs. We are about to have words."

"And what about Dan and Nina?"

"Technically they have broken no laws. Helping them may actually be easier than helping you."

I closed my eyes for a second, hit by a wave of relief. "Thank you."

"I have much to discuss with the Council, I should be on my way," Quintin said.

I stood to walk him the few steps to the door.

He turned and leaned over, looking me deep in the eyes. "I won't let anything happen to you. You have nothing to fear now."

I wasn't a hugger, but this seemed like the occasion, so I gave him a quick squeeze around the waist before jumping back.

A smile lit his face and he squeezed my shoulder before stepping out. As soon as the door closed behind him, it melted into the insides of a tree.

"Wow, that's pretty cool," Dan said.

Nina slapped his shoulder. "Not the time, Dan."

"Oh, right, sorry."

"You okay, honey? All that is an awful lot to take in." Nina patted the bed and I went over to sit back down beside her. She was right, it was a ton to take in. And honestly, I hadn't sorted out how I was yet.

"He seems pretty great," I finally got out.

Dan and Nina looked at each other.

"What?" I asked.

"I don't know," Nina sounded hesitant. "There was just something... off. Like something didn't quite add up."

Dan scratched at his ear, looking like he didn't want to agree but didn't have a choice. "Sorry, kid, but Nina's right. There's something strange about that guy."

"That guy? That's my father!" It came out more defensive than I'd intended, but I couldn't feel bad about that. I'd been wondering about my father my whole life, and now finally here it was. They were just upset because I'd found someone I was related to by blood.

"How do you know that?" Nina asked.

"You know fae can't lie." I couldn't sit anymore. I jumped up off the bed and paced the small room. "If he says he is, than he is."

"Then why is Starren in prison?" Dan asked. "Even if he can't lie, it doesn't mean he's telling you the whole truth. I could say I'm your father and be completely honest. If he was married to your mother at any point, then he's your father, even if it's step-father."

He was right. Everything he said made sense. But this was my father. That I could feel, deep inside. I just knew. As for the rest, I didn't want to think about it. "The Council probably won't let Starren out. You heard him say that they have been causing problems for him."

"That's true. I'm not trying to say anything bad, I'm just saying keep an open eye. That's all."

"Have you seen Wade or Jaden?" I changed the subject.

"No, last I saw them they were with you," Dan answered.

My stomach sank. Where could they be?

We didn't get to continue the conversation, because the door slowly came back into being, announcing that someone was coming. Relief trickled through me. I didn't want to talk about my dad like that. I didn't need another person in my life that I had to question their motives. He had saved me today, and he would make it permanent tomorrow. Totally dad-like things to do.

A fae I didn't recognize pushed a small cart through the doorway, laden with food. And I thought I'd been fed well with my last meal, not that long ago. Now that people were admitting I was the daughter of the King, look what happened.

"I apologize for intruding," the guy said. "I know you ate recently, but the King was afraid it may have been a while for our other guests." He pulled out a small table from the bottom of the cart and began moving food to it. All kinds of things I hadn't seen before, but it all smelled amazing. Oh, and there was that white stuff from the prison. So good.

The man finished and bowed slightly before leaving the room.

"Have you eaten anything from here, yet?" I asked, eyeing the food.

"No," Dan answered. "That all looks pretty amazing. Where are we on the whole humans shouldn't eat food in Faerie thing?"

"Better safe than sorry?" I said.

Dan sighed. "That's my thoughts on the subject too. Granola bars for us then."

Was it coincidence that my dad had sent all this food in? Was there something behind the old stories, or was he just being nice? Only one way to tell, and it wasn't good.

I matched Dan's sigh. "Guess I'll have to eat all of this then, just to make sure they don't know you aren't eating."

Nina rolled her eyes. "What a sacrifice." Oh snap, sarcasm. Not only were they wearing off on me, but I was wearing off on them.

I grinned at her as I stuffed my mouth. Sure, tomorrow I was supposed to die, and my sister was still in prison, my friends were MIA. But right at this moment, things felt pretty good. At least that was what I was going to tell myself. Right up until the moment someone swung the axe.

CHAPTER THIRTEEN

Morning came far too soon, even though I barely slept. Dan had offered to take the floor, but I hadn't let him. Weirdly enough, even the floor was comfortable. The branches that made it up molded to fit me perfectly, and somehow stayed warm, like a heating pad. I wanted to hate this place so bad, but so far it had been pretty neat. Other than the whole imprisonment and execution thing.

I was barely awake enough to see the door materialize. "Dan, Nina, wake up," I mumbled as I forced myself into a sitting position.

"Already up, Trish." Dan sounded like he'd been awake for a while. Maybe making escape plans. Probably not, but a girl could hope.

I was mostly awake by the time the door opened, hoping it was my dad. No such luck. One of the guards. He marched forward and grabbed my arm, yanking me to my feet.

"Hey!" Nina and I yelled in unison. Oh, now she was awake. That was good I guess.

"The Council is waiting for you," the guard said, pulling me toward the door. It was obvious who he thought was in charge, someone that respected my dad wouldn't treat me like this.

Once we were out of the way, two other guards went in for Dan and Nina.

"Hey, isn't this supposed to happen at high noon or whatever? Does my dad know about this?"

The guard didn't answer either question, just kept pulling me along. I struggled a little, looking back to make sure they were treating Dan and Nina okay. We reached what I now was going to call the execution platform way too quickly.

No crowd waited for us, just the Council.

"Trisha Penchant, it is time for your sentence to be carried out," one of the Council members said. Cowards. They were going to kill me without my dad knowing.

"You can't do this!" Nina shouted, slapping at her guard.

Dan punched the guard holding him straight in the face, knocking him to the ground, then went after the one holding Nina.

I struggled with the guard holding me. I wasn't going down without a fight.

Three more guards joined the fray. It took them a couple minutes, but eventually they subdued Dan. Nina, though spitting mad, wasn't much of a threat.

I fought with renewed fury, seeing the fosters get taken down. But it didn't matter. All of my blows seemed to bounce off. Even with all the training I'd done, this guy and the guy that had come over to help him were immeasurably stronger than I was.

Without ceremony, or words even, a guard took each of my arms and dragged me over to the block.

"What is the meaning of this?" My dad's voice, booming out across the platform.

I nearly cried. He really was here for me.

"Trying to get this done early, without my knowledge?" Even without me knowing him, his fury was completely obvious in his tone. He stalked across the platform, flowing cloak dragging the floor, fierce anger in each step.

"Quintin, we knew this would be hard for you to see, so we were just getting it done without torturing you," one of the women said. She must truly believe she was helping, or she wouldn't have been able to tell my father that.

"Truly, you believe that murdering my daughter earlier in the day, rather than later, would be preferable to me?" His eyes bored into theirs, he caught each of their gazes and stared them down until they looked away.

"You forget your place, Quintin," the guy that had boasted about how old he was the day before said. "You really aren't doing well, are you? Both your daughters, now rightfully imprisoned, one about to be executed. It's time for you to realize that your power has waned. Only the will of the Council matters now."

Quintin's face burned red, his eyes in slits, a vein bulging on his forehead. "No. It's time for this to be over, but not time for me to admit defeat. I'm done with all of this."

"What do you mean by that?" one of them asked.

"Come, daughter."

I almost walked over to him, but another shape appeared behind him.

"Starren?" I squeaked.

The guards that had been holding me dropped my arms and turned toward her. I used the opportunity to run back to Dan and Nina.

"What is she doing here?" one of the Council demanded.

"Why has she been freed?" another added.

"My father was kind enough to allow me to be a part of today." Her voice was monotone, her eyes dead. She was way scarier than normal, and that was saying a lot.

"That's your sister?" Dan asked incredulously. "The one we came here to save?"

"Uh, yeah." I took a step back. Something wasn't right. This was the Starren I'd fought, this was how she'd looked when she'd taken Jaime and hadn't wanted to. The violent Starren that turned her feelings off.

She slipped her sword from its sheath, choosing her favorite weapon over the bow on her back. "You really should have reconsidered when you sent me to prison. I was a loyal soldier. Taking the girl was an easy mistake. You were looking for a way to hurt my father, and you found it in me." She stalked along the edge of the platform, swinging her sword through the air, twirling it until it whistled.

Several guards rushed to position themselves between Starren and the Council. Somehow I didn't feel like that was going to be much help.

They only had a second, and then she was on them. Two swings and two guards were down, with three rushing in to replace them. One of the guards tossed a fireball at her, but it dissipated harmlessly when it hit her.

"She's impervious to magic!" one of the Council yelled. "You know that, you buffoons!"

More guards rushed in, trying to move the Council toward the walkway leading away from the platform.

Starren was through two more guards before they'd even started to move. One held his hand out like he expected to choke her, but nothing happened. Another called down lightning, it struck her and bounced off. The guards seemed at a loss without their abilities being able to help them.

The woven vines and branches of the floor were soon covered in blood. I wouldn't have had a chance to help, even if I'd wanted to.

All of the guards were down, and Starren was standing in front of the Council, blood dripping from the tip of her sword.

One of the women began to chant, and the branches around the platform shivered.

A vine flew at Starren. Without taking her eyes off the Council, her sword jumped and it fell squirming at her feet.

More vines and branches started toward her. She dove before they could reach her, plunging her sword into the Council member doing the chanting. As the body fell from her blade, the branches stopped moving.

"Don't you think you should do something?" I hissed to our dad.

"Quite right," he said, looking like he was coming out of a trance. He walked over to stand beside Starren.

"Quintin, you must stop this!" the old fae said.

My father's face twisted, going dark. "And why would I do that? You've tortured my daughters. Attempted to have me dethroned. Were about to execute my youngest for trivial crimes." He tilted his head. "Go ahead, my dear."

One of the men reached for his sword, but my father lifted a hand.

"Stop," he ordered, his voice both hypnotizing and authoritative. The man froze, his hand on the hilt of his sword.

Another of the Council started frantically yelling something in the fae language, but he was too late. With little effort, Starren dropped him before moving on to the next.

"Wait, Quintin, I've always sided with you!" the woman who had tried to tell him earlier that they were executing me early for his own good yelled, her voice hysterical.

"There cannot be any of you left. I'm sorry." He nodded to Starren, who moved forward, blade raised.

Fire shot from the fae's hands, but Starren walked through it unsinged.

I just stood there, frozen to the spot, wanting to scream at her to stop. My sister. My sister was killing a bunch of people, right in front of me. I shouldn't care, they'd been about to do the same to me, but nausea dug through my insides, working its way up my throat.

"Come on," Nina whispered in my ear, tugging me away.

She was right. This was the perfect moment to escape. But I was stuck in place, the picture of my sister murdering people in cold blood forever etched on my brain.

"Let's go, Trish," Dan said, grabbing me by the hand and pulling me in the direction of the portal.

I stared over my shoulder as he dragged me away, completely shell shocked, not able to comprehend what was going on. I'd always known what Starren was capable of, heard so many stories, but this... She'd slaughtered old men and women without a pause.

They finished their work, and my dad turned and saw us making our escape. "Stop," he commanded, and my body obeyed.

Nina joined Dan trying to jerk me free, but I couldn't move.

"The humans can do as they wish. Mareena is staying here."

Starren flicked the blood from her blade and sheathed it. Just for show, I knew. She could have it back out as fast as I could blink. She walked toward us, pulling something from her back.

Dan let go of my arm and moved between us.

Starren looked him over critically while I struggled, trying to get free from whatever influence my dad had on me, but I couldn't even roll my eyeballs. She threw whatever she'd grabbed at Dan's feet, then turned and went back to our dad.

Suddenly my muscles started working again. I looked down to what Starren had left for me. My sword, taken by the jailors back at the prison. "Thanks, Star." It came out kind of weak, but she did look back and nod at me. Progress, at least, even if our relationship wasn't where I'd want it to be.

Had I really expected her to just be my friend now that I knew we were sisters? She'd suspected even when we were fighting trolls together. Nothing had really changed for her.

"You just... you just killed all those people." Nina sounded like she was still in shock. Finding out your daughter's sister was capable of cold-blooded murder did that to a person.

"Now, as I said, Mareena will be staying here. Humans, you are welcome to do as you wish." Quintin made his way to the middle chair up on the dais and sat down. A branch descended, weaving itself into an intricate crown before breaking off the main section. "I'm sure you would prefer to leave Faerie, as it is so foreign to you." He nodded toward Starren. "My daughter will escort you."

Starren looked at me, trying to say something with her eyes that I couldn't understand.

"If we're truly allowed to do whatever we want, then we choose to stay here," Dan said, taking Nina's hand. They hadn't even had to discuss it. Would it ever stop surprising me when they treated me like true flesh and blood?

Better than the flesh and blood I'd had experience with so far.

"How did you get out of the prison?" I asked Starren, after a moment of awkward silence.

"Father came for me." She didn't look at him as she spoke, didn't seem very grateful. There was obviously a story here, but without any of the background I had no idea what.

"Well... that's good." I didn't know what to say. "I'm glad you're out. Do you happen to know a girl there, Nara? She's deaf, about your age."

Starren's face hardened. "No. I never left my cell."

Okay, obviously she was done talking about this. I couldn't blame her. I wouldn't want to talk about it either. Plus, she was probably exhausted. Funny how sitting around in a cell could make you so tired. I wanted to ask about Jaden and Wade, the question burning in the back of my brain, but I was afraid to say anything in front of father. How did he feel about Wade? He was Starren's partner, if not friend, surely he would know that. And the Council wanted Jaden dead, so the enemy of his enemy was his friend, right? Hopefully.

I moved over to stand in front of my father, who still sat on the throne, looking like the cat who ate the canary. At this moment, I realized how little I knew about him. Sure, he was my dad, but I'd just met him last night.

"Now, we feast. Today is a great day for the fae."

Nausea swept through me. A great day for the fae? He'd just had all of their leaders murdered. People they had known for hundreds of years. Would they actually be happy? I didn't know. If they were, maybe the Council really were monsters, maybe they deserved what had happened to them. I knew they were monsters, actually. After what they'd done to me, and to Jaden.

But still. Did that mean they should be murdered right in their job site, or whatever?

Quintin flowed up from the chair. "Let's be on our way then." He swept by me. I waited to see if he would make sure I followed, but he ignored me. It was Starren that waited until Dan, Nina, and I started to follow.

We passed my little cell, winding down a stairwell wrapped around the trees. The steps were fluid, reaching to meet us as we stepped, so Dan with his long stride and me with my short walked at the same pace.

Finally not quite as numb, I got my first look at Nina since the disaster upstairs. Because I knew her, she looked sick to me. But she was hiding it well. My eyes swung over to Dan. Resolute. Probably trying to figure a way out for all of us.

If that was true, I was behind him one hundred percent. Mom had been right about this place.

Somehow we reached the ground within a few minutes. I knew it was a long way to the ground from the platform. I'd fallen for what seemed like forever, and hadn't even gotten to where I could see the ground, yet here we were. Apparently the stairs were helping us like an escalator.

Spread out before us was a clearing, packed full of fae of all kinds. Tall fae, short fae, dangerous looking fae, and even some that didn't look dangerous at all. Those were the ones to watch out for. There were huge tables made of living plants, straining with foods I didn't recognize.

The stairs dropped Dan, Nina, and me to ground level, kept Starren a head above us, and Quintin high in the air.

"My fellow fae," Quintin called, the crowd already eerily silent from the moment we came into sight. "Today is a good day. Today we leave the past in the past, and move on into a brighter future."

My skin crawled at his tone. So relaxed. So... jubilant. After just killing people he'd known for... a really, really long time. Something was wrong with my father.

"The Council held us back. The Council regulated us without reason. As your King, I vow to give you the freedom all fae deserve!"

The crowd cheered, the many types of voices creating a strange din of all pitches. It wasn't just the more human type fae here, but many others. Horns, hooves, wings. Beautiful, but somewhat terrifying.

"Be merry, my friends. Today is a good day. We will see about tomorrow. With my daughters by my side, the fae are headed for a new age of prosperity!" He hung in the air for a moment for affect, then the stairs floated him down to our level.

Show-off.

We moved toward the tables, the crowd parting around us, making me really uncomfortable. I preferred not being seen. Being seen always meant trouble for me. Whether it was being picked on by human kids at school, or the fae Council noticing I hadn't been in for training, it never turned out well. My stomach churned at the thought of the Council. Sure, they'd wanted to have me killed, but Starren's brutality was forever burned in my brain now. I saw the blood every time I blinked.

When we closed in on the table, we were treated like the royalty we apparently were. Wait a sec. I just took that in for a moment. Was I royalty? Not a princess, ew, but daughter of the King meant something, didn't it?

A fae with an extra broad face and wide set eyes tried to sit Dan and Nina a little ways down the table from us. I glared. He paled and moved them closer. Okay, I still hated this, but maybe there were some perks.

But if my dad thought I was staying here forever, he had another think coming. I did want to ask him why, why he'd had those people killed, why he wasn't with my mom wherever she was, before I left, but I would be leaving as soon as possible. I had to get Dan and Nina out of here. Did I want to believe my dad would take care of them because I cared about them? Absolutely. Did I? Absolutely not.

The platters of food in front of us all looked good, but my stomach screamed that anything I put in my mouth would be coming right back out. Starren had killed those people without a thought. No remorse, no hesitation. I put my forehead on the wood table in front of me, starting to gulp for air a bit.

A hand on my back helped a little. "Breathe in, Trish," Nina whispered. "Breathe out."

I tried to do as she said, but my vision swam. Wade had told me repeatedly how amazing Starren was in a fight, how dangerous she could be, but I'd never really stopped to consider what that meant. How many people had fallen to her blade?

"It's going to be alright, Trish. Just breathe. You'll feel better if you breathe." Nina's voice sounded faint, far away. I closed my eyes and sucked in a breath through my nose.

"Trish!" Another distant voice, this one familiar too. Strong arms grabbed me, pulling me into a tight hug. I struggled for a second, until my heart figured out who it was.

"Jaden!" I screeched, grabbing onto him like he was a lifeline. "Where have you been? I was worried sick!" I slapped his shoulder, then hugged him back, hard. "Where's Wade?"

"I'm here," Wade said, leaning around Jaden.

I nearly burst into tears on the spot. Too much had happened in the last few days. In the last year, really. But my dad and sister were here, and I didn't want them thinking I was a wimp, raised by humans with human failings. So I blinked and sucked it up, doing my best to smile.

"I'm so glad you guys are okay. I was worried."

Wade's eyebrows hit his hairline. "Are you okay, Trish?"

I frowned at him.

"You're admitting you care about people. You never do that."

I swatted at him and then scooted closer to Nina, making room for them at the table. She hugged me close, looked me in the eye for a moment, checking the state of my mental health. Better, now that the boys were here alive. Much better.

"Where have you guys been?" I asked. "You're lucky I don't beat the crap out of you for making me think you were dead."

"Ah, there she is," Jaden said. He shared a look with Wade, like for once they were agreeing on something, and slid onto the bench next to me. "We were formulating a plan when your dad caught us."

I snorted. "Formulating a plan? You mean you were hiding somewhere."

"We weren't doing anyone any good if we got caught," Wade protested.

"True, and you were probably doing the right thing, but call it what it was, hiding."

"Fine," Jaden said. "We were hiding just outside the prison." He held up his hand before I could ask. "There was another portal at the far end that goes to a portal in the woods not far from the main one. The guard's housing is outside, so they don't have to live underground like the prisoners."

"Anyway," Wade said, leaning around Jaden again. "Wurt caught us in the woods." I shuddered again at the thought of what could have happened with that monster. "He and I are friends. He told me your dad was back, and that he'd make sure Quintin would find out you were going before the Council. I knew right then that Quintin would keep you safe, so we waited until he came for Starren."

"You didn't go back and try to find us?" Nina asked.

"We did." It was Jaden's chance to protest. "We couldn't find you!"

"Quintin came for Starren. He asked us to make sure things were taken care of at the prison, we did and then we followed them all through the portal, and here we are," Wade finished the story.

Had they seen what Starren had done? Surely they would have stopped her. Jaden, at least.

I cocked my head, glaring at Jaden. He gave me a look back. There was definitely a lot more to this story than Wade was telling me. Whether it was because of where we were, or because he didn't want me to know, I would find out later.

"What's your favorite dish, my dear?" Quintin surprised me by asking. He'd been talking pretty intently with some guy until this moment. "We have a lot to learn about each other." His face went sad. "Only a terrible father doesn't know what his daughter likes to eat."

"It's hardly your fault, father," Starren muttered. She still seemed like she was in a dark mood. She was my sister, but I hadn't known what to do with her in social situations even before all this. Now, after seeing all the blood she'd spilled, I was completely at a loss. Did she still hate me? Hard to tell when her face seemed like it was made out of granite.

A glance over the table told me exactly what I'd thought it would. Other than a couple things I'd been fed in the cell over the last day, I didn't recognize anything. "I actually don't know what any of these are."

Quintin frowned, looking out across the table. "Did your mother not teach you about fae culture?"

"She tried. We just didn't have any of these things on Earth, and she didn't have a lot of time."

"Didn't have a lot of time?" he leaned forward, his eyes boring into mine.

"She went missing years ago. I haven't seen her since I was a kid."

He straightened, looking hurt. "She took you from me, then disappeared, leaving you behind?"

I didn't like his tone. My mom had done her best. "I don't think she wanted to. She got all scared and left me at a children's home. She said she was coming back, but she never did." I swallowed down some more emotions. Way too many of those today.

"Now that the Council will no longer be hindering me in everything I try to do, we'll be able to find your mother. Wherever she is, I'm sure she's been worried about you."

Starren's face went ugly for a second, and then the look vanished, making me wonder if I'd actually seen it there in the first place or not.

"Lord Quintin," Jaden said formally.

"Yes?" Father asked.

"Now that you have punished the jailors at Fairbent Prison, what will become of the prisoners?"

Punished? My head swung nearly on its own toward Starren. Her face had gone that same closed off, emotionless expression as earlier, when she'd killed the Council.

"The prisoners will starve without anyone there to care for them," Jaden said.

No one there to care for them? Had they relieved the guards of duty? Or had they... I looked at Starren again. She stared back, her eyes dead. And I knew. My gut started to churn again. I'd so badly wanted a biological family, and this is what I was getting. I should have left things alone.

"Father."

He leaned in, giving me a small smile. "Yes, my dear?"

"There was a girl with me, in my cell, when I was in that prison." I couldn't stop a small shudder from escaping. "She was good to me. Do you think we could look into it?" What if she was dead already? No, no. I took one of those deep breaths Nina was getting me to take earlier. It had only been one night, at the most. She should be fine.

He smiled indulgently. "Whatever makes your kind heart happy, little one."

My kind heart? That was a first, seriously. No one had ever said anything like that about me ever before. Except... I glanced over at Jaden, who was watching my exchange with my father intently. Somehow even when I was planning on ruining his life, Jaden had seen the good in me. I hadn't thought it was there. In the end I'd tried to give him up to save myself, but it hadn't worked out like that. Would I have actually been able to do it?

Hopefully we'd never find out.

He noticed me looking at him and smiled before breaking eye contact to go back to staring down Quintin.

My cheeks warmed. Then I realized what he was doing and kicked him under the table. No need to antagonize one of our few allies, who just happened to be the King of all the fae.

"I can send a man right now, if you'd like."

Poor Nara would probably get so freaked out if some random guy came and took her out of her cell, dragging her here.

"That's okay, I'll go get her. It isn't like it's far to go with the portal." And this way I would get a look at the prison. The guards being 'punished' scared me.

"You have to be exhausted after going through all this. I'll send you with an escort in the morning, just to be extra safe."

I made sure to not allow my eyes to go to Jaden, to see what he was thinking. I didn't want my dad to know how much he meant to me. I didn't know why, but it felt wrong. "I'd hate for her to sit there with no food or water. I don't mind going, it will only take, like, fifteen minutes." If I waited until tomorrow, everything would be cleaned up and I'd wonder forever what had really happened there.

Quintin sat his cup down on the table, rather forcefully. "I will send someone to feed all the prisoners until we can figure out who should be there, and who was wrongfully imprisoned. You will not be going until tomorrow."

"Yes, Father." I looked down at my plate, pretending to be submissive while internally my blood boiled. He didn't want me to see what they'd done at the prison. That was the only explanation for his anger.

"Today we will eat and talk, take a tour of your new home, and then rest. Tomorrow you can visit the prison, and we can discuss what to do with your humans."

"Dan and Nina," I corrected automatically. Apparently Starren got her disdain for humans honest.

"Yes, Dan and Nina."

Nina reached under the table and grabbed my hand, out of sight. I gripped hers back, probably much harder than I should have, but she didn't complain.

Quintin handed me a dish of something and I moved a small

amount to my plate. Conversation around us resumed, and I realized for the first time how quiet it had gotten for a minute. The fae around us whispered to each other, but didn't seem to be holding any conversations. They were scared. Scared of my father, just like the rest of us.

"You gotta be more careful, Trish," Jaden whispered from one side.

"Don't antagonize him," Nina said out of the side of her mouth from the other. "We know he's capable of horrible things. We don't know how strongly he feels about you."

She was worried about me when she should be worried about herself. If he ever tried to do anything to 'my humans,' I'd lose it. Full on crazy girl. All I could do was pray it never came to that point. Because really, what could Jaden, Nina, Dan, and I do against what we'd seen back up on the platform? Probably not much, if I didn't have my extra helpers.

That was it. If I couldn't convince Father to let me leave with Dan and Nina, I just needed a reason to leave this area, and when the trees were no longer forced to obey whatever leader was in charge, I'd be able to take out my 'escort' or anyone else that tried to stop me.

Feeling a lot better about things, I dug into the food I'd been mindlessly shoveling onto my plate. The prison visit would have been the perfect opportunity, but I didn't really want to leave that soon. I still had questions, and I still didn't know my father at all. Maybe now that the Council wasn't gunning for me, I could do some kind of visit schedule. If I found out he wasn't a monster. He wasn't. He couldn't be. My mom would never have been with him if he was.

Now that I'd been here, I knew I could survive the land. Faerie itself didn't seem that bad. The fae, yeah, just as bad as every story I'd ever heard, but the land itself was beautiful. Maybe the reason my mom had never come to get me was because she was here somewhere, stuck. That portal in the old farmhouse near home still worked, as far as I knew. It hadn't been that long since Starren tried to drag Jaden and me through it. Maybe I could come back and look for her. As scary as my dad was, no one would want to cross him and hurt me.

"Now that you're here, Trish, I'll get to show you around," Wade broke me out of my thoughts, leaning around behind Jaden.

Jaden slowly leaned back. Wade tipped forward and caught my eye in front of Jaden.

"There are so many things to see here. You're going to love it."

Jaden leaned back forward to take a bite of food, blocking Wade a second time.

Wade tilted around behind him again, his face going grumpy for a second. "I can introduce you around. Teach you more about fighting."

I didn't want to know more about fighting. Watching Starren kill those people had pretty much put me off fighting for good. Sure, I needed to be able to defend myself, and Nina, but I would never be able to kill someone. Never.

Nina gave my hand under the table another squeeze. How did something so small make me feel so much better? And I appreciated the fact that her and Dan were just staying quiet. The less attention they brought on themselves the better. I glanced around the table, as subtly as I could, trying to gauge the other fae sitting here. Were they the type that hated humans? Or did they not care? No way to know right now, but I'd have to keep a close eye on things until we got out of here. Some of the sideways looks sent my way were making me uncomfortable. Problem was, I didn't know if they were aimed at me because of my father and everything he'd just done, or my association with humans.

"Is the food not to your liking?" Quintin's question startled me. I was eating the food just fine, why would he ask that? But then I noticed who he was looking at.

"I'm just not used to this type of food," Nina answered smoothly. "It's all new to me."

Quintin grabbed a bowl of the white stuff I loved so much and handed it to Nina. "Try this. You'll love it."

Nina looked at me and I nearly panicked. We didn't know if it would do anything or not. Surely eating some food couldn't bind a person to Faerie, could it? Those were just old stories, like changelings and mermaids. And she was in danger if she didn't, I could feel it. Could see it in the way Quintin's gaze bored into her.

"It's been quite the day, I'm not sure my stomach could handle much right now." Wow, Nina could think on her feet. It might be the truth, honestly, but still.

"Ipsish is very soothing. Trust me, you'll enjoy the flavor, and it will help settle your stomach. This feast took much to prepare. You will cause serious offence if you refuse."

The entire table had gone quiet, everyone studiously looking like they weren't paying any attention, but very obviously eavesdropping. I shoved down a trickle of panic working its way up my chest. This was my father. He loved me. He wanted what was best for me.

"We better just eat some," Dan whispered from the other side of Nina. Hopefully no one else had abilities like mine that made it possible to hear him.

Nina smile-grimaced, then took a spoonful of the white stuff. Quintin didn't blink as he watched her raise the spoon to her mouth. She smiled when she took the spoon out of her mouth. "Pretty good."

I stared her down, waiting for her to start gagging and fall to the ground, foaming at the mouth like what happened in the movies. Nothing happened.

Quintin smiled back at Nina. "Good. I'm glad you like it." After that he passed dish after dish, explaining what things were called and laughing at Dan when one of the dishes was too spicy.

Wait. I'd almost started to calm down a little when something registered. He'd said the feast took much to prepare. He'd known. He'd had a feast made to celebrate. The food I'd been starting to enjoy caught in my throat. Killing the Council had been his plan for the day.

I watched him out of the corner of my eye, doing my best to keep him from noticing. Who was he really? The man here, chatting with everyone around him, or the man that killed without remorse? He could be both. He'd been protecting me, right? That's why he had Starren kill those people, they were going to hurt me.

I had to keep telling myself that.

Somehow we ate most of the day. Conversation flowed and ebbed around me. I didn't join in much, but it was interesting all the same. The tour Quintin had wanted to take me on was pretty basic, just some history about how things had come about. It turned out that the clearing we'd had our meal in was the original glade that the Council had met in, before King Frian had used his ability to create the platforms and walkways above us.

A complete charmer and gentleman, Quintin walked us to our rooms for the night. He put Jaden in his own, Dan and Nina in one, and then gestured for me to follow him to mine.

"Night, honey," Nina called after me. "We're right here if you need us."

Quintin chuckled. "I will always be grateful to them for caring for you when I could not, but now that you're here, you'll want for nothing ever again." He led me into a nice little room, a lot bigger than the cell I'd been not-sleeping in.

He leaned over until we were close to the same height. "Goodnight, dear. Sleep well."

"Father?" I asked, making sure not to call him Quintin.

"Yes?"

"Why did Starren do that today? Kill everyone?" I hadn't had the courage to ask before. In fact, it just kind of slipped out now. But I didn't want my father to be a monster. I didn't want my only blood family to be the kind of people that killed for power.

He lifted a hand like he was going to brush my hair out of my face, but dropped it when I flinched away. "They tried to hurt you, my dear. And they imprisoned your sister. There was no chance of you being safe as long as they lived."

The words made sense as they dripped out of his mouth like honey. He definitely knew how to manipulate people. I'd had plenty of that happen to me in foster care, I knew how to see it and call it what it was. Maybe saving me was a nice side benefit, a nice excuse. But I wasn't sure it was the main reason.

I gave him a small smile. "Goodnight."

He moved to leave. "And just so you know, I am sorry about this part. It's for your own protection." I didn't know what he was talking about until he stepped out of the room and the door closed and faded.

I jumped forward and slammed my fist against the wood. "Hey!" Another cell, seriously? Would he do anything to Dan and Nina while I was in here?

"Don't worry about them," Starren's voice nearly gave me a heart attack. I whirled around to find her sitting in a chair, leaning back on two legs against the wall, very un-Starren-like, her bow and sword across her lap. "He won't risk making you angry. They're safe as long as you're cooperating."

"And what, he left you in here to threaten me? Keep an eye on me?" I snarled.

Starren snorted, dropping to all four chair legs. "Hardly. I'm as much a prisoner as you are. I have been all my life."

I moved over and sat on the bed, near enough to make her feel like I cared, far enough away to jump back if I needed to. She had been so weird since we'd found each other, I didn't know what to make of her anymore. At least before she'd been predictable. "What do you mean you're a prisoner?"

She mimicked locking her lips and throwing away the key. "That's the expression your humans use, right?"

I rolled my eyes. "Not all humans are mine. Just Dan and Nina."

She rolled her eyes back, mimicking me. "Whatever."

"You can't tell me because at some point you told someone you wouldn't?"

She cocked her head. "Something like that."

And I'd thought my childhood had been bad. Quintin may be our father, but he certainly wasn't the fatherly type.

"Why are you mad at me, Starren? I'm here because of you." Sometimes I could be too blunt. I didn't feel like this was one of those times. We needed to get this out in the air. Preferably without her injuring me too badly.

She bared her teeth at me and growled. "Because she took you and left me." She dropped her head, her body drooping. "I know that's not your fault. But it's what I think about every time I see you."

Ouch. Mother had left her here, even knowing what Father was. I hadn't thought of that. I bit my lip. Hard. There was no fixing this. Unless I could give her different memories, make her think of other things when she saw me, not just our mom abandoning her to live here, to be used as a tool. I reached forward and grabbed her hand, something I would have never done if I hadn't spent the time with the Inzas.

"I'm sorry, Star. I don't even understand why."

"Whoever has the girl, wins the war," Starren said.

I stared her down. She was losing it. That didn't follow at all.

"That's what he said. The last fae seer. Father and Mother thought it was me, at first, but it wasn't. It was you. That's why Mother took you and ran."

Was she serious? Mom had only snatched me because of some prophecy? She wasn't trying to protect me, didn't do it so we could be together, nothing like that?

"She didn't need me." Starren kicked at the wood floor with the toe of her boot. "She left me here, with him."

A pang hit me. That's why she hated me so much in the beginning, before we'd even gotten to know each other. It wasn't because I was a law-breaker, it was because I was a family-breaker. "How old were you? Do you remember Mom?"

Her eyes glistened for a second, and it almost made me start crying too. Starren who felt nothing, felt a whole lot more than I'd thought. "Let it go, Trish. It's in the past. Let's leave it there."

She'd called me Trish. This had to be the first time she'd ever done that. Did that mean she was ready to be sisters? Then the other part of what she'd said hit me like the swing of a tree held by a troll. "Wait a second, whoever has the girl wins the war? What war?"

Starren moved over to sit by me on the bed, dropping down to lay with her legs still dangling off the edge. "I'm not supposed to tell you any of this. I'm supposed to be a good soldier, make you feel like family, get you to trust me."

"I think that ship has sailed." My voice was a little high, but I was keeping it together pretty well, or so I kept telling myself.

"Yeah," Starren said, staring at the ceiling. "All I can say is that it isn't here yet. A war has been brewing between two factions of fae for hundreds of years. I don't think it will be long before it reaches a tipping point. That's why the Council wanted your Jaden so badly. Their seer was assassinated shortly after you were born, and another hasn't been found. Except for Jaden."

"He's not my Jaden," I protested. And this was an oh crap moment. The Council had known about Jaden's ability. Did anyone else?

Starren gave me a look, then went back to staring at the ceiling. "Without the seer, the Council was blind. Quintin would have struck years ago if he'd had you around. He was biding his time."

Okay, now I was officially freaked out.

"So what do we do?"

Confusion crossed Starren's face. "What do we do about what?"

"How do we stop the war? Or at least get out of the danger zone?"

Her face lit up. "If we got you away, it would never start. Quintin is only feeling bold enough to get things in motion because of you being here." Then her face fell, going back to the mask I was really starting to hate. "But there is no escaping Quintin. I've tried. And obviously, I failed."

"Yes, but were you trying on your own? This is a whole different story. You've got me, Jaden, Dan, Wade, and Nina is great moral support."

"We're taking your humans?" Starren asked.

"Well, yeah, you used them against me to force me to help you catch Jaden, you think I'd just leave them here in Faerie to die? And stop calling them that."

"It's what they are, isn't it?"

"Yeah, but they don't walk around calling you fae."

"I wish they would. The fae are the superior race, and the humans are far too familiar."

I shoved her. "Stop that. You're going to get to know them, and then you're going to change your mind."

"Doubtful." She sat up, crossing her legs on the bed. "So how are we going to do this?"

"I really want to wait until tomorrow, after I've been to the prison. That girl I told you about, I just can't leave her there. I feel so bad for her, she can't even talk to the other prisoners or anything. It has to be torture."

Starren let out a huge sigh and fell back onto the bed. "You realize we are never going to get away if we have to stop and save every single thing you get attached to."

"Hey, don't insult me like that. Ask Nina, I don't get attached to things." I fell down next to her.

"I doubt she'd agree with you, since you seem to have gotten pretty attached to her."

Fine, she had me there. "So after we get Nara from the prison, then what? How do we escape if we are around father during the day and locked up at night? I don't want to wait too long, I have a bad feeling about him with Dan and Nina."

"Your bad feeling is justified. Quintin hates humans. He feels they are weak, and thinks that the Earth shouldn't be only theirs."

Okay, this was new information. "What does that mean?" Starren mimed locking her lips again. For a fae that hated humans so much, she sure did like to copy them.

"What about your plant power, whatever you call it? Can it help us escape?"

"It hasn't been working. The trees caught me and brought me back when I tried to escape last time."

Starren sat bolt upright. "But the Council was in charge at that point. The trees are enchanted to help the people ruling. We have father's blood. They may not listen to me, but if they already want to help you, then maybe they can force it."

I sat up beside her. "Genius!" I jumped up and ran to where the door should be. I put my hand up, touching the wood, and closed my eyes.

"Trish," Starren hissed after a second.

I peeked out of one eye. The edges of the door were glowing in the wood. "Yes," I pumped a fist. "I just need to get a knob."

"Pause for a second," Starren said, hopping off the bed and coming over to stand by me. "There may be guards out there. We don't want to give this away."

"True, good thinking." I stopped communicating with the tree and the door faded away.

"We can't wait around with this, Trish. We need to get out of here. But if we don't do it smart, we won't get far. We don't know where we'll be tomorrow, we could be totally split up. We need to get out before Quintin gets us separated, using us against each other."

I threw up my hands. "That's what I was doing, and you told me to stop."

"Yeah, going out that door. We need to figure something else out."

I turned my back to the door and slid to the floor. "If we can't go through the door, what's another option?"

Starren paced the small room, which was really annoying since there wasn't much space.

I tipped my head back, bracing myself on the floor with my hands. The wood sunk beneath them, like the tree was trying to help me figure it out.

"What about through the floor?" I asked.

Starren paused. "That would work for the staying out of sight, but how are we supposed to not plunge to our deaths?"

I pushed both hands into the floor, whispering to the trees. Slowly a hole opened. "Remember what happened when we got in that fight?"

"Yes?"

A vine slithered through the hole and grabbed Starren around the waist, pulling her out of the tree. Another came in for me, and I loosened my body and forced myself not to fight it. I'd asked for the help, it was just doing as I'd asked.

It was like a slide, down, and then out the side through a small hole, just big enough for me to fit.

I went airborne for a second, then the vine snapped and I was just hanging next to Starren.

"What now, genius?" Starren sounded annoyed.

Oops. And now I was queasy. "We need to get everyone else out."

Before Starren could answer, the vines pulled us upward, close to another tree. A moment later Nina came sliding out, literally holding her hands over her mouth to muffle her screams, followed by Dan.

"Nina," I whispered. "Nina, be quiet. It's us."

Nina's thrashing paused. "Trish?"

"Yeah, we're escaping."

"Good plan, something is going on here," Dan said.

"Okay then, up, up, and away." The vines snapped and we flew away. I heard an oomph from Dan, and more muffled screaming from Nina. We all stopped in front of another section of tree, swaying in the slight breeze.

"What is happening?" Nina asked, sounding super breathless.

"Trish's other weird ability," Starren grunted, not sounding happy.

She'd barely gotten the words out when Wade and Jaden shot out of the tree, wildly writhing in the air.

"Stop, stop, it's me," I said.

"Make them let us go," Wade said, struggling wildly. "Now, make them let us go!"

"No, they're helping us. You don't want them to let you go right now anyway, it's a long way down."

He closed his eyes and made a weird whimpering noise. Probably PTSD from the last time he'd been caught by a vine.

I actually felt a little bad, even though he'd totally deserved to be squished to death at the time. I wiggled around so I could see Starren. "Now what? Where should we go from here?"

"The portal," Starren answered.

"You guys hear that?" I asked the trees. "Would you please take us to the portal?"

A leaf from the vine stroked my face, weirding me out, but then we were going up. Fast.

We flew toward the portal at alarming speed. Popping over the floor of the platform, I got sight of it, glowing in the dark. And three forms, standing nearby.

"Stop, stop," I hissed at the vines. They snapped to a halt, knocking us into each other, sending everyone careening in wild circles. "Ouch, be more careful. You're going to break one of us."

The vines holding everyone looked sad somehow, drooping like they'd been without water for a week.

"We can't go through there," Dan said.

"Why not? We could take them, easily," Starren said.

"We need to keep it quiet that we escaped for as long as possible." Jaden swung around on his vine until he was pointing at us. "We have got to get as close to the tunnel as we can before morning, when they figure out we're gone."

"We got this," I said. Hey, guys, one more favor. The vines and branches hanging around us swayed over until they were close, almost at attention. Nina was starting to look even more freaked out, and I didn't blame her. I was just getting out of that stage.

Could you grab those guards and hold onto them for me until it gets light out?

Vines lashed out toward the guards. "Make sure to cover their mouths," I whisper yelled.

Apparently the trees heard me, because the guards didn't even have a chance to scream as they were violently pulled upward into the tree canopy.

"Thanks."

Now everyone was staring at me.

"What?" My voice came out a little crankier than I would have liked, but people thinking I was a freak was one of my greatest fears.

"Nothing, honey," Nina said. "Let's get out of here."

I couldn't agree more. The trees felt my wants, and we were lightly deposited right in front of the portal. Except for Wade. He got a little toss. Maybe these trees could communicate with the ones from home and didn't like him.

I headed to the portal first. I still healed, and no one else did, so whether they wanted it this way or not, I didn't care. I hit it full tilt, at as-fast-as-I-could while still being sneaky run.

Instead of the normal weird, water feeling of going through a portal, when I slammed into it at full speed, I bounced right off, almost hitting the ground. I would have, if Jaden hadn't caught me.

"You okay?" his whisper sounded anxious.

"Hunky dory," I groaned out, gingerly poking at my nose. This I had never encountered before.

"The portal must be blocked," Starren said quietly. "Someone else try it."

Wade stepped forward and went through the portal without a problem. He came right back.

"What's going on?" Dan asked.

"Father has blocked the portal for our DNA. He's making sure we don't escape." Starren sounded completely monotone. I'd have been more comfortable if she'd had some inflection at all, even defeat. This no emotion stuff scared me.

"We don't know that yet, you try."

"No," Starren answered.

No use fighting with her when she was like this.

"The rest of you are going to have to go," I said.

Instant protest broke out from everyone but Starren.

"I'm not kidding, guys. I don't think Quintin will come after you. I need you all to safety. It will be much easier for Starren and I to find the tunnel alone than if we need to watch out for the rest of you."

"The girls can take care of themselves," Wade said.

I smiled at him. He was always the first one to believe in me when it came to stuff like this. His number one redeeming quality.

"Can I trust you to deliver my parents to the tunnel?" I asked Wade, looking him in the eyes.

"I will protect them with my life, until you return." His word was binding. This was a serious thing he was promising for me. He leaned in. "Maybe once we meet up again, we can talk."

I nodded, not really promising anything. I had a feeling what he wanted to talk about, and the discussion would not be going well for him if I was right.

"Jaden, will you protect my parents?"

"You know I'll always protect them, Trish, I love them too. But I'm not leaving you."

"When you get to the other side of the portal, go into the jail and find the cell where I was held, down the first hallway. There's a girl in there, Nara. She's deaf, she needs your help. Show her this, and I think she'll go with you." I made the sign that Nara had made up for my name. I hadn't known her long, but her whole situation was just so terrible, it about made me sick. And now it sounded like they might just let the prisoners starve to death in their cells. I couldn't save them all, but I could help her.

I repeated my sign for myself again. "Now you do it," I insisted.

Both boys sighed, but did as I asked.

"One more time."

They did it again.

Almost satisfied, I nodded. "She's going to be totally freaked out, so nice, slow, gentle movements, okay? And if you have the time to do it safely, let some of the other prisoners out, maybe they'll help each other. I don't know what they did, but it can't have made it okay to leave them to starve to death." I described what she looked like, and how to find the cell.

"Is it really wise to free someone you don't know why they have been imprisoned?" Wade asked.

I crossed my arms. "I'm not going home without her."

He shrugged. Okay, that wasn't the best answer when talking with him. He'd already implied he didn't want me going home anyway.

"Wade has a good point. We don't even know why she's in there, honey. She might not be safe."

"No one deserves to die like that. And she's deaf and super shy, how dangerous could she be? She probably just ticked the wrong person off somehow, and they had her thrown in there. Fae can be so petty."

Nina looked at Starren like she expected her to protest. Starren just shrugged.

"You sneak in, grab Nara and sneak out. Then meet us at the tunnel. It will be easy."

"Oh yeah, because it was so easy last time," Starren said. "You waltzed right in, freed me, and we were gone. Five minutes, tops."

I glared at her. "There were guards there last time. There shouldn't be any now. Don't risk your safety, or Dan and Nina's." I hated adding that, but I had to. I wouldn't lose any of the people here to save Nara, but if she could be saved easily, I wouldn't let her die either. "Starren, do you know how to get to the tunnel?"

Starren nodded. "Wade told me earlier."

"This is all a moot point," Dan broke in. "We aren't leaving you, Trish. It doesn't matter what kind of danger you're in, we aren't leaving you."

"I was afraid you'd say that." I whispered to the trees and waited for a second. Vines lashed out of hiding and gripped Dan, Nina, and Jaden, lifting them slightly off their feet and waiting for my command. "Love you guys." It was weird to say it out loud, but I had to. "See you at the tunnel." Then I gestured, and the vines threw them through the portal. "Better get after them," I said to Wade.

He nodded and jumped through.

"They'll just come right back," Starren said, sounding bored.

"They'll try." I called branches to me. They wrapped around the branches of the portal, straining for a moment. Then the supports gave way. The portal snapped and fizzled out of existence.

Starren slid her sword slowly from its sheath. "Someone heard the portal being destroyed. I can feel them coming."

"Feel them, like powers feel them? Or just warrior feel them?"

She gave me a withering look. "I have no powers, except that others powers don't usually work on me." She looked around, keeping her sword ready. "Things like your plants? It isn't magic so they can still get to me, but things like fireballs just bounce off."

"I figured that out after the lady from the Council tried to barbeque you." And did that mean our father couldn't do that weird thing where he just froze people in place to her like he had done to the Council?

"What's the plan now, genius? We're about to be found."

"No we aren't. We just need to get out of here. Follow me." I walked over to the edge of the platform, checked on Starren, and then fell off the side.

CHAPTER FOURTEEN

It took a few seconds, but Starren jumped off the platform behind me.

We hurtled toward the ground, my eyes watering at the speed, my heart leaping, this time with a weird since of thrill instead of the terror last time. Just as the light of some torches came into view, a branch snatched me out of the air, and another caught Starren, setting us lightly on the ground.

"Thanks."

Starren leaned over and vomited. "Are you insane?" she asked, after recovering for a second. "What in the world were you thinking? What if they'd decided not to help you out this time?"

"Whatever. It worked, didn't it?"

She glared at me and looked like she was about to start heaving again.

Whatever. I was right. It was definitely the fastest, safest way to get to the ground. And you guys wouldn't let me go splat, right?

None of the trees answered.

I shivered. Yeah, it had been a gamble. But I could feel my connection with the trees growing. Like we really were learning about each other, getting to know each other. They wouldn't let me die. The worst that could have happened would have been if they'd taken us back up to the platform and deposited us in front of Quintin. But at least then the others would still have gotten away.

"How much work will it be for them to fix that portal?"

Starren straightened, still looking queasy. "At least a few days. The tunnel is only a two day journey from here, we should be there before they can get it operational again."

Two days? Two days walking? With Starren? I groaned. I hated walking, so much.

A torch near the stairway up to the platform burst into light.

"Shhh," Starren said, dropping low to the ground. She waved at me, and took off into the forest, staying down.

I went down too, attempting to imitate her. I definitely wasn't as good at this as she was. Did she train for this specifically, because she was almost out of sight already and I thought I was moving along fairly quickly.

Something made a noise to my left. I jerked right and started running in earnest. There, another twig made a sound.

And then I was ten feet in the air, with my mouth being covered by a tree branch, my heart thundering in my ears.

A figure, beneath me. I could barely make out a shape in the dark, it was more of a sense of movement. A guard must have noticed Starren or me. One guess on which one.

Suddenly one place of movement turned into two, and two to five.

Help Starren, please. I had better not have just gotten a sister to lose her now. If the trees helped me and left her behind, how many guards could she fend off? I'd seen what she'd done to the Council. Supposedly incredibly powerful fae, snuffed out in a few swings of her blade.

A muffled squeak came from somewhere to my right, at the same level in the air I was. "Starren?" I whispered.

"If you don't stop sending these things after me, I'm going to kill you." Her squeak turned into a groan. "Not literally." She started to pant. "Tell your tree I'm not actually going to kill you."

"Ah, she's good, don't hurt her."

I heard Starren gulp in a breath. Thankfully we seemed to be high enough that whoever, or whatever, was looking for us below hadn't noticed what was going on.

"We need to get ahead of them. As soon as Quintin finds out we're gone, this entire wood will be swarming with fae loyal to him, desperate to catch his eye and attention. Once that happens, we won't get away."

"Okay... trees." I'd almost said guys, but I didn't really know how that worked. They might be girls. Or neither. "We need a bridge please." I pointed. "Going that way."

Starren snorted. "That way, you dope." She pointed a different direction than I had.

"Ah, sorry, that way." The trees rustled as the branches moved, intertwining. "Shh, quietly!"

The branches slowed, silently weaving together to form a walkway. Once there was enough for us to stand on, they sat us gently down.

"Are you sure this is okay?" Starren whispered. She sure was not a fan of all this tree stuff. I was beginning to think it was amazing, instead of being scared of it.

"Yeah, they'll take care of us."

Trusting me, Starren took off. Her fast walk turned into a slow jog, and then a fast-paced trot. The trees upped their pace to stay ahead of her, but still kept the rustling to a minimum. Hopefully the guards would just think it was the wind.

I checked behind us. The pathway was dissolving as soon as I passed each section. While looking behind, I misstepped and lost my balance, nearly plunging to the ground. A branch caught and righted me.

My heart nearly jumped out of my chest. I patted the nearest branch. "Thanks."

We were moving quickly when suddenly the bridge stopped weaving in front of us. I nearly ran into Starren when she stopped at the edge, teetering slightly.

"What's that about?" Starren ground out.

"I don't know. Hey, trees, can we get a little help here?"

The words were hardly out of my mouth before a dark object floated by us, at our level. Starren hit me from the side, making me smother a yelp, and slammed us into the closest tree. She put her finger to her lips, and kept super still.

Okay, so many scary things had happened to me recently, but this not knowing whatever it was out there took the cake. I moved my head trying to get a better look, but Starren poked me in the side.

In through the nose, out through the mouth, in through the nose, out through the mouth. The coaching helped a little, enough that I wasn't feeling faint, but it worked a lot better when Nina counted it out for me.

Whatever it was flew silently by again.

After a moment of me not breathing at all, the tree bridge starting building in front of us again.

"What was that?" I asked Starren.

She started jogging forward again. "An owl."

I stopped dead. "An owl? You freaked me out that bad over just an owl?"

She just kept jogging, and I had to book it for a second to catch up. "Here's a great lesson for you. In Faerie, there is never a just in front of anything."

Okay, that seemed valid. "What's weird about the owls here?"

"Nothing is wrong with them all the time, but one of Father's friends can control beasts and see through their eyes. It was looking for us."

So if I'd been by myself I would have been caught after five minutes of running. If someone could control animals, see through their eyes, and I could control plants, could I do the same somehow? Not that they had eyes, but they had awareness, for sure.

Wait, one of Father's friends? "Do you think he knows we're gone?"

"Hopefully not yet, but the owl is a bad sign. You weren't exactly subtle when you destroyed the portal."

True. But I'd like to see her try and destroy a portal in stealth mode. It just didn't work.

We ran on in the dark, on and on and on. Finally, after not seeing any sign for a while, Starren let us slow to a walk. This was one time I really didn't mind hiking in the woods. The more distance between us and Father, the better. Sad, that I still called him father, but I couldn't help it. I'd longed to meet him since I knew what a father was.

All this extra breathing while I ran was making my nose tender. Why would that be? I reached up and poked at it. Ouch. It still hurt from running into the portal. It was healing, yes, but not nearly as quickly as normal.

"Starren, my nose isn't healed yet."

She threw a look over her shoulder. "So?"

"So normally it would have been a minute after I hurt it. And it took forever for me to heal after the guards at the prison were rough." At the time I'd thought it had been something in the prison, but maybe not.

"So your healing powers aren't as effective here?"

I blinked, not sure how honest to be. I didn't want her worrying about me, maybe getting herself hurt because she wouldn't let me take a hit that I could normally take.

"It's because you grew up on Earth," she didn't even wait for me to answer. "I've heard something like that happening, but never seen it for myself."

Oh great. That was just wonderful. Right when I needed this ability the most. At least it hadn't seemed to mess with my communicating with the trees.

Starren made us travel in the trees for another twenty or so minutes, then told me to make them let us down. I asked the tree we were on, and instead of the bridge just going forward, it went forward and down, making a ramp to the forest floor.

We trudged on through the dark for hours, alternating between walking and jogging. I didn't complain, didn't bother Starren. I got the weird feeling that the reason she didn't try to go through the portal was she knew that she could. And if she knew that she could, that meant that Quintin hadn't tried to force her to stay. That he either didn't care what she did, or didn't expect her to try to leave, at all.

And it also meant that she could have went the easy way, but she'd decided to help me make it to the tunnel. Was that out of obligation because I'd come to try to rescue her? Or would we really end up being sisters? Not just sisters by blood, but actual sisters. She'd chosen me over our father, who she had always known, who she'd worked with all her life.

"I can feel you thinking back there." Starren didn't even turn around when she spoke.

"I'm just glad we're together, even if it is here."

She whirled around, her finger coming up to my face. "Don't for one second believe that we are, as the humans say, good. We are sisters, but that means nothing."

I blinked. "But you came with me, instead of turning me over to Father."

"Father," she growled, turning around and marching off, anger pouring out of her body. "Oh yes, Father. Well, 'Father' left me to rot in prison as bait to get you to Faerie."

I stopped dead. "Wait, what?"

"Hadn't you guessed that?" Starren snarled over her shoulder, pausing but not turning around. "He needed you here. 'Whoever has the girl, wins the war.' He let the Council do whatever they wanted to me, to get you to come here. Oh how easily you were manipulated. You have human weakness for family."

He would really do that to his own daughter? What kind of monster was this man? How had I ever wanted to meet him? "I'm sorry, Star," I said softly.

Her shoulders stiffened even more, and she took off again. "It has nothing to do with you. My anger toward you is illogical, you didn't even know what was going on."

Hey, at least she'd made it to the point she could admit she was mad at me. A little progress. But I had no idea what to do now. I'd never been good with any of this emotion stuff, and this was some pretty deep trauma.

"It's okay to be mad at me for a bit, but I hope you can get over it," I offered. "We are sisters, after all, whether that's something you really want or not."

The withering look she sent me came across loud and clear, even in the dark. "We should keep quiet. We don't want anyone hearing us out here."

I followed her lead and let it drop. Who was I to push when

someone didn't want to open up. If Nina had done that with me in the beginning, I probably would have ran. She'd waited until the whole impaled by an arrow thing to start forcing confessions, and by then I'd been a whole lot more willing to tell her stuff. Hopefully Starren and I would get to that point too. Without the impaling. I didn't heal as quickly here as at home. Plus, that seriously, seriously hurt.

We kept up the pace with zero talking for about another hour. I didn't have a watch, and the moon, if Faerie had a moon, wasn't visible through the trees, so I just had to estimate. Plus now that we were out of danger, I was bored enough to start counting the seconds and minutes as we walked.

Eventually the forest began to lighten. I still couldn't see the sky through the tree canopy, but it must be sunrise.

"We should find somewhere to sleep for a couple hours," I said. "And I could really eat."

Starren pulled a fire fruit off a tree and tossed it at me. "We can't stop. They know we're gone by now. We need to get as far away as we can while we have the advantage. They know where the portal led, and they know we will want to reconnect with everyone else. We have to get there first. If we don't hurry, they'll beat us." She thought for a second. "Unless you want to just leave them on their own. They would probably be fine. We could head somewhere I know, where we would be safe. Wade knows the place, he could join us later."

"What is wrong with you?" I asked. "You know I'd never leave Dan and Nina to wander around Faerie alone."

Starren raised an eyebrow. "They have your Jaden, don't they? He got himself out last time, surely he can get them out this time."

"It's a lot easier to get one person out than it is three, especially when two out of the three aren't from around here."

"Jaden's not really from around here either."

"You're making my point for me." I took a small bite out of the fruit, even though I wanted to swallow it whole I was so hungry.

Starren pelted me with more fruit. I only caught two out of the six she tossed at me. "That's what you get for now. No sleeping until we cross the lake."

I took another tiny bite. I'd learned my lesson on these things. "What lake?"

"The lake. The big lake."

Yeah, like that really helped.

"There is only one great lake in Faerie. We don't name things like the humans do. If you say the lake, everyone knows what you mean."

That sounded like a lot of work.

"How are we going to cross this lake?"

"There are several boats left on each side, for anyone's use. We'll skirt the lake until we find one."

Great. A boat. That sounded so fun. Not. The last time we'd been in a boat together we'd been hunting Jaden, headed for Alcatraz. And Wade and Cray had been with us. Which made me wonder, how was Cray doing at home alone? He still wasn't comfortable around humans. Had he gone to school without me?

"How far away is this lake?" I asked as Starren broke out into a jog again.

She took a bite out of whatever fruit she'd picked. I couldn't tell in the dim light. "Only ten minutes, if we can keep up the pace."

So we did. Without me even complaining.

We hit the lake just as some color burst over the other side. So apparently there was a sun. The colors were so different that I stopped to stare for a moment. The light here came across more pastel, with greys, blues, and purples. Nothing like colors at home, but completely gorgeous.

"You coming?" Starren asked after a second.

"Uh, yeah." I moved after her.

She reached the water's edge and turned left, jogging.

I didn't take off after her, the sand caught me off guard. Not like the sand at home either, this stuff looked like it was formed from small pearls, glistening in the new sunlight, beams going through it and creating tiny fractured rainbows everywhere.

It was wild, and the most beautiful thing I'd ever seen, by far.

"Come on, Trish," Starren called from a ways down the beach.

Her voice pulled me out of my nearly mesmerized state. Too bad Nina wasn't here, she would absolutely love this.

"Trish," Starren sounded irritated. But really, when did she not.

I broke into a run to catch up with her.

"Never seen a lake before?" she asked.

"Not one like this."

"The boats shouldn't be far."

We jogged along for a bit, but Starren was right, like always. Several boats made from hollowed out trees waited for us near the water.

"These just sit out here all the time?"

Starren didn't answer, making for the boats.

I joined her, helping her flip one over. I pulled it toward the water.

"Wait." Starren grabbed my arm, jerking me back. "You can't just go into the water. What are you thinking?" She sounded mad, and half freaked out. "Unless you're trying to kill us, of course."

What in the world could make Starren freak out? I'd thought that was impossible.

"Kill us? What's in the water that we can't even cross it in a boat? And what was the point of up stealing this boat if we aren't going to go across?"

"We're going to go across, we just have to ask permission first. This might be interesting." She kicked a rock. "At least I hope we're going across," she muttered.

Okay, that didn't sound really promising. "Who are we asking permission from? And why do they get to decide? Maybe we should just go for it. They aren't likely to notice, and we don't want them to be able to answer questions anyway."

"Oh, they'd know. And they aren't happy with me right now."

"Who is this mysterious person that's so mad at you? And why?"

She gestured at the water. "The mermaids, of course."

"Mermaids?" the word somehow came out both excited and terrified. I had vaguely known they existed. Wade had mentioned it when he gave me my sheath. It was made out of mermaid scales, which kept it camouflaged. But knowing and experiencing were way different things.

"Yes, I may have crossed them. I needed scales."

"You killed a mermaid?" That came out just horrified. "You killed a mermaid to take these scales for my sheath? I thought it was from Wade." Poor Ariel, gone the way of Bambi's mom.

She rolled her eyes. "Wade was trying to get in good with you and I had already made the sheath, so I gave it to him. And I didn't kill anything for it. Mermaids shed their scales like an Earth snake."

"Whew." I let out a puff of air in relief. "If you didn't kill anyone, why are you so afraid of the mermaids?"

She huffed and crossed her arms. "I'm not scared of them. I just have a... healthy respect. And they aren't really happy about anyone taking their scales. They like shiny things. I had to... liberate scales because they wouldn't give me any."

The fact that she would give me the sheath when obviously it was really hard to come by mermaid scales made me grin. On the inside. I didn't want her to see it.

"So you stole mermaid scales, and now they're mad at you," I said.

"More like hate me."

That was going to make getting over this lake really interesting.

"You're sure there isn't another way over or around?" I asked.

"Not if you want to beat Quintin to the tunnel. He doesn't know where you came in, but I'm sure he will be able to guess that you're going to try to hit the prison. If we don't cross here, it will take an extra two days, which means he will be there long before us. The mermaids love him."

"Can't we just tell them you're his daughter? If they love him, surely they'll forgive you."

Starren rubbed the back of her neck. "I wish it was that easy. Fae aren't the same as humans. Every fae is only viewed by their own merits. We aren't seen as family groups. Either you're good with them, or you aren't, it doesn't matter what your family is like."

There were both good and bad things about looking at the world like that. At the moment, it was just bad.

"So what do we do, then?"

"Our options are to try to sneak across, which won't happen, call them up and ask for safe passage, or split up. You go across the lake, and I'll find another way around."

My gut clenched. "No. No way. We aren't splitting up." I'd already lost the rest of my group. Hopefully they'd busted Nara out and were on their way to the tunnel by now. Not hopefully. I would just assume that was true until I learned differently.

"Well then, here goes the chances." She stepped toward the water.

"Here goes the chances?"

She eyed me. "It's a fae saying. You've never heard it before?"

"Where would I have heard it."

She sighed. "I forget how uneducated you are. Here goes nothing. Is that more to your liking?"

It sure was more familiar.

Starren walked to the water's edge. "Avaria," she called. "Avaria, I'm here to ask for safe passage."

The water rippled toward us. With the beautiful environment they lived in, and all of the stories from back home, I couldn't wait to see what popped out of the water. Mermaids were supposed to be so gorgeous.

A head broke the surface of the water, and I had to clamp my teeth to not shriek as I stumbled backward. Abort, abort, this so was not what I was expecting.

It had huge eyes, but with a film over them, like one of those fish that live in caves in the dark. The thing had no hair, just some kind of sharp looking bristle stretching from between its eyebrows, over its head in a mohawk and down its back.

"That's not a mermaid," I whispered to Starren.

She looked confused. "Yes, it is. It's the queen of the mermaids."

"Humans have this one so wrong."

"How so?" Starren asked, leaning toward me so we weren't overheard. The mermaid was still a bit away from the shore, but I didn't know how their hearing was.

"Everything except they live in the water."

The mermaid reared slightly out of the lake. Little pieces of her were missing everywhere, and she was invisible from the collarbone down. It took me a second to realize that the spots where it looked like there was nothing were actually patches of scales.

"Starren," Avaria said. She grinned, baring sharp needle teeth. "So good of you to visit. Come closer."

Starren snorted. "Not likely. Not until we get something figured out. I need to cross the lake."

The mermaid started laughing, water snorting out of her nose as she nearly choked. "Come close and I promise you, I'll get you to the other side of the lake."

"I'd prefer alive," Starren said.

Avaria bared her teeth in earnest, the smile gone from her face. "There we will have to disagree."

Starren pointed at me. "This is Quintin's other daughter. I'm escorting her. You don't want to offend him, so you need to let us pass."

The water around her boiled with activity, looking like a video I'd seen during shark week. More heads burst out of the water all around Avaria, soulless eyes staring at us.

"I will get her safely to the other side," Avaria said. "You though…"

"I need her. My father told her to protect me," I broke into the conversation. "You don't want to make him mad, trust me. He just took out the entire fae Council, he won't give a care about slaughtering all of you."

Hissing and clicking went around the group, the water getting agitated again. I had no idea what they were saying, but it seemed like they were talking with each other.

"Finally," one of the other mermaids said in English.

"Finally?" I asked.

Starren whacked me from behind.

"Yes, finally. He's been planning this a long time."

"It needed to be done," a different mermaid hissed.

They all keened together in agreement, making a completely other worldly noise. But really, I was in another world, so was it this worldly? I shrank back a little, before Starren glared at me and I straightened up, trying to look confident.

"Because of our friendship with your father, we will get the girl across the lake," Avaria said to Starren. "But if either of you touch the water, you will die."

"Only if we touch the water?" I asked.

Avaria cocked her head. "Yes."

"So if we stay in the boat, we're fine?"

"Yes."

"And you won't tip the boat over, or pull us into the water?"

"Agreed."

Too easy. Like that totally wasn't some kind of weird trap. Fae and their strange deals.

Starren gestured to me, and we stepped back away from the water. "There's obviously a scheme in here somewhere. Last chance. You can take them up on their offer and be perfectly safe getting across the lake."

"No way. Between the two of us, we got this."

Starren looked blank. "We got what?"

"We got this."

She still looked confused.

"Never mind. We'll figure out whatever they throw at us, together."

After a second of staring, Starren nodded and led the way back to the water. "Deal. If neither of us touch the water, we will be allowed safe passage."

The mermaids all started cackling as one, a couple of them jumping out of the water like dolphins until they all went under together, disappearing.

"Welp. I think you were right about this being interesting," I told Starren.

"And it hasn't even started yet." She moved over and shoved one of the boats. I went to help, but it was much lighter than I'd expected, and she had the front touching the water right after I grabbed on. I jumped in, being careful not to rock the boat. The fae were sticklers for details. Did a drop of water being splashed around count?

Starren gave the boat a light shove, and jumped as it moved away from shore, sending us bumping around. Surprisingly though, the boat barely moved side to side. This thing was solid craftsmanship, which even I could tell without knowing anything about boats.

Starren wordlessly handed me a paddle, looking like she was on high alert. I didn't blame her.

I dipped my paddle into the water and pulled. We shot forward, the weight of this water so much different than at home.

Both of us were completely tense as we moved across the water, the entire world around us silent. I repeatedly told my muscles to unclench. They obeyed, but a few seconds later I'd be right back to where I'd started.

We were well over half way before the silence got the better of me. "So. So far, so good, right?"

Starren didn't answer. I looked back over my shoulder. She looked like some weird statue where only the eyes and arms moved. The rest of her was stone still.

"Star? We're almost there."

She nodded, face white. Drowning would definitely be high on my list of ways I would not want to die, so I couldn't blame her. If we got drug down into the freezing depths, I'd be fine. Her, not so much.

I was still turned around, not really paying attention to anything but my sister, when something grabbed my paddle, ripping it out of my hands. "Starren!" I screamed, but it was too late, scaly, nearly invisible hands reached out of the water and latched onto her paddle.

Starren leaned back, putting all her weight into keeping the paddle in the boat, rocking us all over. A mermaid popped out of the water, wheezing out a gurgling, choking laugh as water spewed out of her mouth.

I scrambled to the back of the boat, supporting Starren with one arm, and grabbing onto the paddle with the other. There, the unnamed mermaid's hands were slipping a little.

Then three more mermaids burst out of the water, flopping all over each other in an attempt to be the one to pull us overboard. Both of us lurched forward leaning dangerously over the water. I let go of the paddle and grabbed Starren with both arms, pulling her over and toppling us to the floor of the boat.

Starren shot right back up and had an arrow nocked before I could blink.

"What are you thinking? You made me lose the paddle!"

"I was thinking I shouldn't let you die," I yelled back.

Starren rolled off me and let her head fall to the bottom of the boat. "Now we're both going to die. It will just take a lot longer."

I sat up and looked over the edge. Grinning faces floated just beneath the surface, laughing up at me. Stupid mermaids.

"No, we aren't going to die." I kicked her with the toe of my shoe. "Seriously, between the two of us, we'll come up with something. No mermaids are going to outsmart us."

Starren raised an eyebrow. Her haughty look was actually pretty funny coming from the bottom of the boat. She sat up, looked over the side and spit in the water. Decidedly the least polite thing I'd ever seen her do.

I laughed. It came out a bit hysterical, but it made the side of Starren's mouth tip up. "So genius. How do we escape this one?"

What a great question. One I had absolutely no answer for at the moment. I looked around, but an answer didn't present itself. There were no currents. The shore sat taunting us, not that far away but far enough that we had no chance of reaching it before being snatched if we tried to swim for it. There wasn't even any debris floating that we could use as paddles.

Speaking of. One of our paddles popped to the surface, about ten feet from the boat. Much too far to reach, but close enough to be tantalizing.

"They're taunting us," Starren said. She stood and moved back to her seat, falling heavily onto it. The other paddle drifted up and hit the surface on the opposite side of the boat. "Where are your trees when we need them." Starren's voice came out muffled with her head cradled in her hands.

If only. No way any tree had branches long enough to reach us this far out. I stared down into the water. The mermaids must have gotten bored, because there were none in sight. That, or they were trying to lull us into a false sense of security. Starren took her light jacket off and started on her boots.

"Ah, what are you doing?" I asked.

"No reason for both of us to die. They'll leave us here until we starve to death or Quintin finds us. I'm not very happy with either option."

"Are you kidding me? You're just going to be like Jonah or something and toss yourself over the side for your sins?"

A crease appeared between her eyebrows. "Who's Jonah?"

Okay, bad example. I didn't even know the story that well, I'd just heard it once when I went to church with Dan and Nina. "Some guy that didn't listen to God and… whatever, he jumped off a boat in a storm to save the other people. Or something."

She had one boot off and started on the other. "I guess I am like Jonah then. This is a consequence for something I've done."

"Nope. You put your boots back on and give me a little time to think. Plus, if anyone goes into that water it will be me. I can breathe under water, so they can't drown me."

Her eyebrows went up in surprise. That may have been the first time I'd ever told her to do something. But it was for her own good, so she had better listen.

"Just because they can't drown you doesn't mean they can't do worse. Doesn't matter anyway, if you touch the water it nulls our deal with the mermaids, and the second you hit it they can swarm the boat."

I hadn't thought of that. But it was true. "Just be quiet and let me think."

She grumbled something under her breath, but pulled her boot back on. "You have one hour. I'll be watching the sun. We can't waste time."

"Waste time? Saving your life is wasting time?"

She just looked at me with no expression on her face like she always did when she was hiding her emotions.

I sighed. Stubbornness must be genetic, because genes were the only thing we'd shared. Same parents, completely different upbringings.

Ugh, if only a breeze would start up, or a slight current. If it could get us close enough to shore, the trees would be glad to help us.

Checking to see if the mermaids were still there, I got my first real sight of the water while it wasn't all stirred up.

The section of lake we were in wasn't as deep as I would have thought. In fact, I could see the top of some seaweed. I sat bolt upright. Seaweed. Something like that had helped saved me from the trolls.

I glanced back at Starren. She looked like she was about to have a breakdown. Her face twisted, trying to keep the fear from showing, but her mask had cracked. Not a good idea to mention this to her, just in case it didn't work.

Anything down there? Could you help me out, please? I need to get to shore.

I waited a second.

Nothing.

Hello? I don't need much, could you just push the boat toward shore, please? The closest shore? This was all for nothing if the plants did decide to help but sent us to the wrong side. Oh well, at least we'd still be alive.

Slowly the boat started gliding forward. I leaned over the edge, trying to get a look.

A mermaid jumped out of the water, screeching in anger. The boat slowed, and she came back up, tossing some seaweed stuff at me. It wasn't seaweed in fresh water, was it? Now was not the time.

"What's going on?" Starren asked.

Thank you. Thank you for trying. Please, help us.

The boat started forward again, faster. A slapping sound made me look over the edge again. More and more plants were grabbing on, shoving us forward enough for the next set to grab on.

"We're moving," Starren said, her face in shock.

"Sit tight," I answered.

Mermaids broke the surface around us, taking up a keening, angry call. They frantically boiled around the ship, ripping plants up by the roots and bringing them to the surface to throw at me.

I'm so sorry, please, keep us moving.

At this point we were hurtling forward. I moved to the bottom of the boat to make sure my clumsy self didn't fall overboard. Starren joined me, gripping the sides with white knuckles. "What's going on?"

"Underwater plants listen to me too."

She nodded, so apparently that was enough of an explanation for her.

Avaria broke the water in front of us, blocking the way.

We kept up speed, flowing toward her far too fast to stop.

"Keep your word," I shouted at her. At the last second, she dropped below the surface. All of her friends did the same and there was almost instant calm. The underwater plants still rushed us forward, which I didn't mind since I didn't really trust the mermaids to not come up with another way to get around the fae binding of a promise.

We bumped the shore, and it didn't take five seconds for both me and Starren to bail out of the boat. I crawled a safe distance from the water and collapsed on the pearl sand, which didn't smell fishy. Huh.

Starren walked up and plopped down beside me, laying on her back to look at the sky. "That was almost really bad."

"No kidding," I groaned out.

"But it was almost nice to be on the same team again." She got up and started walking away, something I was thankful for because it meant she missed my mouth hanging open in surprise. I had to agree with her though, being on the same side again was pretty amazing.

CHAPTER FIFTEEN

We walked and walked and walked and walked until finally Starren thought we could take a short break. I slept a little, but not much. Something about being hunted and knowing everyone I cared about could be in danger or dead at the moment made a person have insomnia.

The woods took a weird turn as we walked. While there should still be plenty of light, the light seemed to get sucked out of the air, leaving everything gloomy. The trees here felt different, stalkery, giving me the heebie-jeebies. It didn't seem to have the same effect on Starren. Because she couldn't feel the trees like I could, or just because she was Starren.

She kept us on a path through the woods. It was the first real path I'd seen since I'd made it to Faerie. Different enough to be kind of weird. Not that I minded, it seemed like the safest option at this point. I moved up closer to Starren, keeping an eye behind us. I got the feeling that these trees wouldn't be helping us out of a bind. Like they might even be the cause.

"What's with there being a path here?" I asked. "Everywhere else we just walked through the woods." I didn't add the whole I wouldn't want to walk through these trees anyway part, because I didn't want her to think I was a wimp. And I didn't know if they were listening.

"You don't want to walk through these woods."

So much for not saying it out loud.

"What's that supposed to mean? Why can't you ever just explain stuff?"

Starren gave a longsuffering sigh. Did that make me the annoying little sister? Okay, that was a role I could totally get behind.

"There are fae that live in these woods that you don't want to mess with. Less... humanoid fae, for lack of a better description."

"So like the hyran we met?"

"Worse."

Okay, yeah, I would be avoiding those woods for sure. Especially with my diminished healing ability right now.

We kept on through until finally the path opened up into a small clearing. It ended here, because on the other side the woods didn't look so weird. Back to the more open trees, with plenty of space to not need a path.

Starren slammed me down into the grass.

"Hey-" Somehow she managed to kick me even though we were both on the ground.

"Movement, in the trees."

I looked to where she was pointing. Sure enough, a flash of blue. Wait, wasn't Jaden wearing a blue shirt? I jumped up and waved my arms. "Over here!"

Starren jerked me back down. "Are you an idiot? Or just insane?"

"It's our group, let me go. No one here wears those kind of colors."

And I was right. Nina was first to run out of the trees. She saw me and burst into a dead run, arms outstretched.

"What are you guys doing here?" I yelled as I ran forward and jumped into Nina, pulling her into a bear hug and nearly taking us both to the ground. "You were supposed to meet us at the tunnel."

"Wade knew you had to go through here to make it to the tunnel, so we decided to meet you instead of going on."

Wade came over and acted like he was about to give me a hug, then changed his mind. "I was afraid that if we camped outside the tunnel, someone would notice. And the firnen don't make camping inside seem like a good idea either."

Dan came over and gave me a huge hug, lifting me off the ground. "I was so worried."

"Yeah? Me too." Well look at that. I'd admitted an emotion to Dan. That was new. Nina, sure, I'd gotten there a while ago. But now Dan was starting to feel like my father, since I'd met my actual father and he was awful.

Jaden had hung back, so I waved at him. He waved back, smiling pretty big.

I looked around. "Wait a second. Where's Nara?"

"She took off," Wade said. "As soon as we went through the portal from the prison to the forest, she was gone."

Okay, a bit disappointing, but I could totally understand why she wouldn't want to hang around with a bunch of strangers. Not with everything she'd been through.

"That's fine, thanks for getting her out."

"You know I'll do whatever you need," Wade said. I hated it when he said stuff like that. It made me think of better times, when things had been good between us.

"Are you done with all of this, then?" Starren asked. She sounded bored. I wondered if she portrayed herself that way to cover the fact that no one had been excited to see her. Fae didn't have family the way humans did. I would just have to teach her what being in a family felt like. Dan and Nina had done it for me, time for me to pass it on.

"Yep, all set."

She stepped off toward the tree line without a word.

Nina gave me a slightly weirded out look. I shrugged. Starren wasn't much different than I had been before I'd figured out what it was like to have someone care if you lived or died. Wade had given her a nod, but that was it. Kind of surprising since he'd set this whole thing up, to save her and all. I'd have thought he'd be a bit more excited to see her, but they were fae, and so, weird.

Everyone fell into place in line. Wade made his way back to walk beside me. He reached out and grabbed my arm, slowing us down until we were out of earshot.

"Hey," he said, giving me a smile. A smile that used to melt my heart. "How do you feel about Faerie now that you've been here? Not such a bad place, huh."

I tipped my head, considering for a second. I hadn't really thought about it in a bit. Wade loved it here, and I was to the point that I didn't want to hurt his feelings anymore. "It's really beautiful." And full of crazies, death, and insanity, but I didn't add that out loud.

His smile broke into an all out grin. "I'd hoped that would be the case. Do you think..." he trailed off. "Is it possible..."

I raised an eyebrow. Wow, I needed to practice this to get as good as Starren.

"Is there any chance of you staying?"

Um, what? That came out of nowhere. I'd never given any indication whatsoever of wanting to stay here. Never. "You know I have to go, Wade. I love Nina as much as I ever loved my real mom. And Dan has been more of a dad to me than my actual father ever was. They're my family."

Even if I'd wanted to stay here, which I didn't, Dan and Nina wouldn't want to, and I didn't want to live anywhere without Dan and Nina.

"But not your only family. Your dad is here. And me."

"I'm sorry Wade, it just isn't going to happen. I know technically I was made for here, but I just don't feel it. This isn't my home. Dan and Nina are my home right now."

A flicker of extreme anger went across his face, catching me off guard. But then it was gone, and the small smile back, making me wonder if I was losing my mind.

We walked in awkward silence for a while.

"I'm going to go scout ahead," Wade said, then jogged off without me giving him a chance to answer. I really didn't know what to say anyway. I didn't want to hurt him. I'd finally forgiven him for the whole shooting me thing, once I'd stopped being so hurt and thought it through.

I watched him for a second, until Jaden dropped back to walk with me. It surprised me how happy that made me. I still cared about Wade, even after everything, so it was all so confusing.

"Did you have an interesting time getting this far?" Jaden asked.

"You have no idea," I answered. "Did you know mermaids are really mean?"

He laughed. "Yes, actually."

I shuddered. "Hopefully I never see another one of those again."

We walked quietly for a few minutes. I scanned the trees, hoping to see Wade. I didn't want him to feel like I was turning him away too, just because I wasn't a fan of Faerie.

"Still have feelings for Wade, huh." Jaden startled me out of my thoughts. "Don't look so surprised. It's all over your face when you look at him. Confusion, anger, but something else too. And the anger part has faded away quite a bit, compared to back when you were helping me, Mom, and the girls."

"What do you think you are, my therapist?" I snapped.

"Nope." He kicked at some grass. "Just someone who cares. I knew I would care someday, I just got surprised by how quickly it came. I was really worried about you while we were split up."

"Yeah well, you knew Starren was with me, so there wasn't any reason to worry. I bet Wade wasn't worried."

"I've seen the future, Trish. If you feel like you need to be with Wade right now, that's fine. Do what you got to do. But I'll be waiting for when he betrays you again." Then he just walked away, leaving me here with my mouth hanging open like an idiot.

He'd said something, a while ago when Cray and I'd had him trapped in that alley, before I'd decided to help him instead of sending him back to the Council, about how he'd seen I had a good heart. Apparently that was from seeing the future. That fate had us being together. Stupid fate. That wasn't fair. It couldn't decide stuff like that for me.

But the more I thought about it, the more I realized, it wasn't fate, was it. I liked Jaden. I liked Jaden far more than I liked Wade. The feelings for Wade had faded, like to an annoying older brother. The love I felt for him wasn't the same kind of love it had been before, that was part of the reason I was so confused. And I'd never fully trust him again. Jaden's statement about betrayal, was that because he'd seen something or just because he knew Wade? And was I really going to let the fact that I was stubborn and didn't want to follow what was supposedly my fate keep me from being happy, just because I didn't want to follow some cosmic plan for my life?

Not when my fate had a great smile and an amazing heart.

I ran to catch up to Jaden and gave him a shy smile before falling into step with him. He looked a little surprised, but smiled back.

"I'm going to scout too," Starren said suddenly from the front. It had been pretty quiet. Even Dan and Nina weren't really talking, which meant they must be pretty tired.

Or didn't have anything to say that they didn't want overheard, because as soon as Starren loped off into the woods, they descended on me.

Nina looped one arm through mine. Dan edged his way in on the other side. Jaden seemed to get the hint, and moved away a bit.

"So, honey. What's the plan now?" Nina asked.

I looked at her. Was she okay? We'd already discussed the plan like ten times and it hadn't changed.

"We get to the tunnel, get through it, and get home to Sanctuary. No one can bother us there."

She tipped her head, like she was considering. "So you aren't thinking about staying here?"

"Are you kidding me? I don't want to stay here!" Where in the world would she have gotten an idea like that? I'd told her repeatedly how much I despised Faerie, and most fae.

Nina let out a whoosh of air. "Oh good. Wade suggested you might be happier here, with your own people, and I just... I was a little worried."

What was Wade's problem? I'd told him over and over that I didn't want to be here. I'd been nice about it, but that wasn't going to last if he started telling people I was staying. "Nope. All I want is our family." I peeked at Jaden's back. Mostly.

We marched on and on until I felt like we should have passed the tunnel about four times. Starren and Wade came back to check on us occasionally, make sure we were still going in the right direction, but they always went back out 'scouting,' always separately.

Dusk fell when Starren came back for the night. We sat in an odd semi-circle, without a fire to stare at.

"So, what's the plan?" Dan asked after a bit.

Jaden and I looked at each other. "The plan hasn't changed," I said. "You okay?"

Dan looked confused for a second. "Oh yeah, just making conversation."

I shrugged it off. Dan and Nina did seem a little uncomfortable with the silence.

"The tunnel is only an hours walk from here," Starren said. "It will be easy to find. In the morning, I'll take my leave."

I sat up, fast, "What? To go scout, you mean?"

She shook her head, not looking me in the eye. "Faerie is my home, not Earth. I won't be going with you."

I scrambled to find a better seat, trying to get her to look me in the eye. "Are you serious? You can have a home with us. You're my sister."

Then she did look me in the eye, and I almost wished she hadn't. "That means less than you think. I've told you that, many times."

"But it means something to me." I was putting myself on the line here, being way out of character. I didn't let people know I cared about them, and I never, ever, did without knowing what their response would be.

"I'm sorry. It's not meant to be. Is Cray adjusting well?"

Oh sure, she asks about him and stops talking about us. "He's doing great, which means you could too. Just give it a try, please?"

Then she got up and headed to where she'd made herself a bed in the grasses, not even answering me.

Why that... my face heated up and hot tears filled my eyes. No. I would not cry. I'd done far too much of that lately, I was going to lose my reputation.

Nina threw an arm around me. "I'm sorry. I know that's not what you hoped for when we came to rescue her."

No. No, it wasn't. But at least she was still breathing. As long as she was alive, we still had a chance.

"Do you know anything about mother?" I asked, without moving from beside Nina. I hadn't wanted to bring up a sore subject too early, but it looked like this might be my last chance.

"Nothing you don't." Starren didn't even roll over to look at me when she answered. What a jerk. It really didn't affect her at all, not going with us. She just didn't care.

I pulled my legs up and held on with my arms, locking my hands on my wrists. I couldn't say this whole trip had been for nothing, because my sister was still alive, but it would have been better to keep dreaming of a dad who wanted me just because I was his daughter. To keep hoping I'd be able to catch Starren someday, and she'd know where our mom was. But it wasn't to be.

"Should we be worried about the other guy?" Nina asked. "Wade?"

I hadn't really noticed he was still gone. "No." I didn't elaborate. They didn't need to know what was up between us. Whatever he did next was his choice. He'd said he would get us safely to the tunnel, and had to keep his word, but he'd probably be gone as soon as we were close enough for his fae blood to believe he'd fulfilled his oath.

I went and tossed my sleeping bag down by Starren, mad at her, but afraid this would be the last chance I had to really be around her. Our bags had been at the prison, and the boys had grabbed them while springing Nara, thankfully. Not that I needed it temperature wise, but it was amazing for the feeling of security it gave me.

Starren didn't say anything, so I followed her lead and kept quiet. Goodbyes were horrible. No use going through one now, and then again in the morning.

I woke up and rolled over. One eye opened a slit. This whole not healing as well as normal thing was really starting to bug me, especially now that I needed an actual night's worth of rest.

Dan and Nina were packing their stuff. Jaden just sat there, staring at me. Kinda creepy. "What?" I asked, my voice still growly with sleep.

"Sorry, Trish."

I sat up. What was he sorry about? And why was Nina giving me the sad face? And where was Starren?

Oh.

I sat up, blinking away the sleep, groggily trying to take stock.

"She's just going to the bathroom or something, right?"

Nina shook her bag, shifting her sleeping bag down a little more forcefully than was necessary. "She had already left when I got up. That's been almost an hour."

She might as well have punched me in the gut. It probably would have hurt less. Starren had just left? Not even a goodbye. Family really did mean nothing to her. Family was horrible.

I stood and picked up my sleeping bag, violently shaking it in the air to dislodge anything it had picked up in the night, then crushed it into my backpack. It was all good. She didn't need me. I didn't need her. We both were fine. If I'd stopped to think about what would happen after we got her out, this was really the only scenario that I would believe.

But she could have said goodbye.

"Are we going, or what?" I asked.

The other three just stared at me, making me uncomfortable. This was stupid. Starren and I didn't even get along. It wasn't like I wouldn't be functional with her gone.

I took off without waiting to see if any of them followed. First Wade, now Starren. I was made for people to leave me. How long until Dan and Nina got tired of me? I glanced over my shoulder at them, rushing to catch up. That was a stupid thought. They'd come to an alien land, not really to save my sister, but to keep me safe. They weren't going anywhere. Someday I would believe what I knew to be true over my baggage.

Slowing down so they could catch up, I readjusted my bag over my shoulders. "Has anyone seen Wade?"

"No." Jaden's answer was short. He looked like he didn't know what to say. I didn't blame him. I didn't even know what I wanted to hear.

I nodded to let him know I'd heard him.

It was quite a relief that the tunnel wasn't far from here. Leaving this place would be amazing. No wonder my mom hated it here. Nothing but heartache and back-stabbing. The fae were all she had said, and more.

"The tunnel is only a mile or so from here," Jaden said after walking quite a distance in silence.

I did my best to smile at him, but barely felt the corner of my mouth twitch. Normally I could fake my feelings a lot better than this, but today...

We were in a wooded area now, which made me feel safer than being out in the open. Dan had held Jaden back a bit ago, and they were discussing something quietly, getting farther and farther behind, until they were pretty much out of sight.

Nina just rolled her eyes when I cocked an eyebrow, asking what was up without words. So they were probably talking about me. What else would I expect on a day like today.

We only made it a short distance in the trees before a crack broke the stillness. An unnatural sound, completely out of place here.

"Was that what I think it was?" Unfortunately, I knew the sound of a gunshot intimately. And that was definitely a gunshot. I turned to see what Nina was thinking, but she wasn't there. My heart jumped out of my chest, breathing going ragged.

I tore grass out as I ran, flinging my backpack off somewhere.

"No, no, no, no," I dropped beside Nina on the ground, my heart thundering so loud the words didn't even come through my ears. She was on the ground. Why was she on the ground? Blood oozed out of a hole in her abdomen. I put pressure on the wound, as hard as I could, but it didn't help. "Tell me what to do, Nina!" Hot tears dripped off my face. I was never the one doing the first aid, I was always the one wounded. "Nina!" I shouted when she didn't answer me.

I looked around frantically for help, but no one was in sight. "Dan!"

She looked up at me then, face white, and blinked, not really focusing. "Trish?" Her voice was weak, unlike any time I'd ever heard her. I pushed harder, afraid to hurt her, but more afraid to let her bleed out. My hands slipped in the blood and I readjusted, tears dripping to mix with all the red. I couldn't live without her. Couldn't.

"Yeah, I'm here. Keep talking. Tell me what to do." My voice broke, the words barely making their way through the sobs. "Dan!"

She reached her hand down to grab mine, but they were both slick with blood and it slipped away.

"It's okay," she said, and closed her eyes.

"No! No, it is not okay! We made this far!" I lifted my hands for a second, and the deep red of a fatal wound flowed steadily out of her abdomen. "It is not okay!" I reapplied the pressure, tipped back and screamed in anger. I couldn't lose another mom. I couldn't. "Dan!"

My scream, or Nina's pain drawing him like a magnet, brought Dan bursting out of the trees. He took stock with a single glance and rushed over, practically falling beside us.

He didn't ask how bad. He must have seen it on my face.

He pulled her head over and cradled it in his lap, tears dripping down his face as well, tearing what was left of my heart into tiny pieces. Who would have thought I'd care about another's pain as much as mine. Nausea burned through my stomach. They were here because of me. They had come to help me save Starren. And save her we did, with Nina as the sacrifice.

"Nina, hold on. We're going to get help." I looked wildly around, catching Jaden's eye. I hadn't seen him come up, but a flood of relief hit me. He would know what to do. "Jaden, go get help!"

He came forward, not running off like I'd expected.

"What are you doing? Hurry up! Nina needs help!"

I bent back over her, putting all my weight into stopping the bleeding. She stopped moving.

I pulled my hands away, and the blood had all but stopped flowing. A bad sign. A really, really bad sign.

I grabbed her shoulders and shook her, but it did nothing but make her head loll to the side. I screamed again, my insides tearing themselves apart. This couldn't be the end. It couldn't just happen like this, couldn't be that one second I had a full family, the next, not.

I stumbled back away from her, caught by someone behind me. I thrashed for a second, but Jaden turned me around and held me tight, tears in his eyes as well. He held me while I beat on his chest and wailed. This far. We'd made it back to the tunnel. After all the times we should have died, we'd made it this far.

"What happened?" Jaden asked, his voice thick with tears.

"Starren." I gulped, my face heating up, nausea burning its way through my body, anger clogging my throat. "It had to have been her. That's why she left this morning. She must still be working for Quintin." I couldn't even call him father anymore. He'd wanted me to stay. Had tried to force me to stay. Because of some stupid prophecy.

Jaden jerked, looking at the trees around us. "Then we need to go. She'll be back for Dan."

I looked over to where Dan was kneeling, cradling Nina, tears pouring down his face, his forehead on Nina's, her face so pale. "I don't think he's going anywhere. Can you go take a look around?" I pushed away from Jaden and went back, wiping blood onto my jeans that for once in my life wasn't mine. I wished it was. I wished it was more than anything I'd ever wished in my life.

Not knowing if Dan wanted me there, I stopped myself from taking her hand. But he noticed me, reached up and pulled me closer. I dropped to my knees, and then leaned down to cry on Nina's still chest.

CHAPTER SIXTEEN

Seconds? Minutes? Hours? Eternity. That's how long it had been since Nina had been shot. Since she...

I wouldn't think that. Couldn't think that. My body began to warm, terror and anger battling for dominance. How could I survive? Nina had been there for me since the second we'd met, no matter what it was, something small, or something as big as rescuing my sister. Whatever I'd needed, she'd provided, whether I wanted her to or not.

I tried to care that someone may be out in the trees, watching. But one moment I was numb, and the next my world was shattered. Jaden would find whoever it was. And when he did...

The heat flowed through my body even stronger. All of the anger I'd held for the last few days, all of the hurt. I didn't know what to do with it without her here to help me. This much rage needed an outlet, but I had nowhere to send it.

"Uhhh, Trish..." Jaden's voice barely registered. Apparently whoever had done this was gone. I hadn't heard Jaden get back. Something about his tone was off. I'd never heard him sound like that before. I ignored him, my skin hot enough it should be blistering.

"Trish!" Jaden's tone broke through the fog, just a bit.

"What?" I asked, snot dribbling down my face, my eyes still closed.

"You're... glowing," Dan answered for Jaden. I felt him shifting back a bit from Nina, her body slipping to rest on the forest floor instead of in his lap. Her body.

I pried my eyes open, gritty from leftover tears. What did it matter if I was glowing? What did that even mean? I didn't care what happened to me now. It didn't matter without Nina. I ground my teeth, doing my best not to snap at him, to let loose everything I was feeling, even though he was hurting as much as I was, or even more.

Deep breaths. Relax. Nina's voice, inside my head. Nothing supernatural, just the advice she'd given me before, helping me calm down.

It took a second, but then I noticed my skin. Dan was right. A light glow covered my torso, and was working its way down my arms, the heat moving with it.

"What are you doing?" Dan whispered, like I would know.

"I don't know," I whispered back. The burning light reached my hands, which desperately clutched Nina's.

It didn't stop when it reached the tips of my fingers.

I looked wildly from Nina to the men, but they just seemed mesmerized, staring at the unnatural aura around me.

The light flowed through me, and into Nina's still warm body, giving her a rosy glow. At first, nothing seemed to happen. But then, her body jerked limply. I panicked, trying to drop her hands, to scramble away. What was I doing to her? But I couldn't let go. My fingers were open, but melded into her flesh.

"Jaden!" I screamed.

My voice snapped him out of his stupor and he jumped forward, grabbing me under my armpits and pulling with all his strength. He pulled me away, but Nina came too, almost ripping my shoulder out of socket. Nina and I were fused together by light.

Pain exploded across my abdomen, followed by the familiar warmth of blood flowing. I sucked in breath after breath, the air crushing my lungs, almost glad to have something to think about other than my mom, lying on the forest floor.

Instinctively I grabbed at the wound, the pain taking my breath away, but my hands were still occupied.

"Trish's been shot!" Dan jumped to his feet, wildly looking toward the trees. "Why didn't we hear anything? Jaden I thought you checked the perimeter!"

He arrived at an explanation far quicker than my foggy mind could. Shot. It was fitting, even though it wouldn't kill me, for me to take a bullet after Nina had.

Nina.

Nina's body jerked again. Then she sucked in a breath, and her eyes flew open. At that moment the light binding us winked out, and my hands dropped from her abdomen. She grabbed at where the hole was, eyes wide.

"What happened?" she asked.

I nearly fainted. From the pain, of course, not because of my mom coming back to life. Jaden settled me back in against him on the ground. "Nina?" I managed to croak out.

"Trish?" Nina's voice went up an octave. Oh, how I'd missed that high squeaky, freaked out voice. I went limp against Jaden for a second, my eyes glued on my foster mom.

Dan was trying to hold her, but she was dragging herself over to me, and me, well, fainting sounded really good about now. I closed my eyes and did the whole in through the nose, out through the mouth thing, desperately trying to figure out if Nina was really alive or if I'd actually been shot and was hallucinating because of blood loss.

"Please let her be real. Please let her be real," I panted out, my stomach roiling, pain clouding my vision. I would not survive thinking she was okay if she wasn't.

Arms grabbed me and pulled me close. Much more feeble than the squeezes I normally got after a bad wound, but recognizable anyway. My eyes fluttered open and there she was, pale, but breathing. I bit my lip until it bled to keep a yelp of pain from escaping and mashed down the joy trying to work its way up from my chest, too afraid to believe what my eyes were telling me.

After holding me for a second, she pulled her shirt up. Dried blood. Enough to make me nauseous again, with little floaters going across my vision.

But the wound wasn't there. Gone. Completely.

Had I done that? How had I done that? I looked to Jaden, who was still propping me up. He shrugged, obviously spooked but still holding on to me.

Nina shoved her shirt down, and jerked my shirt up, gave me a grumpy glare, then went back to checking out whatever had happened to me. I really, really wished I was healing like normal at the moment. Because it hurt just as bad as when it had first happened. The blood still flowed out of a small hole in my gut. Yeah, it definitely wasn't healing like it should, stupid Faerie.

But slow healing I could handle. Physical pain, that I knew how to handle too. Nina was alive. I could deal with anything else. This I could do. Absolutely. But now seemed like a good time to pass out.

I woke up to grumpy muttering. How long had I been unconscious?

"Nina?" I rasped out.

She was by my side instantly, checking my forehead in some weird mom ritual.

"What happened?" I asked.

"We think somehow you took Nina's wound." I hadn't even noticed Jaden sitting behind me, cradling my head. I craned my neck to look up at him.

"Ah, what?"

Nina leaned back and pulled her shirt up a little, just enough for me to see completely unblemished skin. The wound had closed without a trace.

"Not even a cool scar," Nina said.

I snorted. "Only fair. I never get any either."

She smacked my shoulder lightly. "Then stop getting hurt. I've told you that a hundred times. And now that I know what getting shot feels like, I'm going to be even more mad if it happens to you again."

"Try an arrow. It's worse." Anticipating what I'd want, Jaden helped me sit up. My midriff was bare, and there was definitely still a wound there. I gritted my teeth as the pain hit me. I shouldn't have looked.

"From what we can tell, you are healing, just very slowly," Dan said.

"Stupid Faerie," I managed to get out from behind gritted teeth.

"We built a stretcher of sorts, to try and get you home where you can heal faster." Dan paused, giving me a sympathetic look. "Moving is going to hurt. A lot. But you won't heal for at least a week at the rate you're going, and it's a big risk for us stay here with Starren knowing where we are. We waited to see if the healing would speed up any, but it hasn't."

Starren. My gritted teeth started to grind. She'd done this. If I ever saw her again, it wasn't going to be pretty. She'd almost taken Nina from me. She'd been insisting that we weren't family since we'd escaped together. Apparently even with all we'd been through, that hadn't changed.

Jaden dragged the stretcher thing over and laid it beside me. He gave me an apologetic look. "This really isn't going to feel good. I'm sorry."

"As if I haven't been shot before. I know it hurts."

Dan helped me roll to the side and Nina shoved the stretcher underneath. Little black floaters went across my vision, and I nearly passed out again.

"Deep breaths," Nina said.

I wanted to yell at her that deep breaths didn't fix nearly as much as she thought, but I couldn't get in a full breath to do it with. I gritted my teeth to keep myself from screaming.

"Okay, all good?" Jaden asked after about three seconds of getting situated. "I know we've sat here for a while, but whoever tried to kill Nina might figure out she's rejoined us in the land of the living. We need to get a move on it."

He was right. He was always right. "I'm ready."

Dan took the section at my head, Jaden at my feet. I couldn't contain the yelp that came out as they did their best to lift me gently.

Nina instantly took my hand, tearing up. She was far too soft-hearted for this kind of thing. I really was an idiot for bringing her, no matter what she'd pulled.

After a second to let me adjust, the guys started forward. First they went slowly, then picked up speed after a few steps.

I closed my eyes and leaned back, exhaustion rolling over me. At least the stretcher was fairly comfortable. Problem was, lying here gave me a chance to think. At this moment, thinking was not good for me. Or for Starren, for that matter.

If I wasn't lying on a cot right now, being carted through the woods, she'd be dead. Dead for hurting Nina. Dead for trying to kill Nina. She knew how much they meant to me, but she hadn't cared. There was no one else in Faerie that me staying would benefit, just Quintin, and because of that, Starren. That crazy man had more of a hold over her than I'd thought.

"Don't let your guard down," the words came out a little slurred. "Starren is ruthless."

"We don't know that it was Starren," Jaden said. "Maybe you should give her the benefit of the doubt."

I forced my eyes open to glare at him. "Who else would have motive? Only my father, and he couldn't have gotten here this quickly. Even if he had, he would have come to grab me after taking care of Nina. No, it was Starren."

I must have passed out again for a couple minutes, because I woke up with the others talking. Dan was starting to a huff a little. I wasn't that heavy, but this was a lot.

"We're only a few minutes from the tunnel," Jaden told me when he noticed my open eyes.

"How are you feeling?" Nina asked.

"I'm alive." I gave her a strained smile. It wasn't possible for me to lie, but I didn't want her feeling guilty.

She caught me on my non-answer. I could see it in her face. But she didn't call me on it.

A wave of nausea hit me as I swayed back and forth. "Hold it," I managed to get out before leaning over the side and vomiting all over the beautiful Faerie grasses. That's what they got, they should have protected Nina. The grass around me wilted, like it was ashamed.

"Trish," Nina sounded next to tears. The guys sat me down and let me have a second.

"Yeah, you better feel that way," I managed to get out. I spit and rolled back into the stretcher. Nina's eyes filled with tears. "Oh, not you. I was talking to the grass."

Nina sent a worried look to Dan, that I almost missed. Couldn't say I blamed her though, I probably sounded pretty crazy.

"Trish?" Wade's voice. I blinked, confused. Wasn't he gone? Where'd he come from? A large, warm hand gripped mine. "Trish, what happened? I was looking for a safe way through the tunnel. How did you get hurt?"

"Gunshot," Dan said. He didn't sound like himself. But then, I was only half with it.

Wade's head whipped around. "Gunshot? Here? Who would do that?" He settled back on his heels, not letting go of my hand. "Fae don't have guns. Only fae that travel to Earth."

Exactly. "Starren," I muttered.

"Starren?" Wade sounded shocked. "But you came here to rescue her."

"Family doesn't mean the same thing here." I'd quoted Starren, but they didn't know that.

An arrow whistled through our group, hitting Wade in the shoulder and knocking him away from me.

"Wade!" I shouted, struggling to see how badly he'd been hit.

"Get back," a woman's voice snarled. Starren. Just hearing her voice made my stomach clench. She'd figured out she'd failed, apparently.

Wade said some things in the Fae language that I was really glad Nina couldn't understand.

I growled and forced myself to my feet, pulling my sword. Jaden's sword popped out too, and Dan moved between Starren and Nina.

The trees around us started to sway, twisting where there was no wind, my anger whipping them into a frenzy.

"Come back to finish the job?" I hissed at Starren.

Branches clawed at each other, fighting their way toward Starren, every one of them needing to be the one that claimed the prize I so desperately wanted at this moment.

Starren oomphed loudly as the trees gripped her, fighting over her like sharks after bait, forcing the air out of her lungs.

"Hold," I yelled at the trees. They froze, instantly.

I took a step toward her, Jaden jumping forward to help. I waved him off. A glance showed Nina caring for Wade's wound, but watching me.

"I asked you a question." The words poured out like acid, my anger not having anything to hold it in check.

"I would never do such sloppy work."

If I'd thought I was angry before, I had no idea. Her words sent the trees whipping around hysterically. I could hardly hold them back from ripping her limb from limb. They felt my anger, and they wanted it to go away.

Starren started to struggle for air. I could hear her labored breathing from where I stood.

"Think about this, Trisha. Would I use a bullet? Am I such a coward that I would hide in the woods and shoot your human from afar? I'm not the one who took the shot. It was someone that can't aim with a bow."

It took her words a moment to bleed through my wall of anger. But they did. And she was right. She was never one to run from a fight, never seemed to care about anyone's feelings. And she couldn't lie. I deflated, the anger still burning, but at a more controllable level. But if it hadn't been her, who had shot Nina?

"Think you could tell this thing to let me go, now?" Starren grunted.

"Oh yeah, sorry." I waved my hand and the branch dropped her.

She stood, brushing herself off. "That's getting really annoying."

"No kidding. Stop making me do it to you. Do you know who shot Nina?" It might not have been her, but she hadn't been here to stop it either. She'd ran out on us. A vine slithered toward her again, feeling my renewed fit of temper. I glared at it, and it dropped to the ground.

Her eyes darted away. "No."

"But you have your suspicions. You're pretty sure you know."

Now her eyes went over my shoulder. Wait.

"You shot Wade!" I turned and awkwardly shambled to him, holding my wound. The hate had dulled the pain for a few moments, but moving brought it roaring back. Wade was on his feet, the arrow pulled already. He was pale, but seemed fine.

I got to Wade and shoved him in the chest, my hand jerking down to hold the wound closed. "Tell me it wasn't you. Tell me you didn't do this." If I'd thought he was pale before, I was wrong. I now knew what pale actually was. "Well?"

He knew I wasn't going to leave it alone. "I can't tell you that, Trish."

"Trish? Trish? Like we're friends?" I shoved him again, hard, with both hands. The pain meant nothing now.

He stumbled back, nearly falling to the ground. He would have, but Dan caught him, his face twisted in an anger wouldn't have thought him capable of. He righted Wade, then hauled back and punched him in the face, sending him sprawling on the ground.

Jaden ran forward and bent down, searching him. "No gun. He must have stashed it somewhere."

Wade shoved Jaden away and stood, spitting out blood. "You were supposed to come here and love it. You were supposed to stay," he yelled in my face.

"Stay with you? After you killed my mom? Are you crazy?" I screamed back. I'd thought I'd hated him after he'd shot me. But I hadn't. That had been mostly hurt, some confusion, and some anger, all mixed together. This was not that.

"You were supposed to see how beautiful it is here compared to Earth, how amazing. You were supposed to stay of your own free will." He looked at Nina, an ugly expression on his face. "You're choosing these humans over me? Over what we had?"

The anger that I'd directed at Starren came back full force, building until it blew the previous amount of hate out of the water. Starren I could understand. I could hate her, but I could get it. She had our father to try and please. But Wade? He was supposed to love me.

"Quintin was in on this, wasn't he." Starren asked quietly, though it didn't really sound like a question. "It was the reason I was arrested in the first place. The Council didn't care that I broke Sanctuary on a half fae kid. Quintin just needed a reason to get Trish to Faerie."

"I'm truly sorry about that, Starren," Wade said. "We didn't see another way. And he isn't ready for the humans to know about us, so we couldn't just take her, especially not from Sanctuary. Some of the more powerful fae he doesn't want to antagonize still believe in it."

Starren's face was cold, but she didn't look surprised. She'd probably figured most of this out before. His whole confession was just sad confirmation.

"You'd better run," I choked out. "Because I'm about to kill you." I hadn't killed anyone before. Never even really wanted to. But I did now. How easy it would be.

"Don't say that," Wade pleaded. "I still love you."

"Love me?" I let out a short bark of laughter. "If this is what you think love is, you need help. Serious help." The trees started to whip around, the branches reaching. "I was serious. You're about to die, whether I mean for it to happen or not."

An arm threading around my waist startled me. "Don't hurt him on my account," Nina whispered to me. "Killing him will only make things worse. He just admitted we're safe in Sanctuary, let's just get back there."

Angry tears leaked from my eyes, my face burning so hot they were gone before they could drip off. "I don't know if I can stop it."

Wade looked nervous. He should be terrified. A branched lashed out, breaking free of my control and snapping across Wade's cheek, drawing blood. He tried to jump out of the way, but another branch grabbed him, jerking him into the air. Vines and branches lashed around his arms and legs, curling around his neck. Then they all started to pull.

I started to cry for real then. "I don't think I can stop them."

Dan came up behind me and wrapped both Nina and me in his arms. Jaden came up on the other side and grabbed my hand.

"Hey," Jaden said. "Think about something else for a few minutes. Just until you calm down."

I forced my eyes off of Wade, away from the picture playing through my mind of Nina laying on the ground, dead, and into the dark eyes beside me.

"What's something that makes you happy?" Jaden asked. "Sunsets? Your sword? Your family?"

All of those things. A little of the anger leaked out.

"How about your friends from school? Cray? So many good things."

I glanced at Wade. The vines had stopped pulling, but he was still stretched tight, a vine down his mouth gagging him, his eyes impossibly wide with terror.

"If you have to think about Wade, think about the good times. It sounds like there were plenty of those."

He was right. Wade had been a good boyfriend. I'd truly loved him, the only other person I'd ever loved except for my mom at that point in my life. He'd helped me, changed me, made me feel loveable again for the first time in years. He'd gotten me through some pretty tough times. Without him loving me, I might not have accepted Nina when I had.

I folded in on myself, and would have dropped to the ground if Starren hadn't been there in a flash to catch me and gently help me to the forest floor. The pain in my abdomen, forgotten in my anger, came back full force.

"Let him go," I whispered, and the trees obliged after a moment's hesitation, dropping Wade to the ground.

He sucked in air like he was dying. He almost had. I gave him a second.

"Get out of here," Dan said.

Wade struggled to his feet, watching us. "Trish-"

"No," I said, looking up at him. "You don't get to talk to me anymore. Get out of here. I never want to see you again." All the energy I'd put into my anger had burned everything I had. I felt nothing at the moment, hollow.

His face flushed in anger. He took a step toward me, but a tree lashed out again, marking his other cheek. "You should have let them kill me," he snarled, then took off into the woods.

I probably should have. But what would that have made me? A murderer, killing an unarmed man. Dan and Nina looked past all the strange things about me that were just me. But me being a murderer? That would be a harder thing for them to swallow.

"Thank you," I told Jaden.

I squeezed Nina's hand.

"Now what?" I asked Starren. "Now that you know for sure what father did, you can't go back."

She stared in the direction Wade had left. "I couldn't have gone back anyway. Not after helping you get away."

"Then why did you disappear? Where did you go? Why did you come back?"

She rolled her eyes and settled into the grass next to me. "I left because I'm a danger to you, being around. I didn't really have a place in mind. I was trailing quite a distance behind you until you got to the tunnel when I heard the gunshot."

"You knew what happened, didn't you."

"I was afraid I knew what happened. You had said many times that these two humans were why you stay on Earth. I suspected Wade of helping my father, but I never thought he would do something so foolish, or I wouldn't have left."

I reached out and squeezed her arm. "Quintin is our father. I know he wasn't good to you, but still. And more importantly, Wade was your best friend, your partner. This had to be incredibly hard, especially since we don't always get along that great. Thank you."

Starren looked at the ground. "You're my sister."

I couldn't help the grin that popped on to my face. It didn't last long before a wave of nausea hit me. I laid down into the grass and closed my eyes.

"We shouldn't stay here long. If Wade is helping Quintin, he'll be getting backup."

"Stretcher time." Dan's voice.

I groaned.

I poked lightly at my abdomen, then about yelled at myself. That was pretty stupid. No new bleeding, but some pretty intense pain.

They rolled me back onto the stretcher, and we were off.

I closed my eyes for what seemed like a second, and we were at the tunnel somehow. "Wha...?" I asked groggily.

"Nothing, just take a nap," Nina answered.

But the tunnel... it wasn't safe because... I couldn't remember. All I could think about was sleep.

CHAPTER SEVENTEEN

The next time I woke up, it was sunny. Like really bright sunny, not like Faerie sunny at all. I squinted up at the sky. "Are we home?"

"Not home, home, but back on Earth," Dan's voice answered.

I sat up quickly, with only a second of dizziness. "Wait a second. We're already through the tunnel?"

"Yep," Jaden said, grinning at me from the front of the stretcher.

"How?" I asked. "I thought we were all going to die in there."

"Jaden was right," Nina interjected. "The firnen didn't bother us when we were trying to leave Faerie, only when we were trying to go there. Someone must have them there as a security measure." She kicked a giant rock. "Just like this stone thing."

I couldn't tell without it moving around if the rock she'd kicked was actually a part of the golem or not, but I'd give this one to her.

"Where's Starren?" the fact that she was gone almost sent me into a panic. I jumped to my feet, anxiously searching for her.

"Right here, you idiot," she said from over where she was leaning on a different rock. "Take it easy. You might be healed now, but you aren't even close to recovered."

"Hey!" A voice I didn't recognize yelled. "That's a not public area. None of you are authorized to be here."

All of us jerked toward whoever was speaking, Jaden pulling his sword, Dan's hand going to his gun which he must have grabbed in the tunnel, and Starren unslinging the bow she'd used to shoot Wade.

A kid with a nametag saying he worked at the Red Rock Amphitheatre raised his hands above his head, his face going pale. "Sorry, sorry!" He turned and ran.

"And I think that's our cue to go," Dan said, taking his hand off his gun.

"I think you're right," Nina said. "Trish, how's the.." she made a weird little movement with her head and pointed at her abdomen.

What in the world? Oh wait, the wound. I poked at the bullet hole. "Gone."

"Yes." Nina pumped her fist in the air. "Score one for Earth."

I poked at myself again. Only a slight amount of pain. It would be totally gone before we made it to the car. We started toward the parking lot, leaving the stretcher behind. Good. I hoped I never had to see one of those again.

"Doing okay?" Nina asked, hovering on my right.

"Don't push yourself too hard," Jaden said, hovering on my left.

"I can cause a distraction if you need a little extra time to get away," Dan said from the front.

I ground my teeth, trying not to yell at anyone. Being injured was fairly normal for me, they were just going to have to get used to that. At least Starren just rolled her eyes and took off. She believed in me. I hoped.

"There they are!" That guys voice. He came at us from around a huge boulder, a whole group of security guards with him. That was really fast.

"You guys really should get out of here," Jaden said. Then I realized he was invisible again. Funny how a few days in Faerie seemed like years. All the stuff here didn't feel real at the moment.

"Time to go," Dan said, dragging Nina away.

We tore off across the edge of the parking lot, at least twice as fast as we'd been going before. I made it a short distance before getting dizzy.

"You okay?" Jaden asked, supporting me on my left side.

"Yeah, just haven't been healed for long."

"No excuses. We have to get out of here." Starren slipped my arm over her shoulder on the right.

Together they half dragged me away, which probably looked pretty weird to anyone watching, with Jaden being invisible.

I never thought I'd be so glad to see a mini-van in my entire life.

Dan hit the remote locks, starting when we were still about ten rows away and continuing until he got the driver's side door open. Nina jumped in the passenger side, and Starren shoved me into the side sliding door. Then she backed away.

"What are you doing?" I shouted. "Get in!"

She looked hesitant.

"We'll have time to talk about whatever your problem is later. At the moment, a bunch of security guards are headed our way."

She shrugged and went invisible.

"Whoa," Dan said from the front seat. "That's still neat. But we really need to go before they get our plate number."

I grabbed Starren's partly translucent hand and jerked her into the van.

"Go!" Nina yelled as the guards came around the fence and started dodging cars headed in our direction.

"Wait for Jaden!" I shouted.

"Jaden?" Nina asked. She sounded confused.

"Yeah, he's invisible again since we're home."

"Oh, right."

Jaden jumped in beside me. "Okay, go!"

I slammed the sliding door while Dan gunned it and we flew out of the parking lot.

I watched out the back window as the guards shouted to each other. It wasn't long before they were out of sight. We squealed around a couple curves before Dan started driving like a normal person. "Everyone okay?" he asked. "I'm going to slow down. Better to not call attention to ourselves."

"They've probably already called this in," Nina added. "We'd better stay on some back roads until we're a ways away." She popped out the map she always carried, since the whole Chicago incident, and bent over it, trying to figure out a good route home.

I just leaned back into the chair and closed my eyes for a second. Talk about exhausted. But it was a good thing we were back, or I'd still be in much worse shape. What Wade had done...

I'd forgiven him when he shot me, even when he didn't know about my healing thing. I would never forgive him for shooting Nina. The second betrayal hurt even worse than the first. I'd given him another chance. Look how that turned out.

"Doing okay?" Jaden asked, like he could feel the turmoil going on inside me at the moment.

I guess that wouldn't be hard. I was angry enough to make a troll cringe, and they were so dumb. "I'm fine," I answered.

"Who are you talking to, Trish?" Dan asked, looking in the rear-view mirror.

What was with the old people the last few hours?

"Jaden," I answered.

Starren was looking at me funny.

"What?" I snapped.

She didn't answer, just turned to look out the window. Jaden was the only not weird person right now, including me. At this point the only thing that would get me to go back to Faerie would be if I could get Wade thrown in a cell for life. How else was I supposed to handle this anger?

Nina was fine. But every time I closed my eyes, I could still see her lifeless face going slack, could still feel her body cooling as I laid there and cried.

This would be with me forever.

"Do you guys mind if I take a nap?" I asked.

Starren's eyes got wide. "Leave me alone with them?" she whispered.

"Not alone. I'm right here."

"Trish!" she hissed.

"It's fine, Starren. We can talk about growing up in Faerie," Nina said, smiling back at both of us. Her smile made everything that happened come back and I almost zoned out for a second.

Starren looked like she was about to have a panic attack. "It wasn't great."

Nina's smile dimmed. "Well then we can talk about something else. What would you like to talk about?"

My eyes drooped.

Starren kicked me.

I ignored her and snuggled up in the seat as best as I could. This coming back from near death had to stop, it was exhausting. Better than the alternative, but still.

We drove pretty much straight through without stopping. When we did, it was only to get gas and switch drivers. Being out of Sanctuary made everyone anxious. Even Starren would only be safe there now, which seemed pretty ironic.

Listening to Jaden get yelled at over the phone by his mom was funny for the first bit, but got old fast. It would be a while before Rebecca forgave him. And by extension, me.

Crossing the city line went about like the first time went, except this time I thought to have Nina driving instead of Dan, so we didn't have the repeat of the near accident we'd had when we'd moved here. Jaden had popped into existence with Rebecca at the wheel and it hadn't gone well.

"Whoa!" Dan yelled when Jaden became visible. "What just happened?"

I frowned. "It's Jaden, Dan. You knew this would happen." He'd heard the story about Jaden only being visible inside of Sanctuary about four hundred times. What was with him?

Relief washed over Dan's face. "Oh right. It just happened really quickly. So weird."

"How's the wound?" Nina asked over her shoulder.

"Gone, Nina. I'm fine." Moms and their asking the same questions five-hundred times. Or was that just my mom?

It was late enough that we just dropped Jaden off without going in. We got back to the apartment and the familiar scent of Nina's detergent and Dan's aftershave almost made me tear up. Almost. I went straight to find my phone. Yep, Cray had thrown it on the bed. A ton of texts, something that I would never have thought would happen before. Mostly my friends asking where I was.

Jaden had texted me shortly after we'd dropped him off to say everything was good at his place. Which was a relief, actually. I hadn't been consciously thinking about it, but without Jaden here Rebecca and the girls were vulnerable.

I answered a few messages telling my friends that yes, I was still alive and I'd see them ASAP.

"Where's Cray?" Starren asked, startling me from behind.

Good question. I left my room and headed to his, knocking on the door.

Cray, hair tousled and eyes wild, with no glasses, threw open the door, grabbing me and pulling me into a surprisingly tight hug. "You're back! I was starting to think you were dead!" He squinted over my shoulder. "Starren!" He dropped me and went over to hug her.

She didn't look thrilled, but she allowed a short squeeze.

"Dan and Nina?" Cray asked.

I pointed at their room.

He tore off to check on them. So weird, considering a month ago he was terrified that they could see him in Sanctuary because his charms didn't work here.

"Well all the bedrooms are taken," I said to Starren. "So I guess you're bunking with me?"

She raised an eyebrow. "I'll take the couch, thank you. Just for tonight. Tomorrow I'll figure out what I'm going to do."

She was lost. Adrift. Without people to call her own. Exactly where I'd been, not that long ago. "Or you could just stay here. We'll figure something out. I don't think you'd like school, but we could find you a job of some kind."

"A job?"

"Yeah, sure. We'll get you going somewhere. Dan will help."

She looked confused. "Why would Dan help me?"

I beamed at her. "I went through the same thing. It's something they do. You're family now, so you'll be taken care of. I don't get it either, but it's awesome."

She still looked confused, but she followed me in to the living room, where Dan, Nina, and Cray had moved.

We told Cray about what had happened in Faerie for a good hour before Nina looked at her watch. "Bedtime. You have school in the morning."

I groaned, though it was mostly for show. I wouldn't mind seeing everyone, wouldn't mind things getting back to normal. Though I also wouldn't mind one day sitting around at home, either. "Seriously?"

"Seriously." She shooed me toward my room. "Get Starren something to sleep in."

I sighed, but did what she asked, digging through my drawer until I found something I thought would fit. I turned to take it back out to the living room, but Starren was right there when I turned around. "Whoa, you startled me." Again. But I didn't add that part. "You know you don't have to stay beside me all the time, right?"

Her face went blank, like she was processing. "But they are your humans."

Okay, now I was the one who was confused. "Uh, yeah?"

"So you understand them. It would be better if we didn't have a miscommunication."

I tossed the pjs at her and crossed my arms. "There had better not be any miscommunications." I did air quotes, which just made her look confused. "They're good people and I expect you to be good back to them."

She cocked her head at me. "What does that mean?"

"I mean be nice. And don't hurt them, ever, under any circumstance, that's rule number one. Got it?"

She nodded slowly. "What's rule number two?"

Ugh, I'd forgotten how much she liked rules. "No hurting anyone else, either, unless they are trying to hurt you or someone in our family."

"Our family," she repeated.

"Yes, our family."

"Just like that?"

"Just like that."

It was my turn to shoo. We went back out to the living room, where Nina had already set up blankets and pillows on the couch. She smiled when she saw us.

"Here you go, Starren. Until we can figure something else out. We might be able to fit another bed into Trish's room."

"No need," Starren said, moving over to stand at attention near Nina. "I don't plan to be staying long."

A pang hit me. I hadn't even gotten to truly know her yet, and she was already talking about leaving. No use arguing tonight. She had that look that I knew meant nothing I said would get through. Maybe tomorrow she'd be in a better mood.

With a chorus of goodnights, I went in and collapsed on my bed. Even with all the stuff flowing around in my brain, I fell asleep faster than it took me to heal an arrow wound.

Breakfast the next morning definitely made me miss Nina's normal cooking. Most of the stuff in the fridge had spoiled while we were gone, so we got a lot of good food, it was just kind of a mashup. It was quiet though. No one had much to say.

When I left for school, Dan was getting ready for work, Nina was cleaning up the kitchen, and Starren was watching TV like it was the strangest thing she'd ever seen. She had to have seen a lot of screens with all her visits to Earth, but this was probably the first time she'd ever just sat and watched something. Goodbyes took a little longer than normal, and seemed just a little more important.

Since I'd lost Nina, I'd figured out what I had at stake in life. And I wasn't going to take it for granted again.

When I got to school, I was mobbed.

"Trish!" Rosie shrieked from across the parking lot as I pushed my bike into the stand. I turned around in time to oomph as she hit me at full speed, pulling me into a hug. "I almost cried when I got your message last night, I was so worried! And I wasn't sure I could trust a message, but here you are. Where were you?"

"Ah, an, unexpected family trip." True. Just my family wasn't a normal family. "We didn't have any service." So true, but also so not in any way she would believe me. "What are you doing here? This isn't even your school."

She shrugged, but still looked at me funny. "I don't know where you live and you didn't answer my messages last night, after the first one. I wanted to check on you. Next time give us some warning before you fall off the face of the planet."

Ha. If she only knew.

"At least your parents called the school, I have a friend that goes here, she asked Mr. Yamen where you were he said you'd be gone a few days, but didn't say anything more than that."

Leave it to Nina to think to call the principal, even without much notice.

I tried to say that I was fine, but the words wouldn't come out. Okay, so obviously I wasn't fine. "Well, as you can see, I'm completely healthy." I gave her a fake smile. Physically I was healthy. Emotionally, apparently not. But it would come. If I could convince Starren to stay.

Rosie and I talked for another couple minutes, but then I heard the bell ring and we had to say goodbye.

Coming back to school was a little weird, after seeing so much of Faerie. And what I had seen had probably only scratched the surface. If it wasn't for all the crazy, I would have loved to go back. The beauty there was indescribable.

I fidgeted in class all day, every hour getting a little worse. Starren hadn't been too happy to be left with the humans. Would she even still be there when I got home? Hopefully she hadn't killed anyone.

And where was Cray? I hadn't seen him all day.

I buzzed home as quickly as I could once I got out of school, dropped my bike outside the apartment building and ran up the stairs. I burst through the door, and let out a huge breath of relief. The first thing I saw was Starren, sitting at the counter eating cookies. She hadn't run.

"Star! You're still here." I dropped my bookbag at the end of the counter, grinning at her.

She didn't grin back. My smile slipped. She looked like someone had killed a puppy.

"What's wrong?"

"Oh," Nina said, turning away from the fridge. "Hello."

"Hey," I answered, not really paying attention. "Star?"

She twitched her head toward Nina, her eyes looking like she wanted to panic. What was going on?

"Everything okay, Nina?" I asked, still staring Starren down.

"I'm truly sorry, Trisha," Starren said. And she looked like it. But what I couldn't figure out was what she was sorry about.

"Yes, everything is great, thanks for asking," Nina said. Okay, now my eyes shifted to her. What was with all the formal talk? "Trisha, was it? Is she a friend of yours?" Nina asked Starren.

"My little sister, actually," Starren answered.

I let out a nervous chuckle. "You know that, Nina."

Her brow wrinkled, her face going into intense concentration for a second, then smoothing out. "How would I know that? Have we met? Oh wait, you're Lucy's friend, aren't you!"

"What's going on?" the words would barely come out of my mouth.

"You didn't let them eat anything while you were..." Cray paused. "There, did you?"

I hadn't even noticed him sitting in the corner. "Why? What was wrong with the food?" My voice was high, so high it took a second to process that it was me speaking. "All that stuff about the food is just legend, right?"

"What food?" Nina asked, frowning.

No, no, no. This couldn't be happening. "Starren?"

"I've only heard myths. It isn't like it has been tested in hundreds of years." She was being intentionally vague because Nina didn't know what was going on. Because Nina didn't remember.

"Nina, why did you move to Fort Wayne?" My voice still had a hysterical note, but it was much more under control. There was a way to fix this. There had to be a way.

Nina's brow furrowed, like she was trying to figure something out.

"Dan's job?" It came out as a question, like she didn't quite believe her answer either.

"You knew this would happen?" I asked Starren, my voice hardly audible.

"No, no, it isn't like that. I didn't know."

"But you suspected." It wasn't even a question, so I stated it as fact.

"Yes, but I didn't see any reason to make you panic if it wasn't real."

She'd suspected. I leaned on the counter, gripping the edge so tightly that my fingers ached, my breaths starting to come out in pants.

"Why are you kids in my house?" Nina's voice snapped my attention back.

I took a step closer. "Nina, it's me."

Nina looked nervous and my stomach churned. It was the look I'd most dreaded from her, fear of me because of what I am. But it wasn't over what I was, I was causing her fear just by being in her apartment. Our apartment.

"I think you should leave." She'd never used that tone of voice with me before, not once. No recognition, no warmth. Even when she was mad at me and chewing me out, I always knew it came from a place of love. But this?

When I didn't head for the door, she crossed her arms. "I've asked you to leave. If you aren't going to comply, I'm going to call my husband."

Yes! A small flicker of hope burned through the despair. Maybe Dan could set her straight.

"And as soon as I hang up with him, I'll be calling the police."

The police? My mind blanked and I froze. I was pretty much human here, but that didn't mean I wanted the attention. And attention on Cray or Starren could be bad. Really bad.

"It's time for us to go." Starren stood, grabbing me by the shoulder. "Thank you very much for your hospitality. I'm sure we'll be seeing each other again."

Cray grabbed my other arm, reached down and picked up my school bag before the two of them drug me from the apartment. None of us spoke as we stumbled down the stairs, and outside, moving to an alley that ran by the building.

There was a way to fix this. There had to be a way. There was a way to fix anything. "What do we do?" I asked Starren.

She stared blankly back.

"How do we fix this? We have to be able to fix this."

She looked at me, but didn't say anything.

"Come on, tell me how!" I grabbed her arm and jerked, like that would force her to spill some answer. "Why aren't you answering?"

"Because she's trying to figure out a way to tell you that it isn't possible." Jaden. Jaden was here. He was walking up the alley and I'd been too busy attacking Starren to notice.

I ran to him and buried my face in his chest. He wrapped his arms around me. "Aren't you supposed to be at work?" It came out muffled with my head smashed into his coat, but he understood me.

"Yeah, but Cray called. He told me what's going on."

Him showing up had been a moment's distraction. But now that he was here, I couldn't keep it together any more. I burst into tears, gripping onto his coat like a lifeline. He pulled me in tighter, and just held me, not saying anything.

"We have to get them back, Jade. Everything I ever needed, ever wanted, that's them." The words came out clogged, and my tears were starting to freeze to my face.

Starren looked completely miserable. Probably at my show of emotions. "I know family doesn't mean a thing in Faeire, but it means a lot to me," I snapped at her.

She looked at the ground, not making eye contact. "It isn't that."

I glared at her.

She glanced up, then went right back to looking at the ground. "You're in this situation because you helped me, and I'm not sure how to fix it. I wish I could."

Her admitting she didn't know something would have come as a shock to me at any other time. At the moment, all I could hear was no cure. Dan and Nina didn't know who I was. Would never know what I was supposed to mean to them, would never know what they meant to me. How was I supposed to live with this?

"Jaden?" I asked. "Have you seen anything?"

His face crumpled and for the first time I noticed he had tears in his eyes too. "No. I haven't seen anything about them in the future at all. Which means…" he trailed off.

I leaned back, staring up at him. "Which means?"

"As things are, they will probably never be a big part of your life again. Because I will be, and I haven't seen any interactions with them. I dreamed in the van on the way home from Colorado, but I thought it was just a dream."

I let the fact that he was going to be a large part of my life whiz right over my head. I did not have the emotional energy to go through that thought right now. "Who else can we ask?" I looked back and forth between all three of them. Cray was keeping quiet, no doubt trying to stay off my radar, but no one was getting out of these questions until I found an answer I liked. "Who would know what to do?"

Jaden shook his head. Starren looked uncomfortable.

I zoned in on her. "Star?"

"If I could go back and change things, I would change everything. But I can't. I don't know how to fix this, and I'm sorry." She just kept repeating the same thing. Why didn't she come up with something better? She was the one that always took charge, always knew what to do.

Something in the back of my mind registered the fact that she was sorry. Everything about her screamed that she was in pain over this too, but I could barely cope with my own pain at the moment. I hunched into myself, and nearly fell to the ground. I didn't have anyone now. Everything I'd finally gained, I'd lost.

"Come on." Jaden slipped an arm around my waist and started pulling me toward the street.

"Where are we going? I don't have anywhere to go." The tears were starting up again, but I was too exhausted for anymore straight up crying.

"To Mom's. She'll know what to do next. She always does."

He pulled me toward his truck. Starren started to follow, then stopped. I didn't have the energy to care.

Cray moved past us and threw a couple bags in the bed of Jaden's pickup. "I packed up our stuff," he said awkwardly. We didn't have much at all, having just moved here, especially Cray, who hadn't had a single thing except for the clothes on his back when he'd moved in with us in November.

"Come on, Starren. You're a part of this family now too. Time to figure out what that means," Jaden said over his shoulder.

She followed without comment, helping him stuff me in the truck and cramming herself in beside me.

"I'll bring her bike. You guys go on," Cray said. I barely heard it through the haze.

Why had Jaden said family? It wasn't fair to call this a family without Dan and Nina. They were the first family I'd ever had. Yeah, the Martan's felt like family now too, but it wasn't the same. Even in a biological family, it wouldn't be the same. I'd lost my parents today. They weren't dead, but to them, I was. Worse, I'd never existed. They wouldn't miss me. Wouldn't mourn me. Wouldn't even know that they had once loved me enough to risk everything and follow me to Faerie. What a mistake that had been.

I lolled my head over to look at Starren, my eyes aching from the tears. Had it been worth it?

Starren caught me staring, and it was like she knew what I was thinking. She shook her head no, and looked like she wanted to cry with me. And here I had thought she wasn't capable of such emotion

We pulled up in front of Jaden's building, me still a blubbering mess. No matter how hard I fought to control it, I couldn't. Fighting seemed to make it worse, so I stopped trying.

Jaden parked and came around to help me out. I held it together, shrugging him off while there were other people around, but as soon as we were inside the apartment building the tears flowed again.

Starren followed behind me, trailing along like a lost puppy. I wanted to hate her, but I couldn't. She was all I had left.

Jaden pushed the door to their apartment open and Rebecca rushed forward, pulling me into a crushing hug. "I'm so sorry, Trish. Jaden told me what happened."

I buried my face in her sweater, mostly so she couldn't see it. Her body shook a little as she cried for me. Even with the amount of crying I'd already done, I teared up. "I don't know what I'm going to do," I admitted, my voice small.

Could I just leave Fort Wayne? But what if someday they remembered, and I wasn't here? But maybe if I did leave, I could find a cure.

But if I didn't go to school, Social Services would be notified. Dan and Nina would be in trouble, and wouldn't even know why. Would the interviews and questions jog their memories of me?

I didn't know. I had no answers for anything. I started to crumple, but Jaden caught me under my arm and helped me to the couch.

"What is she doing here?" Lucy's voice asked from somewhere.

I looked up, ready to glare at her through bloodshot eyes, but she wasn't looking at me. She was staring at Starren.

"Don't think we don't recognize you," Lucy hissed. "We saw you at the gas station, remember? You're the one who took Jaime."

I so was not in the mood for this. I could understand Lucy's anger, but I just couldn't deal with her right now.

Rebecca's attention whipped from me, to Starren, to Jaden. "Jade?" she asked.

"It's complicated," Jaden answered.

"Complicated?" Lucy asked. "How complicated could it be? She kidnapped Jaime." Her entire body seemed to vibrate in anger. I was a little worried she'd jump Starren. That probably wouldn't turn out well. If Starren fought back, Lucy didn't stand a chance. If she didn't, I'd have to step in.

"Let it go," Rebecca said. "Jaden wouldn't bring her here unless she's safe to be around now." And then she gave Jaden a look that totally shouted they'd be having a discussion later.

"Rebecca." It came out as a whisper, so much weaker than I'd expected. "What am I going to do?"

The anger in the room dissolved instantly, and I was back in Rebecca's arms getting squeezed to death within a second of the words leaving my mouth.

"We'll figure it out, honey. There has to be an answer. This isn't how it's going to end, I promise you."

I buried my face in her jacket and didn't answer. Jaden could see bits of the future, and he didn't agree with her. Maybe he just couldn't see anything to do with Dan and Nina for another reason. He still couldn't control his power much at all. But my soul told me that he was right. As things were now, they would never know me again, never know everything we'd been through together.

"We don't have much room, but of course you are staying here until we find somewhere else," Rebecca said.

I didn't answer, not knowing if I should be relieved or not. Not on the streets was a good thing. Especially this time of year. Staying in a cramped apartment, with Lucy here to boot, not so much.

"She," Rebecca nodded toward Starren, "has to go though. I don't want her here any longer than is absolutely necessary."

I caught the slight twitch that crossed Starren's face. No one else seemed to.

She turned back toward the door without a word.

"Star, wait!" I pulled away from Rebecca and went after her. She slowed, but didn't stop. I grabbed her from behind and twirled her around. "Wait. You can't leave. You're the only family I have left."

She eyed the Martan's over my shoulder. "I am less family to you than they are."

I crossed my arms and gave her my best staredown. "Nope. It isn't that easy. You aren't going anywhere, promise? Not until we figure out what we're doing?"

Starren sighed and reached up, pinching the bridge of her nose. "But what are we doing, Trish? Playing house with these humans, because we have nowhere else to go? That might work for you, but we are very different people. It can't work for me."

I reached out and grabbed her hand, tugging on it until she looked at me again, my heart stampeding in my chest. She couldn't leave too. Dan and Nina were gone. It wasn't their fault, it wasn't fair, but I was still angry about it. I couldn't lose my sister too. "Please?" The whisper came out broken, hardly audible.

But she must have heard it, because she looked me straight in my teary eyes, and sighed. "Fine. I'll stay until you're settled. But that's it."

Nina must have really been rubbing off on me, because I jumped forward and gave her a quick hug. "Thank you." That was good enough for now. She would see this wasn't such a bad life. She'd stay. She'd have to.

"Can someone tell me why Trisha is hugging the enemy?" Lucy asked from the living room.

Ugh, how could one person be so annoying? "None of your business, mouthy," I called back at her. "Just stay here for a minute, Star." I stared her down for a second to make sure she would listen, then went back to the living room. "So. Any ideas on how we can do this? I'm not old enough to do much, and Starren doesn't have any ID, obviously."

"There's an empty apartment on the floor below us," Jaden said. "Mom would have to sign the lease, but it could work."

"How am I supposed to pay for that?" I asked. Who would hire a sixteen-year-old without some kind of parental permission or something? Maybe Rebecca could pose as my mom. How was I supposed to do school and a full-time job? Not really possible. The job wasn't optional though. If Nina was in her right mind, she'd freak out if I said I was thinking about dropping out of school.

But she wasn't. So it didn't really matter, did it? But somehow it did. She was still my mom, even if I wasn't her daughter.

"I can work," Starren said from behind me.

If I wasn't so emotionally exhausted that I couldn't find anything funny at the moment, I would have snorted. "I know I said last night that we'd find you a job, but your skill set probably isn't going to be easy to sell around here. I don't think people have other people bumped off that often in this area."

She looked offended. "I can do other work."

I crossed my arms in front of my chest. "Yeah? Like what?"

"I can get her a job," Jaden offered. "Off the books, like me. It isn't great, but the pay is decent."

I'd forgotten that he couldn't get a real job either, since he was technically dead. Being dead was really inconvenient sometimes.

"You're welcome to stay with us," Rebecca answered. "You're family." My heart rose for a second, but then she nodded toward Starren. "She is not. And I'd prefer she not stay any longer right now."

It was unfortunate for my heart that it had started to ascend, because it fell right back down, splattering on the bottom of whatever.

"She's my sister. I can't do that to her."

"Your sister?" Lucy yelled. "That explains so much!"

I ignored her, pleading with Rebecca with my eyes.

She sighed. "You've done so much for our family, Trish. And your parents as well, even if they don't remember. Between both Jaden and me working, I can get the down-payment on an apartment, and maybe first month's rent. It'll be tight, but we can do that." Her eyes went to Starren. "The problem is, I'm not sure I want her living in the same building."

Apparently some good deeds did count for something. Now to convince her that Starren wasn't a threat to her family. "Do you promise not to hurt anyone from their family, Star? Or kidnap them? Or do anything like that?"

Starren got a mutinous look on her face for a second, but it melted almost instantly. "Yes."

"That you won't hurt any humans without my permission?"

And I'd thought her look had been bad before. She looked from me, to Rebecca, and back to me.

"Or to save a life. Yes."

I looked back over at Rebecca. "See, what else could you ask for?"

Rebecca didn't look happy, and she wasn't answering me. After a moment of silence, I started to get worried. More worried, actually, but who's calculating.

"Fine. But you have to promise that if I ever tell you to leave, you will leave, instantly."

Starren considered her for a few seconds. "Deal."

"I don't know what to do about tonight though." Rebecca tipped her head toward Starren without looking at her. "She isn't sleeping here."

I'd sub-consciously known that, but it still freaked me out hearing it out loud. It was freezing outside, and I didn't have anywhere to take her.

"A hotel is out. Starren looks like a minor and doesn't have any ID. Even if we got the room for you, someone might notice two young girls staying alone and call the cops. The last thing we need is the human authorities finding Starren here," Jaden said. "What about those friends, Trish? The ones you were getting pizza with."

Stay with Rosie? Ask her not only to keep me, but my sister she'd never met? What kind of story could I make up that was close enough to the truth that I could say it that wouldn't sound crazy?

"Let me think for a minute," I said.

"Just tell her you need to get away from your parents for a night," Lucy said from her perch on the back of the couch. She'd been so quiet I'd almost forgotten she was there. Quiet was so weird for her.

"Seems legit," Jaden said. "Teens do that to their parents all the time."

A knock on the door sent my heart flying into my throat. Maybe whatever had happened to Dan and Nina had worn off. I rushed to the door and flung it open without checking the eyeslot. Oh. Cray.

He gave me a wobbly smile. "Made it."

He was without a home too, at the moment. He'd given up everything to help us, without a reason I could see. And now he was out in the cold right along with us.

I moved out of his way, wordlessly. If I tried to speak the disappointment would suffocate me.

"Oh, Cray," Rebecca moved over to give him a hug. "I'm so sorry." I crushed down resentment. They were my parents. But he loved them too, whether he'd admit it or not. "You can stay here tonight, in Jaden's room."

"Thank you," Cray said. "What about you two?" he asked me.

"Rosie," I croaked out, hit again by the fact that I wouldn't be going home tonight. "I just need to call her." Surely she'd let me stay. We were friends. That's what friends were for.

We all stood in awkward silence for a minute, no one knowing what to say or do.

"Better just call her," Jaden said.

I sighed and pulled out my phone, no longer able to stall. I'd never even called her before. We just talked by text. 'Hey. A friend and I need a place to spend the night, would it be okay if we stayed with you?'

It was an agonizing three seconds of silence before my phone buzzed. 'Of course!!!! Come on over' followed by an address.

Cray leaned over my shoulder. "Only a few miles from here."

I looked at him weird.

He shrugged. "I like maps. It's not like I have a social life."

True. So tonight was handled. Telling Rosie enough to make her feel in the loop and like I trusted her without letting on that both my parents had sudden and permanent amnesia would be interesting, for sure.

Tonight I would mourn. Grieve, quietly. But tomorrow? That was a different story. There was a way to fix this. I didn't know what it was, but there had to be. And I was going to find it, no matter what it took. I would have my family back.

ABOUT THE AUTHOR

Growing up, it was impossible to catch Cassie Greutman without a book in her hand, even at the most inappropriate times. Since then with the rise of ebooks, it's only gotten worse. With her full-time job of caring for over thirty horses, some of that has changed to audiobooks, but you can bet there is always some type of story rattling around in her brain. She has always loved stories in any format, whether that is a movie, video game, or book form, and hopes to tell stories that catch a person's imagination and interest like so many have done for her.

A finalist in the Cinematic Book Competition with Screencraft out of over 1200 entries, and five star ratings with Reader's Favorite, and a win with The Indie Author Project, Cassie has been throwing all of the extra time she has into building worlds for everyone to enjoy. When she isn't stuck in a book, of course.

Ready to see what comes next? Check out book three in the Penchant for Trouble series, Anamnesis!Follow me on Facebook and TikTok for updates on new stories!

https://www.facebook.com/cassiegreutman/

https://www.tiktok.com/@cassiegreutman

Or join my newsletter for a free short story about Trish first coming to live with Dan and Nina:

https://dl.bookfunnel.com/pq98nn1jof

If you'd like early access to stories as I write them and behind the scenes posts, check out: https://reamstories.com/page/lh4u19l5l3

www.ingramcontent.com/pod-product-compliance
Lightning Source LLC
Chambersburg PA
CBHW070503300726

48975CB00007B/2308